D0734407

SNITCHERS

SNITCHERS

STEPHANE DUNN

CINCO PUNTOS PRESS

An Imprint of **LEE & LOW BOOKS** Inc.

New York

Cinco Puntos Press, an imprint of LEE & LOW BOOKS Inc.,
95 Madison Avenue, New York, NY 10016
leeandlow.com

Manufactured in the United States of America
Printed on paper from responsible sources

Edited by Jessica Powers and Stacy Whitman
Book design by Sheila Smallwood
Typesetting by ElfElm Publishing
Book production by The Kids at Our House
The text is set in Baskerville
10 9 8 7 6 5 4 3 2 1
First Edition

Cataloging-in-Publication Data is on file with the Library of Congress

CAUTION

FOR NADIR

IN MEMORIAM:
IDENE WARD, ANGELA WILLIAMS (DUNN),
GRACIE BRADLEY FOR EMBODYING LOVE & GRACE

CHAPTER

1

A lady on this talk show I saw once told a story about a time she had died. Her heart stopped beating, and the doctors shocked her chest like three times and still no heartbeat, no pulse. They pronounced her dead. Then she coughed, and the doctors and nurses about fell out. She said dying was like sinking back into the womb. But who remembers that? She saw a light, but it wasn't the kind that blinded you. She called it angel light. After that, I would try to imagine the light as I lay on my bed, looking up at the ceiling, wondering if Daddy had seen the light when he was dying. I closed my eyes and put my arms flat on each side of my body, hands palms down with my legs pressed together and my feet parted in a small Y. I made my body a mannequin and breathed in through my nose, pressing my lips tightly so no air escaped. *One thousand one, one thousand two, one thousand three, one thousand four, one thousand five, one thousand six . . . one thousand ten. One thousand thirteen . . .* My chest tightened. Colors twisted and spiraled out of control in my head. I began to drift off somewhere but whether to a light or warmness, I didn't know. I panicked and opened my nose and mouth, glad to be gasping air.

The thing was, I didn't want to die 'cause I knew there was no coming back from being truly dead. The lady on TV had maybe glimpsed the angel light. I hoped it had been there for my father and he'd gone to heaven like everybody said, though it was hard to picture millions of people somewhere way up beyond the clouds, above gravity, chilling every minute in some paradise with streets paved with gold, and I couldn't imagine the opposite either, every single sinner in the world, millions of them, burning forever every day in a lake or a furnace so enormous it could hold them all.

The last time I was with my father, I didn't wrestle sleep away to do more than hang a lazy arm around his neck as he hugged me and kissed my cheek. Then he whispered, "See you later, Bright Eyes," and left. I didn't know that was the last time I'd see him, so I hadn't taken the chance for one last bear hug. Mama's and Daddy's voices drifted in and out as they talked outside my door before heading downstairs. It was a Wednesday night in August and supposed to be his night off.

"I don't know why they gotta call you all the time like you the only paramedic they got."

"Come on now, Dot-Baby. It's not always me, but my boy need me to cover for him. Ain't like he asks a lot."

"All somebody gotta do is give you a sad story, and while you working, they off partying. You too soft, Les."

"Now, I didn't hear no complaints a little while ago. You just focus on keeping that bed warm till I get back."

"Black man, hush." My mother actually giggled. "Get on outta here."

I knew they would kiss before my mother shooed him out and locked the door. I had dozed off with the memory of us laughing over the stuffed lamb Daddy had won her at the carnival. The thing was ridiculously big and very pink like the color of this medicine for an upset stomach, so Mama had given the stuffed animal the same name, Pepto Bismol.

Our last day together wrapped around me like the comforter I slept with during winter months. If there was a sign of what was to come, I didn't catch it.

For a long time after Daddy's death, I stayed on the lookout for catastrophic events whose sole purpose was to catch me off guard. I understood then that terrible, out-of-this world bad stuff could actually happen to me. I was sure there had been a sign I'd missed. Maybe it was Daddy coming into my room to check on me and give me that quick kiss. If I'd woken up, given him a real hug and looked into his eyes instead of lying there half-asleep and cozy, I might've seen it. But I didn't have the gift.

Mother Willis at church was eighty-something years old. She had the gift. Her bones creaked (her words) and her mind became troubled when the good Lord was letting her know it's going to be a bad winter or a summer storm or somebody she knew was secretly going through serious drama. Sister Creshia, the head deaconess, had the gift, too. Her signs were dreams. They told her if she shouldn't go out or when one of her grown kids was in harm's way before it even happened. If she dreamed about fish, then somebody was pregnant. It didn't make any sense, but next thing you knew, there'd be rumors or an announcement and Sister Creshia would be right. A baby was on the way. She and Mother Willis were about as good as detectives on the crime shows I liked watching, only instead of finger-prints, license plates, and digital surveillance, they relied on the Spirit, which I didn't have. I only had my weird dreams and a future plan to become a detective who solved crimes better than Nancy Drew did. That book series that had been a needed escape for me during the worst time in my life.

Six months after my father's death, our then next-door neighbor Mr. Carter brought a gift over. Actually, it wasn't a real gift. It was a box of old books. Mr. Carter explained to Mama he thought I could put them to use since I liked to read so much. The school library was expanding and reorganizing and so some of their older books were being donated or sent to recycling.

The books were dusty and ancient. Most had a picture on the cover of a red-headed young white woman wearing capri pants or an old-fashioned dress. The girl's reddish hair curled up into a flip at the ends like the white women in some of those black-and-white movies Nana Mae loved to watch and like the lady in *Bewitched*, another one of those old TV shows I'd watched with her and Mama before. The green-eyed girl on the book cover smiled in a way that made her look like she was up to something, which it turned out was true. The book titles all said *Nancy Drew* followed by the mystery or secret of something or the clue in someplace dark and scary. The books were numbered, but they weren't in order and most of them were missing. The highest was fifty-four. There was no number one through eighteen at all.

Over Christmas break that year, I got bored. I'd already read all the books I had checked out from the library, so I went into Mr. Carter's box. I started reading the lowest number in the box, nineteen, *The Quest of the Missing Map*, and over the next month, I read every book.

I liked that she always solved the mystery and how even though her life seemed pretty perfect, it wasn't completely. Nancy Drew's mother was dead, had died when Nancy was really young. I marveled at how it didn't seem to hang over her like a big shadow. She had her dad and the house lady and her friends. She seemed cool with it. After I read all the ones in the box, I checked out some more from the library, and Nana Mae ordered me some off the internet.

Two years, ten months, and five days after Daddy died, I was standing in front of the mirror on the beauty shop back wall, weighing something else I couldn't make happen as fast as I wanted. I hunched my shoulders back and forth, trying to see what position would make me look less like a twelve-year-old. Not a one. From the front, there was just not much to see, and from the side, I could be mistaken for a boy. Unless there was some serious super growth before summer was over, I was doomed. I would be the most flat-chested girl in high school, same as always. If I was the genie on this ancient show Mama watched sometimes on the classic TV network, I'd blink myself some boobs, perfectly balanced ones, not big but definitely not too small. But I didn't have magic either. Even if I did every "bigger boobs" exercise on the internet seven days a week, nothing was going to sprout, not in ninety days or a hundred and eighty. The *G* in my red GIRLS ROCK T-shirt reached toward the half a mini mound on the left. The end of the *K* grazed my barely AAA on the right. The mirror refused to lie no matter how hard I stared and wished.

Across from me, Mama paused and tilted Ms. Torrence's head up by the chin. "Excuse me, Ms. Nancy Drew, there's no mystery in that mirror, but I am wondering why you are not where you're supposed to be?"

I checked her reflection in the mirror. One perfect black eyebrow arched up into an upside-down U. I knew exactly what that meant. It was reserved for when she was thinking deep about something she wasn't going to talk to you about or a warning for when she was on the way to being annoyed. In this case, it was B. I glanced at the clock over the mirror. 9:05 A.M. I was late.

When I turned fourteen, I had begged Mama to finally let me babysit for extra money. Before she said yes, she'd laid down the law and she'd been laying it on me ever since.

"When somebody paying you," she had said, "you gotta be on point and on time. You need to do a good job, understand? No ifs, ands, or buts about it, understand?" She'd paused, waiting for the expected answer.

"Yes, ma'am," I had chirped on cue. Silently, I celebrated the future money I'd make outside of the little bit I received for my only other job, sweeping hair and answering phones in the beauty shop. So far watching Little Petey had been my first and only regular babysitting job, but I was slowly amassing savings in hopes of buying a phone for whenever Mama gave the okay.

I surveyed my book bag. There were Skittles for bribing Little Petey if he was having one of his trouble-minding-me times or I just needed to chill him out, strawberry Twizzlers for me, a story with plenty of pictures to read to Little Petey if I could get him to sit still long enough instead of chasing his little butt on the bike or kicking the soccer ball like the boy could do forever, and I had a book for me just in case he shocked me and got tired enough to take a nap, which was rare. If I dared to take out my book and start reading, it was like Little Petey's radar kicked in. He'd pop up, begging "Read to me please," and then I'd be imitating choo-choo train sounds or some magical animal. It was a pain in the butt, but he was a cute little boy and kind of sweet. Like when he was fresh out of the bath, smelling like Johnson and Johnson's baby lotion and coconut oil, or the time he reached out to me with one of his little hands and offered me his Elmo with the other. And yeah, I hugged Elmo because Little Petey insisted that both me and Elmo needed a hug.

It was the same way the minute I turned to one of my shows while he seemed focused on his toys. He'd have all kinds of questions, including some that definitely weren't for his teenage babysitter to answer. The last time I'd baby-sat was a prime example.

On the way to switching to something a little kid

friendly for Little Petey to watch, I'd discovered a rerun of one of my favorite crime-solving shows. The coroner was right in the middle of explaining how a victim died to one of the detectives on the case.

"Nee-ah, why people dive?"

I didn't even look away from the TV. "How they what? Dive in the water you mean?"

"No!" He'd giggled. "Why people diiive?"

"D-i-v-e?"

"Nooooo, they go away."

That was what I got for sneaking a minute to watch a show where almost every episode revolved around somebody getting murdered.

"Oh *die.*" I'd tapped the arrows on the remote, looking for *Sesame Street* or a kiddie cartoon to save me.

"Yeah, why people dive?" He was in a circle of Hot Wheel cars on the floor.

Why do people die? It was a question I wished somebody could explain. Of course, I understood that everybody did it, but how and when was the messed-up part.

"Why, Neeeah?"

"It's diiiiie, not dive," I'd stalled. "And you know, people's bodies stop working and—"

"Why?" Little Petey had looked up at me with big brown eyes and long curly eyelashes. Mama and Nana Mae were always cooing about how they were wasted on a boy. It was too bad he was so curious and cute. He never got tired of *why this* and *why that*. My question was why you asking me all these questions? But he was only five years old. I couldn't get too mad.

"I guess people's bodies just get tired." I'd cranked up the volume on the TV.

"Why they get tired?"

"I don't know. Ask your mom or your grandmother."

Then I'd sped through channels and was finally saved by Elmo. And that's why I resolved to be extra armed whenever I was babysitting and had my book bag full of an arsenal designed for maximum distraction.

"Soon as Shayla hit that door, you come on back by the house and grab those sandwiches, then straight here. You hear me?" My mother droned on, her perfect black eyebrow threatening to arch into a U position again. She held a piece of Ms. Torrence's thin purplish black hair in one hand, while the fingers on the other, the one with Daddy's ring, gripped the hot flat iron.

"Oh, okay," I answered, rushing to the door.

"Oh, *okay*?" The eyebrow arched.

"Yes, ma'am. Bye, Ms. Torrence," I quickly added, and stepped out the door before Mama could fuss, but not fast enough to totally beat Ms. Torrence's mouth.

"The bible say train 'em up in the way they should go—" The Diva's sign rattled against the glass door, drowning the sermon out.

I could walk MLK Drive from Diva's to Little Petey's

blindfolded. Dontay, one of my best friends, lived farther down past my house, and Little Petey lived with his mother, Shayla, at his grandmother's house on the corner of MLK and Ralph D. Abernathy. My other best friend, Miracle Ruth, lived on the same street a few houses from Little Petey.

When my grandparents moved there long before I was a thought, MLK Drive was named something else. That changed after one in a long line of white guys who was mayor for like twenty years got shamed in public. A local freelance newspaper reporter who had since lit out for bigger stories in Atlanta made his mark by writing a story about how Train, Indiana, was the only city in the whole country with a population of over ten thousand that did not have a street named in honor of Dr. King or any other big-time civil rights leader. The street me and Dontay lived on proved the least disruptive to change after two years debating, which couldn't be changed lest they disturb the city's history or whether to have two names on the street—one preserving the dead white guy's name already there, and an honorary one for Dr. King. It was ultimately deemed too little, too late to do the latter when the city had gotten such bad national press from one little article. Later on, the cross street that Miracle Ruth and Little Petey lived on was renamed Ralph D. Abernathy.

Halfway down the sidewalk, a deep bass and words too fast to catch vibrated in the air—rap music, or what

Nana Mae called "disturbing the peace" when it was too loud. The words under the heavy beat sounded like they came from under water, then both dropped.

POP. POP. POPPOPPOP.

I pulled up midstep and ducked down to my ankles before my brain even sent the message. My heart cartwheeled and somersaulted up high, then dropped hard into the bottom of my stomach. The only sound I could make sense of was the banging against my ribs, the same as when I ran the track full out and everything—people, noise—got suspended in time, and it was just me, the wind filling my ears, and my heart hurting my chest. *Breathe, breathe, breathe.* I tried to follow the command, but the pounding was all I could hear.

It was not a firecracker or a car backfiring. I knew this, so I was supposed to A) lie down flat on the ground or hide low behind a tree or a car, depending on the circumstance; B) run, sprint, or crawl to the nearest house or building; or C) run home or to the shop, but only if that made sense. Mama had laid it all out to me after a safety drill we'd done at school for just in case somebody lost his mind and came busting in shooting, like this white boy did last year a thousand miles away. It had been the one thing to almost make her waver on the cell phone issue and let me have one sooner than she planned.

But I couldn't do any of those things. I couldn't move. My legs were rubbery like they were burning after a hard run. They felt about ready to pop off as easily as the legs I used to twist off a Barbie doll. Had the shots come from behind or ahead of me? Was it over, or would I get shot if I moved—or if I didn't?

I blinked and zeroed in on where the white tip met at the purple canvas on my low-top Chucks. My book bag dragged the ground.

Move.

The muscles in my legs had better sense and stayed put a few seconds longer.

There was a stillness, like a tornado suddenly gone totally quiet. You hope it means that the storm fizzled out, but you know it's what the weather guy on TV calls the calm before the storm as he's happily tracking the dots on his map. The tornado has already touched down nearby and is playing hide-and-seek until it hurtles your way and it's too late to take proper cover.

The terrible squeal of tires scraping asphalt broke the pause and got me standing. Before I could take a step, wild screaming took over like somebody overacting in a horror movie. *Breathe, breathe. Now walk.* I raised one foot and hit concrete. Once I got going, I walked fast and got close enough to see just beyond the intersection at MLK and Ralph D. Abernathy. People ran toward a growing crowd by Little Petey's grandmother's house. I took off sprinting.

I pushed through bodies, no *excuse me*s until I stood

right in front of Shayla. She was screaming breaking-glass loud, on her knees bent over Little Petey, who lay face up beside her, unmoving. His short stick leg poked out of tan khaki shorts, and a small foot missing a shoe hung over the curb. Little Petey's eyes with the long lashes opened wide like he was busy taking in the whole world.

"Baby, PEEETEY," Shayla screamed again and again, tugging at his hand. Little Petey didn't move. His favorite thing, the dark blue bike, rested on one side, the front wheel jutted up in the grass, and the other wheel dipped over the curb just above his head. The fingers of his free hand reached toward the handlebar. The smallness of his hand surprised me.

"Baby, baby! No, baby. No, no . . . Peteeeey," Shayla whimpered.

Little Petey paid her no mind. Women grabbed Shayla, rubbing her back, trying to pull her up and away. She wasn't having it. She shook her head over and over and held on tight to her son's little hand. She was a part of the concrete sidewalk and kept on calling his name and wailing.

MOVE. Come on, Little Petey, I pleaded in my head. *Get up now, little boy*. But he was content to ignore my demand and lay there staring a hole through me. His deer eyes asked a question I could not answer: *Why?*

Now you get up. You hear me? You hear? This was my grown warning voice I used outside whenever he was getting too far ahead of me on his bicycle or running, while I trailed behind him trying not to look like I was chasing after a little boy I had no control of. Or when we were inside, and he veered too close to the stove where his hot dog was boiling for lunch. Really, it was my panicking voice.

Mama had drilled me so much when I started watching him. "Little children got no regard the first for danger. Half-grown ones neither, most of the time for that matter. You listening?"

"Yes, ma'am."

I was on instant autopilot, hearing enough to respond when expected while thinking about the money that would go into my cell phone fund.

"A little child will get excited seeing some blossoms growing on a tree or a butterfly. They'll take right off after it, down the street, around the corner in a store just that quick, wherever. You gotta watch 'em at all times."

"Yes, ma'am."

"While they busy looking at the flowers and checking what to get into next, you gotta have eyes on them. Understand?"

"Yes, ma'am."

Little Petey's eyes continued to stare at me while he stayed still on the ground.

I'm not playin', little boy. Right now.

I channeled all of my brain and breath right at him. *Please, God.*

All right, I'mma count to five.

He ignored my silent commands and just lay there with a dark stain spreading across his chest. A big hand, a man's, reached down and covered the top of Little Petey's face. When the hand lifted, his eyes were closed.

"My B-B-BABY . . . my baby, my . . ." Shayla whispered hoarsely, then collapsed backward into the arms and hands that had been trying to pull her away.

The splotch of dark red soaked through Little Petey's baby-blue T-shirt right where Batman dove off a skyscraper saving Gotham. My insides relaxed their long pause and a million backed-up bubbles cut loose, filling my stomach and threatening to spill out. The impatient ones popped and burst.

I backed up, bumping into a body way taller and thicker than mine, without taking my eyes off Batman drowning in the red pool on Little Petey's chest. The body I fell into tilted forward from the force of the crowd. I turned, pushed my body from head to toe against the tide, and pressed through, pushing blindly against unfamiliar hands and arms, bodies without faces.

Home. I had to get home.

On the outside edge of the crowd, I stumbled into Ms. Torrence. She grabbed at my arm. She was still wearing the black smock from the beauty shop. A limp piece of hair flopped down the middle of her forehead. The rest pointed east, west, and every which way. Her head rotated from side to side as if she was a toy with a messed up on-off switch. Her lips moved, but no words came out.

Mama ran up behind her, blinking back tears. My bag swung from one of her arms, and her other hand clutched a wide-tooth comb. I didn't remember dropping the bag at all. I dodged them and kept going. I didn't care about the sirens whirring closer. I heard Dontay yelling my name. I didn't stop.

When I was very little, I thought I might follow in my father's footsteps someday and drive an ambulance. But that was then. The last thing I wanted to do was stick around and see that stretcher coming out and the paramedics doing what they did on TV and what my father used to do in real life, breathe into the victim. There was no need. No amount of breathing was going to help Little Petey. I had witnessed his eyes staring into mine while Batman drowned in the puddle of blood.

That night after Mama sat with me and rubbed my back for some time, I fell into fitful sleep and dreamed. *I run to Daddy's red-and-white shiny ambulance. Daddy sweeps me up, his overnight whiskers tickle my cheek. I'm grinning and pointing. Daddy carries me. I'm in the ambulance laid out on a stretcher. A plastic cup* covers my nose and mouth. Daddy presses two fingers on my wrist, then clasps his big hands together. They hover high over my chest, pumping air. One, two, three. One, two, three. Daddy's lips move. He laughs, kisses my forehead. He saves me. I grin, chase him out of the ambulance, and jump on his back. I'm laughing, laughing so hard my arms fall from his neck. I slide back. My head flops upside down. His giant hands hold tight to my legs. And then we disappear. A face flickers . . . in . . . out. Snaggle-tooth smile. Little Petey. Little Petey, Licorice raindrops fall fast . . . A maroon pool spreading out, out. A black shadow runs on the edge. Black girl shadow running? Hair braids flying like tail wings, stick legs running, bare feet skipping edges of a red velvet pool. Where to? Where to?

As-salamu alaykum.

Dear Alima,

Somebody shot Little Petey, the little boy I babysit, in front of his house. I think I mentioned he was five in one of my letters. He was lying on the ground. His eyes were open, and I felt like he was looking right at me. That night, I had that dream about my father again. His face was so clear, he looked alive. Usually, I can't see him clearly; it's like when you're watching a show and the signal goes out and you get a dark blank screen or fuzz. In the dream, me and Daddy were laughing like, having a good time just like all the other times. But this time the dream changed and suddenly, Little Petey was in there. He was smiling too and me and my father disappeared. Then there was like this shadow of a girl running. Anyway, my mother just came in my room again. She keeps checking on me like I have the flu. She can't cure what's wrong, but knowing Mama, she'll try.

That means some nasty cod liver oil, so I better go for now. I hope things are better where you are.

Peace,

Nia

PS: Do Muslims believe in spirits like they do in Christianity? Is the heaven and hell in the Quran the same as in the Bible?

CHAPTER
2

Miracle Ruth went on and on, pretending it was a regular Sunday after church service, and that if she kept talking and talking, it would change something. But it wouldn't. It had been two days. Everything was the same. Little Petey was dead. Miracle Ruth was the closest thing to a sister I had, but she was working my nerves recounting who was down at Little Petey's grandmother's house the night before and that morning and who had fallen out and who was crying and anything anybody said. Ugh!

She sat there at my brown Goodwill desk playing some game on her cell with the Disney pink cover. Dontay sat knees up on the floor leaning against my bed with his purple Lakers hat hiding his face, phone in hand, and his camera slung across his shoulder as usual. I was laid out on the bed squeezing my pillow as hard as I could. My father, Little Petey, and the running girl in my weird dream flitted through my mind's eye like a digital flipbook.

"You know what everybody's saying, right? They probably won't ever get who did it." Miracle Ruth paused and dropped her head. "Vengeance is the Lord's," she said, like she was one of the first ladies at church.

Dontay moved his hat back a little. "Who's everybody?" he asked.

"You know, people, *everybody*," Miracle Ruth answered.

Probably this meant Ms. Torrence. To Miracle Ruth, everything her grandmother said was gospel. But that didn't mean what she was saying right then wasn't true. We understood it probably was.

"That ain't right," Dontay said, pulling his hat off. "Nobody ought to get away with something like this."

"Maybe the police will catch who did it. Faith is the substance of things hoped for and the evidence of things not seen." Miracle Ruth was a walking Bible, but she couldn't help it, being around Ms. Torrence all the time.

"Yeah, right." Dontay came back sounding like his dad. "The police are gonna break they necks trying to get him."

His comment reminded me of Mama's frequent complaint when we watched the evening news. "They must line 'em up to make sure they got enough mug shots for the news." The faces involving crimes were usually young and Black, and the reports were often about somebody getting shot. Little Petey was the first child I'd known up close who'd been killed and one of the youngest that I'd ever heard of. Mama and Nana Mae counted the reports about people killing or being killed every day and the Black faces in them, and determined if there was more of those or good news. The bad news outnumbered the good news about 90 percent of the time.

It was insane. How could people like my father and Little Petey get murdered for no reason? Why run around with guns hurting people that weren't bothering anybody, people they didn't know—and kids, little ones, too, like Little Petey? Nothing could stop it, not the police or the president or anybody. Nobody wanted the violence, supposedly, but it went on and on anyway.

Damn.

I wouldn't say it aloud. I didn't like the stupid boys at school who strutted around dropping the F-word in every other sentence and the equally idiot girls that had to be the center of everybody's attention at all times. The B-word stood in for *hello* with them. Dumb. But when I got to thinking about the stranger who'd taken Daddy away from us, going about every day, knowing he was the reason my father was in a box underground, bad words and evil thoughts rushed into my head and tore at me.

At church, they preached about forgiveness, how it's wrong to hate, how you gotta love everybody, even your enemies, like Jesus and Dr. King taught. But they were killed, too. My father had been trying to help someone that night. But it didn't matter. He was gone, and the killer was like this shadow haunting me, Mama, and Nana Mae. I didn't have a face or name to hate or forgive.

I pressed my face down hard into the pillow, glad Dontay and Miracle Ruth couldn't see what was in my head. The killing going on everywhere made no sense. And people did get away with it all the time like Dontay said. It was the same where Alima, my pen pal in the Middle East, lived. Once she wrote in a letter that her grandmother says, "There are children and old people, and then the many dead between them."

I couldn't stand it.

"Somebody could find out" popped out of my mouth before my brain let me know I was going to say it.

Dontay twisted around to squint at me. Miracle Ruth looked up from her pink phone.

"Find out what?" Dontay asked.

My pillow just missed Dontay's head as I scooted off the bed. My room was so small, I was standing on top of them. "Sometimes you gotta do what needs doing," I said. It was something my grandmother had said to me a thousand times, usually when I was dragging my heels about some uncompleted task.

"Who is *you*?" Dontay demanded, frowning.

"Me. You and Miracle Ruth. We could find out who killed Little Petey."

Dontay laughed like a talking animal in an animated movie. "You still reading those stupid Nancy Drew books?"

"Let her finish, Dontay," Miracle Ruth said, sliding the phone into her pink purse.

"Well, she's not talking sense." He stood to confront me, hovering above my head. "You know you're not Nancy Drew right? This isn't some made-up story, Nia. This is real."

"I know that, Dontay. I saw Little Petey die, okay?" I forced myself to meet his gaze. "What I'm sayin' is this can't just happen and then nothing. If the police and everybody else around here can't or won't do something, then why shouldn't we at least try? For Little Petey." I prayed neither one could hear my stomach gurgling up like one of those playground fountains.

"He was killed, Nia—murdered," Dontay said. His hot breath about spit in my face. "Now, I don't know by who, I don't know for what, but this is real, all right? We can't be playing detective. We just teenagers—"

"Kids our age marched, sat in, and went to jail during the Civil Rights Movement, with their parents, sometimes without them," I offered.

"True, true," Miracle Ruth answered. She stood up and made a triangle out of us. We had just come off a semester on the Civil Rights Movement, though Nana Mae had been telling me parts and buying books about it forever. "We're not really that young either," Miracle Ruth pointed out. "We'll be eighteen before you know it."

"I got like two and a half years." Dontay enjoyed

reminding us he had Miracle Ruth by a month and me by almost four.

"You mean you got like three years," Miracle Ruth shot at Dontay.

He ignored that point and went right on. "That don't change nothing. This is craaazy, all right? We can't be running around playing like we no detectives."

"'And a little child shall lead them.' Isaiah chapter eleven: verse six," Miracle Ruth quoted.

"That's what the Bible says," I said as if that decided matters.

"So how do we find out?" Miracle Ruth asked, joining with me in trying to ignore Dontay's protesting.

I've been called mature for my age when it came to my good grades and staying out of trouble at school and home, and not embarrassing Mama with my manners in public. But when words came out of my mouth that Mama deemed too grown for my own good (her words), she'd say I was getting beside myself, which was what I was feeling right then. Miracle Ruth's question slapped me right out of flow. How *would* we find out? That part I wasn't sure about.

Dontay shook his head and caught his hat as it slid off. "Whoa, you serious? We supposed to find out who shot Little Petey somehow, then what? Turn 'em in? What exactly?"

"Dontay, relax for a minute." Miracle Ruth turned to me.

I thanked her silently but couldn't find my words just yet, especially with Dontay looking at me as if I was La La, who everybody knows wasn't right in the head and who was always trailing two or three steps behind her mother, talking to herself or to birds and trees or folks nobody could see but her. "You don't want to know who? And why?" I asked Dontay.

For an answer, Dontay dropped his gaze.

"We just figure it out, okay?" I was pretty much calming myself down while I worked it out. "We keep this strictly between us. We search for clues, put 'em together, and . . . and that's the first thing."

"Kinda undercover," Miracle Ruth filled in, nodding. "Not snitches the way people think," she added quickly, noting Dontay's scowl. "We're on the right side fighting for what's righteous . . . snitchers for justice."

Okay, whatever. Miracle Ruth was down for the cause and that was what mattered. Sometimes we talked about teaming up with our careers, me the detective finding the evidence, and her the forensics scientist that would test it.

"Except this ain't no episode of *Law and Order* or *CSI*," Dontay muttered.

Okay, you going there, Dontay. He knew watching those crime shows was one of my things.

"Dontay, Little Petey was just a baby, and somebody killed him." I let this sink in. "We taught him to ride his bike. You remember that?" I could see the blue bike on the ground and Little Petey's small hand reaching for it.

Ignoring the bubbles churning up, I continued. "We figure it out. I mean, this is Little Petey. In our neighborhood. That's not okay. We agree on that, right?"

"Right," Miracle Ruth said. "I still can't believe this." Her voice caught. "You know if it happened to him, it could've been one of us."

It was a thought I kept pushing to the back of my mind. I was supposed to be with him. I really could have been the one shot and dead. Or maybe I could have helped save Little Petey. If I had been there five minutes earlier, we might've been inside and Little Petey wouldn't have been shot.

That day of the shooting after I'd run home to the bathroom, I was hunched over the toilet when Mama came looking for me. I hadn't thrown up, though my body wanted to. The sweat had stuck my T-shirt and triple-A bra to my skin, and my stomach burned all the way to the top of my rib cage. I couldn't get rid of the image of Little Petey looking at me, with blood spreading like a map across his body.

That day, Mama bent down and pulled me to her. "Baby, you all right? Lord Jesus, thank you, thank you . . ."

The truth of what she hadn't said hung there as loud

as if she had finished the words. I shivered, then went back to hot. It could've been me dead on the ground. It sure shouldn't have been Little Petey. I couldn't stop the thought on repeat in my brain: if I had been there on time, 9:00 A.M. sharp, he might still be alive.

Dontay's glare brought me back to the present, "I ain't no snitch," he said.

"We're not either, Dontay. We just trying to find out what happened."

"You want us to go around getting in people's business and tellin' on 'em. Or what would be the point, right? Sound like snitching to me." His tan face went a little red.

"Dontay," I said quietly as I could, though I was screaming in my head. "It's not snitching." Snitches were often guilty people just trying to stay out of jail themselves.

This had been made crystal clear to me one day a while back when I was definitely not trying to eavesdrop on a conversation between Dontay's big brother, Ahmad, and an old high school acquaintance of his. They were on the front porch talking while I waited for Dontay just inside the door. The friend said, "Man, they got Busy for that shooting at the park a couple of months back."

"I heard it was two or three people involved in that. They just got him?" Ahmad had asked.

"They got two so far."

"I don't know what they was thinking. Why be randomly shooting at a park? That girl got killed for nothing."

"I ain't saying they was the ones. I'm not saying they didn't. What I do know is somebody tricked on them niggas. Police got Busy and his brother. Ain't that some shit?" the guy went on.

"Man, it's kids here and Pops hear you, he's coming out here—" Ahmad complained.

"My bad, it slipped out. I'mma keep it PG. They snitched, so the police got Busy."

From my vantage point, I couldn't see their faces, but I pictured Ahmad with that serious look he had when he was rapping or talking about politics with his dad. "Those people ain't no snitches," Ahmad argued. "See, people don't understand that. A snitch guilty just like the person he's telling on, but he's sharing information, maybe even lying to the police to save his own neck. Now *that's* a snitch. Those people you talking about *eyewitnesses*."

Thinking back on that conversation, I tried to break it down to Dontay now. "Snitching is like when you part of the crime, and you tell to cut a deal for yourself. That's not what this is."

"Don't matter what you call it. It's trouble either way you go," he said.

Of course, he was right. People didn't tell, and most agreed you shouldn't. We remembered the last time there was talk of somebody snitching. One got murdered in prison and nobody knew for sure where the other guy was, but everybody assumed dead. Eyewitnesses who were innocent, well, they faced the same kind of danger.

Maybe I was asking my friends for something that was just too big. In which case, I was on my own because I didn't think it would ever let me go unless maybe I did this. Little Petey came to my mind in perfect color. I saw him squeezing my neck too hard while I breathed in that sour-milk smell of his after he'd run around outside in the heat or the peanut butter he loved to eat so much with strawberry jelly.

I wanted to tell Dontay and Miracle Ruth how I hadn't gotten there on time, how Little Petey's eyes had looked into mine, asking that unanswered question, but I couldn't.

"I have to try, at least" was all I managed to say. Nobody said a word.

Miracle Ruth broke the silence. "Maybe we can get some justice for Little Petey. And if we figure it out, we can stop somebody else innocent from getting killed."

Her words made me think of my father instantly.

"The Bible says," Miracle Ruth continued, reciting like it was a Sunday school lesson she had practiced and committed to memory, "an eye for an eye." Since she shut up and left it right there, it was perfect.

Wa alaykum as—salam.

Dear Nia, my friend,

I love that your name means purpose.

My grandmother Fatima gave my mother a book of poetry. She would read the poetry to my brother, sister and me. This is how I came to know Mahmoud Darwish.

One day, in the many long days after my mother and sister were killed, I was crying and my grandmother came to me. She gave me the book of poems she'd once given to my mother.

When Mahmoud Darwish was a boy, younger than you and I, his village was destroyed and his family was forced to escape. He still believed, "On this earth is something worth living for."

Despite all that has happened, despite the settlements and checkpoints, and so many lost, this is true. You agree?

Alima

عَالِمَة

CHAPTER

3

The week following Little Petey's death, I mostly stayed in my room. Sometimes I listened to music with my headphones on. When I wasn't, I sat in my father's favorite chair downstairs in the living room, a book I'd already read in hand. But an hour at a time would go by without me noticing or turning a page. I tried to push back moments with Little Petey that I hadn't realized were recorded in my memory. They came like unexpected rainstorms, pouring over me and flooding everything else out. Then I forced myself to think of other things like my pen pal Alima, whose letters I would reread. Alima lived in Al-Khader, which was close to Bethlehem where Jesus was born. I reread some of her letters and wrote mental ones back.

In the first quarter of eighth grade, our social studies teacher, Ms. Lexie, came up with what she called her grand project. We would communicate with teenagers who lived in the Middle East the old-fashioned way. She wanted to get us offline, exposed to more cultures outside our own, and writing more than texts and emails. Ms. Lexie used to teach somewhere not far from Al-Khader so she teamed up with a teacher friend of hers there. She said it was a shame people didn't write letters anymore. It was a forgotten art form, she said, which was partly why so many of us had such bad writing skills. So, she resurrected an ancient pen pal assignment, which everybody pretty much thought of as a punishment except for me.

I liked to write and had notebooks from way back to when I first was learning to write sentences in kindergarten to prove it. I wrote in my diary faithfully until Daddy died. Ms. Lexie told us the point was to get us writing practice and more connected with people from out of our own orbit. Our pen pals did not get to live online like we could. Alima and I went on writing to each other even though the school year ended and we didn't have to anymore.

I hadn't gotten a letter back since I'd sent my last two. But I kept her letters and especially liked the couple with the poems. That was something that made us friends. We both liked poetry. I taught her Langston Hughes. My father used to read his poems to me. I sent Alima "I, Too," his favorite. She really liked it. She sent me poems by this

Palestinian poet her mother loved. *I like to be loved as I am / not as a color photo / in the paper, or as an idea / composed in a poem amid the stags.*

I didn't know what stags meant at all and I looked it up online. It still didn't make much sense to me, but when I woke up shaking, thinking about Little Petey, it was one of the things that crowded into my mind. I needed some direction for beginning the search for Little Petey's killer and I couldn't even go anywhere.

Whenever I walked to Miracle Ruth's again, there would be no escaping what had happened. It would not be like the hundred times before, including a couple days before the morning of the shooting.

Little Petey was looking out the window, nose pressed against the screen. I was across the street walking to Miracle Ruth's.

"NEEAH. Hi. Hi, NEEAH," I heard him call.

He was so excited, jumping up and down like a brown bobblehead. There was no ignoring him, so I crossed the street just as his grandmother opened the door for him. Little Petey ran out and hugged me around the waist, looking up at me with a baby-tooth gap grin.

"Hi, NEEAH." He pulled my hand and tried to drag me into the house. I had to promise I'd come by and see him the next day, but I forgot.

There'd been other times when he'd been the one coming or going with Shayla or his grandmother and called to me as I went pass his house.

"HI, NEE-EE-AH. HI. HI . . ." He continued to chant even after I'd waved for like five minutes.

"That's enough, baby," his grandmother tried to intervene.

But it didn't matter to Little Petey. *NEE-EE-AH* followed me down the street every time.

That was never going to happen again either. My stomach bubbled at the thought.

The only thing I could do for Little Petey was to try and find out why he was gone. After a little more debate—from Dontay mostly—we decided to put the search in motion after the funeral. I stayed in my room, avoiding funeral talk and the fact that there was no way I could go. I lay in bed instead, studying the shifting shadows on the ceiling that snuck in as the sun went down.

Like clockwork, Mama tapped on the bedroom door before she went to Diva's in the mornings and first thing when she got back. It was pretty much the same back and forth.

"You okay, baby? How you feeling?" Mama asked, searching my face.

"Fine."

"You sure?" she persisted. Her left eyebrow hiked up and a crease upset the smooth plane of her forehead.

"I'm okay."

What was I supposed to say? Crappy. Sick to my stomach. Scared, pissed off (the latter of which could earn me the threat of a whipping any other time). The truth: guilty. There, that was most of it right there, but of course, I wasn't going to say that either.

The whole week was really the slow march to Little Petey's funeral. I overheard Mama on the phone with Mrs. Torrence when I crept down the stairs, catlike, for a snack.

"She don't have to go," Mama said. It was Wednesday. The funeral was to be that Saturday afternoon. "If she want to then fine, but I'm not making her."

"I been to enough funerals for ten people," Mama revealed once. It was at Diva's and the talk was about who had died and who was on the way. I was supposedly lost in my hair sweeping duty.

Mama wasn't one to talk much about Flint and Battle Creek, Michigan, where she grew up, only that people were always dying way too soon, mostly from getting shot.

"You know, it was so bad, summer I turned fifteen— never will forget it, seventeen people I knew got killed."

"Ooowee, you lying," Ms. Torrence said.

"No, ma'am, sure wish I was. Wasn't no family

reunions or high school ones. We had funerals. That was where family and everybody got together." Mama laughed. There was no smile in it. "Seem like that was every day." That was why she moved away from Battle Creek after her mother died of cancer. She couldn't stand it.

"Lord, Lord, Lord. That's just a disgrace. I know the Bible say it's a time for everything but look like it ain't never a time for no killing," Ms. Torrence grunted.

My mother can be a little scary. Not like child-abuse scary, just serious. I learned this early on. She does not play when it comes to doing right. But at the same time, she makes me feel safe, too. You don't mess with Mama. After Daddy was killed, I couldn't sleep in the room by myself. For two months, I slept right in the bed with Mama. That was the only time I wouldn't wake up crying or screaming.

When she finally decided it was time I went back to sleeping in my room, Mama stayed in there with me, at first right in my bed and then after a time, she'd sit there by my bed until I was asleep. I'd wake up sometimes, dreaming, about to freak out, and feel her hand rub my back or her fingers gently brushing my cheek or forehead. She turned my sweaty pillow over and straightened the sheets.

She did it again the night Little Petey died, and her hands and whispers calmed me. She came into check on me every night after, sitting awhile. I was never asleep, but I lay there still faking it, so she would think I was getting good rest and feel okay about going on to bed.

It occurred to me that my mother was afraid Little Petey's funeral would take me back to the day we buried my father. Truth was, I didn't remember much except waves crashing against one another in my stomach and this feeling of not being able to swallow, like rocks were stuck in my throat. Other than that, memories were flashes— Mama's black hat falling off her head. Nana Mae leaning on Mama, crying with no sound. People singing and saying stuff I couldn't make out. The preacher reciting "Ashes to ashes, dust to dust . . ." and my old school friend Fernando whom I hadn't since he'd left in the third grade pressing a folded paper into my hand outside the church before we got into the limo. And the cemetery, the worst part. Somebody handed me a red rose. I didn't want to, but I copied Nana Mae and put it on top of the white casket. We left Daddy waiting to go in the ground and be buried by all the neatly gathered dirt circled around him.

I kept looking back, and before we made it back to the car, I pulled away from Nana Mae's and Mama's hands. I did not want Daddy going down into that ground where I really would never see him again. Hands pushed me into the limo. The paper Fernando pressed into my hand lay on the seat beside me. I picked it up and unfolded it while my eyes searched out the window for the square green canopy standing over the box with my father in it. Mama and Nana Mae got in. The car pulled off. I looked down at the paper. I couldn't make out what was there at first. I blinked through wet eyes and saw my father's face there in pencil, eyes smiling, mouth laughing. He looked alive, unlike the stiff-faced photo of him in uniform the TV news kept showing in the days right after he'd been killed.

That was all. I don't remember anything else.

The local TV news stations were covering Little Petey's murder, showing a picture of him like they had with my father after he was killed. That was another reason to hide in my room instead of hanging downstairs watching TV. I listened to the same song several times in a row every day. I don't know why I was so drawn to it since the promise repeated in it over and over wasn't true. *This too shall pass.*

It was an old gospel song my grandfather loved. When I was little, he would play it on his ancient stereo every Sunday when Mama, Daddy, and me came over for dinner. I didn't remember much else about my grandfather except what my father and Nana Mae used to share, but I remembered the song, and for some reason the special way he picked me up on my own. My grandfather was very tall and slender but really strong. He'd swing me up just over his pointy elbows and hold me above his head by the arms, my legs curled above him for a beat. It kind of hurt my arms where his fingers squeezed, holding on to me so tight, but I never cried or demanded he put me down. I liked being up high, able to see over everybody's head. After what seemed like forever, I'd uncurl my feet and stand on his shoulders and wait for the best part, the mini roller coaster ride, flipping over and down, safe within his claw grip to my wobbly feet, where'd he'd let go and then laugh very loud. Everybody laughed. Daddy and Nana Mae, then Mama, finally, after shaking her head and her eyebrow easing out of the U.

I wasn't more than maybe four years old when we used to go over Sundays and my grandfather played that gospel song with the line that repeated throughout, alternating the verbs. *This too will pass.* Mama and Nana Mae can't believe I remember that since he died before I turned five, though he wasn't even old. The voice singing the song was rough, almost hoarse, like he was wrung out after having sung so long and hard without relief. He could only lay low out in the wilderness and trust God's ear. Then he'd surprise me, grunting and chanting up out of the deep into a call that demanded response. Soon as the choir answered him, he'd test them like an acrobat dropping into a whisper, then just above into the sweet chant again, then returning once again to the rough wilderness. *This too will pass. This too will pass.* The woeful words pulled at my insides.

When I was little listening to it, I wanted to crawl into Mama's lap and be cradled against her while she stroked my face or patted my back. Sometimes I did it, too. When my grandfather passed, Nana Mae had the choir sing the song at his funeral. I didn't remember any of that either, but Mama requested that the same song be one of the ones sang at Daddy's homegoing. I can't say who sang it.

My father dying, being murdered, would never pass. For the first year, every day, every single time, I thought about it, my throat clogged up like the swallowing-rocks feeling all over again. I didn't think it would ever change. Then one day that feeling stopped, but not the stab of pain in my chest when I thought of him dying and missed him. That never *all* went away.

Back then, I didn't even know the rest of the words to the song or that the guy singing was James Cleveland, who'd been a famous preacher and gospel singer from Chicago, until recently when I'd researched it online after the choir sang the song during a Sunday church service. I downloaded the song onto my MP3 player at the same time and hadn't listened to it more than once since until Little Petey was killed and there was no getting over it or how I'd been late that morning, and how maybe he wouldn't be dead if I had been.

The song matched my mood. Though it seemed to promise the bad things would pass, if pain was a sound, it was that song. I didn't want to face anybody and didn't feel like I could go to that funeral.

Hiding in my room as much as I could didn't save me

from Nana Mae. She and I were so close, talking wasn't always required when she wanted to get a point across. I wasn't used to hiding out from her. That wasn't our thing. Her eyes across the dinner table worked on me and she'd say things like, "Sometimes we do what we got to do not what we want to," so there was never really any chance of escape.

It took me until the Wednesday night before the funeral to tell Mama that I was going. Nana Mae didn't say a word, just nodded at the confirmation. Mama informed Miracle Ruth's grandmother Ms. Torrence the next morning, and that was the wrong thing to do. She had me committed to being a part of the funeral along with Miracle Ruth five minutes after talking to Mama. She said Shayla and her grandmother especially wanted me.

How was I to say no if Shayla wanted me? I didn't know why she would. I couldn't believe she didn't think of Little Petey outside the house that morning on his bike, waiting on me.

CHAPTER

4

Little Petey's wake was Friday, the night before the afternoon of his funeral. Nana Mae went with Ms. Torrence while Mama and I stayed home. I'd already seen Little Petey dead and was glad Mama and I were on the same page about not needing to attend the wake. The name *wake* didn't even make sense. The person was gone. Waking up was the last thing that was going to happen. Nana Mae had explained, saying something about people watching and bearing witness over their loved one. But what was the point? You were in a room with somebody dead, somebody close to you even, hanging out for hours with a bunch of people coming to look at the person's body lying unaware in a box, some of them freaking out when they saw the person really was dead. A wake was creepy and sad.

I had not attended my father's almost three years ago. Instead, I'd visited him the day before his wake when I announced to Mana and Nana Mae that I wanted to see him.

Mama and Nana Mae were in motion 24-7, coming and going to the funeral home, on the phone planning, or huddled at the table writing the obituary. I mostly stayed quiet up in my room. Mama and Nana Mae whispered about me being in some kind shock as they watched over me. At some point, it hit me how much I wanted to see Daddy, and not with a bunch of people staring at him and me, so I went to Mama and Nana Mae and made the demand. They had a last appointment with the funeral director before the next day's wake.

"I want to see him."

They looked up from the kitchen table where they sat working on more plans for Daddy's funeral service, which would follow the day after the wake.

"What, baby?" Nana Mae asked, looking at me over glasses perched on the tip of her nose. Her eyes were darker than usual and red at the bottoms.

Mama's face went blank at first, then her forehead crinkled up.

"I want to see him. I want to see my daddy."

Mama held out her arm. I came and took her hand, standing right between them. Nana Mae rubbed my back.

"Baby, your father—" Her voice dropped.

"I know. He's not alive. I want to see him."

"Okay." Mama nodded.

When we got to the funeral home, the funeral director left us in a small open room with the casket where Daddy lay with the top open.

"Nia," Mama said. "You don't have to, baby. It's okay."

We stood by the door just feet away from the coffin. My feet stuck to the carpet. But I wanted to see him so badly. I ignored the bubbles in my stomach and took a baby step forward.

"You want me to go with you?" Mama asked. The tears in her light brown eyes made them glisten more than usual.

Nana Mae wrapped her arm around my shoulders.

"No," I answered, and eased out of Nana Mae's arms.

At first glance, Daddy could have been sleeping. I'd had this stupid thought that he might wake and say, "Hey, Bright Eyes." The whole thing about him being shot and dead would turn out to be a horrible lie. But he didn't wake up. I crept closer. My body grazed the pearl-white coffin. He did not look like himself exactly, but the resemblance said it really was my father.

He was in a dark blue suit I'd never seen. The chocolate brown of his skin drowned in a fading powdery tan. His face looked plastic. The stiff hands alongside his body did, too. The only thing shining was his silver wedding band. There was no sign of my father, just a dummy kind of lookalike in his place. *My father is a sleeping mannequin.*

"Daddy," I whispered, and then all-out bawled until snot ran out my nose. I couldn't stop. Maybe I was loud. I don't remember. Mama picked me up like only Daddy had, despite my legs being too long, and rushed me right out of there.

I shook the devastating memory off. Now there was another death to deal with, and there was no escaping Little Petey's funeral the day after the wake, the seventh day after he'd been killed outside his grandmother's house. Outside the church, sweat zigzagged down my neck, disappearing down the center of my tiny bra. My stomach couldn't make up its mind what to do and so it took turns spinning, twisting, and gurgling. It was a good thing I had refused the toast and eggs Mama tried to get me to eat.

Adults in bright white and nondescript black wore sunglasses. They were hiding from the sun and one another's red eyes. I tried to concentrate on how many people I recognized to distract myself from sweating and from something sharp on the collar of my new white dress that kept pricking me in the neck. I couldn't reach up because of the white gloves we were forced to wear and the bouquet of white flowers Ms. Torrence had given me, Miracle Ruth, and the other four flower girls to hold. She had drilled us a hundred times on how to walk once we got into the church, and how to hold the flowers cradled in both arms, and where to stand, which coincided with the direct path of the sun. It beat down on us as we stood there concentrating on not violating Ms. Torrence's directions. Stupid. Flower girls for a funeral. But that's what Ms. Torrence said Shayla and her grandma wanted . . . though I suspected it had been Ms. Torrence's idea.

Ten minutes past the start time, we were cooking in the sun. I didn't mind. It was better than being in the church. An usher brought us little paper cups of cold water. We shifted our flowers and gulped the water down quickly so the usher could immediately take the cups as we waited for our cue to go in. One of the church ushers had shared that the car bringing the guest preacher had pulled up to its appointed parking place in the back of the church late and that then the guest preacher and the pastor of the church retreated to his office for some preservice meeting and prayer.

The funeral staff and a few church members milling around us made half-jokes, but they weren't fooling any-body. Nobody was smiling. There was nothing that wasn't sad about a funeral for a five-year-old.

"Umph, some folks don't know how to start nothing on time. They just slow."

"They ain't slow, just too big to be on time. Gotta make an entrance and be seen is all."

"Count on it. They gon' be late to their own funeral."

"It's a sin before the Lord. Always on CP time, don't matter what for."

The top of my head felt hotter. The trickle of sweat made its way down my belly to the top of the itchy white pantyhose we were forced to wear. I hadn't been in them five minutes when a snag split high up on one thigh. I shifted my weight onto the left leg, then to the right one, and got pricked in the neck as a reward. My feet hurt. I should've walked around in the house and broken in the white sandals—with a real heel for once. They were cute. Perfect, had they been for some other event. The left sandal already bore a black scrape across the toe.

I looked to the side and behind me. Miracle Ruth stood calmly at the end of the line, the fifth flower girl. On her, the white dress looked made with her in mind. She could've been a young bridesmaid posing in a wedding magazine. Nothing looked uneven on top or too flat or too big either. She looked grown-up yet sweet, with her sandy hair gathered into a curly ponytail (with a pink scrunchie of course). I was sure if I examined her shoes, they'd looked fresh out of the store and not one speck of dirt anywhere except the bottom soles. I prayed my own pantyhose tear wouldn't stretch below the hemline.

We got our cue from the solemn funeral home direc-tor. It was time to head down the center aisle, between the rows of staring people, and lay flowers on the coffin where

Little Petey would be forever. I wanted to stay outside melting under the sun, watching the people going in. Dontay came with the last line of mourners filing past us to go into the church. He was sandwiched between his dad and his brother, Ahmad, who wore dark sunglasses. All three had on gray-striped ties and black suits. Dontay's jacket hung too far below his wrist in preparation for him to grow into it and wear to more funerals. We were only an arm's length apart, but I was confined to my position with my fellow flower girls. Dontay and I glanced at each other and dropped our eyes at the same time. He disappeared through the doors, hands crossed in front, head down, like his brother and father. Then it was my turn.

Before she'd gone inside to sit down with Mama and Nana Mae, Ms. Torrence prepped and fussed over us one last time. "Keep your eyes on the good Lord," Ms. Torrence advised us.

It was another one of those things that adults liked to say when things didn't make any sense and they didn't really know what to say but saying nothing wasn't an option. I didn't quite believe the Lord was really close by at all times like people said or that he was with Little Petey in the casket at the front of the church. He had not been with him last Friday morning when he needed saving.

"Just remember to breathe so you don't pass out," Nana Mae added.

Mama nodded in agreement. "You doing okay?" she

directed to me. I knew I had only to say no or nothing at all and she would snatch me right out of the flower girl line and probably away from the funeral.

"Yes, ma'am." I nodded back. This was about Little Petey.

I was the third flower girl in line. Someone inside the sanctuary was really showing out, hollering and crying, drowning the hum of voices drifting out the double doors, which were propped open. Greater Grace was the biggest Black church in town. I'd been inside a couple of times with Nana Mae, once on a New Year's Eve and the other time to a church anniversary service. I could see down the aisle to the casket and the easel off to the right side of it with a poster-size picture of Little Petey.

I felt a cold flush on my forehead and my stomach gurgled some more. At first, the burgundy carpeted aisle seemed to stretch on without end. The girl in front of me shifted, blocking my view. My forehead flushed thinking about that poster. A slow gurgle in my stomach chimed right in on cue.

I resolved to keep my eyes fixed on the white heels in front of me. I copied their smooth side-to-side stepping as the choir hummed then sang the Lord's Prayer. The crying swept from one side of the sanctuary to the other in no time as if the sight of us girls in matching white dresses carrying matching flowers unleashed something.

The howler was down front. For a minute, she made

me forget to keep my eyes parked on the white heels ahead of me. She sounded like a wolf under a lonely moon. At first, the choir competed with her, singing to drown her out, but then they got together, the choir settling for answering her call. The howl alternated with a screech every few seconds. The choir went soprano high right along with it. Finally, she flopped backward into some kind of a fit, shaking and moaning. A white handkerchief floated out of her hand and landed in the center aisle right where the heels in front of me were stepping. Hats and black dresses shot up, and the quickest nabbed the handkerchief. The lady sitting in the pew right behind the woman hugged her arms around the weeping woman's neck. A church deaconess in a bleached-white nursing outfit took up position in front of her and started waving a paper fan to cool her off. I directed my eyes back to the white heels leading me to the head of the sanctuary.

Too soon, the girl in front of me placed her burden of flowers on top of the casket and swayed off fast to the left. My eyes traveled up from the metal legs of the casket to the top. Everything became a noisy fan in the background. The gray box shone so it was the silver of a brand-new coin. It was surprisingly small up close, too small, I worried, to hold Little Petey comfortably. But he was in there.

He didn't care for the dark. He slept with an Elmo night-light on. Little Petey gazed out from the easel. He wore his pin-striped blue-and-white linen suit with a little white bow tie. It was from the studio pictures Shayla set up for his fifth birthday in April. He grinned, showing a tiny gap from a bottom baby tooth he'd lost a little early. He was so happy because of his party later that afternoon, and that five meant going to kindergarten where his big cousins went, at my old elementary school.

Arms out. A layer of the white flowers almost covered the top. *Flowers down.* I placed them in the center, stepped back, and turned sideways. When I passed by, I could've touched the wailing woman, who had settled down to whimpering. I finally saw it was Little Petey's great-grandmother, the one he called Grandma. A church deaconess rubbed her back from the pew behind. A light-skinned lady in a huge wide-brimmed black hat sat next to her, holding his grandmother's hand. I recognized her from pictures in the grandmother's house—Shayla's mama, who lived somewhere in California. I didn't know what Little Petey called his biological grandmother. I slowed my steps and resisted the urge to zoom to our assigned pew off to the right of the center.

Shayla sat zombie-still on the other side of her mother, staring out of empty eyes. Like Little Petey on the ground that day. Little Petey's dad, Big Pete, sat next to her wearing pitch-black sunglasses with a single big diamond glistening on each side. Big Pete was over six feet tall, but that's not why he was Big Pete in the street. He was the kind that Mama and the church people did not like having around.

Big Pete's huge arm hung like a heavy crowbar halfway around Shayla's shoulders. She tilted forward slightly, leaning away from him. Her trademark fake eyelashes were gone. There was no heavy makeup that changed her skin from yellow to a cakey beige. I noticed freckles I'd never seen dusting her nose and cheeks. Her blonde weave with the streaks of brown and black was pulled back into a tight ponytail. She looked like a girl my age—but then, twenty-one really wasn't that much older.

All of it was terrible. Shayla paralyzed, the ladies in stark white, the men in their gray and black, the pulpit with the men sitting in high-backed chairs and long robes, and the choir in the background, a single mass clothed in black, murmuring in unison below the mural covering the back wall. A chocolate-brown Jesus with black locks flowing out on either side of his long face was rising above the world, head bowed in prayer over his clasped hands. Jesus was weeping. A splash of teardrops spilled onto his cheeks under each brown eye. Scattered faces, Native American, Black, and Asian spread out below his hands.

I made it to our designated bench without passing out and slid into my seat. The flower girl behind me was right on my heels, then Miracle Ruth lay hers on top of the pile on the casket and marched away, still in time to the music.

"No, he didn't."

"Uh-uh, no."

A figure strutted up the center aisle, his bald head

cocked slightly to one side in dark glasses and black clothes save for a humongous gold chain circling his thick neck. His sheer black T-shirt flashed a muscular chest, bulging out through the open suit jacket. His pants tapered off into black leather Air Jordans. He was nothing but action-movie-hero swagger, ignoring the building murmurs as he moved closer to the front. Some kind of tattoo, orange flames it looked like, snaked out from under the black T-shirt up the side of his neck.

Out of nowhere, deacons swooped forward from both sides of the pulpit and caught him right before he was up to the second center row. Then Big Pete was up on his feet, big body turning super-fast, abandoning Shayla. Two other men, one tall and muscled like Big Pete, rushed over, putting their bodies in front of Big Pete, talking to him while they backed the newcomer down the aisle from the direction he'd come. He threw his arms up goalpost style and grinned, mouthing something at the men. A policeman in uniform waited on him at the end of the aisle. The man walked right past him and slapped the double doors open with both hands.

Everybody twisted around, breaking their necks to see. Except Shayla. She sat there unmoving during the whole thing. I scooted over a space as the fourth flower girl and Miracle Ruth took their seats. A thought briefly distracted me from the fact of the funeral and the itchy collar. *Maybe the one we were set on finding had just found us.*

Miracle Ruth read my mind. She squinted at me. Her mouth opened slightly into a knowing O, code for *uh-huh*. I committed the funeral crasher in black to memory. I glanced at Shayla. Big Pete whispered something in her ear. She never moved or spoke that I could see.

I looked back at Miracle Ruth. She had her little pink Bible on her lap and her lips were moving. She was saying scriptures, I knew. Several of the flower girls sniffled, and the one in front of me started crying softly. An usher brought us travel-size Kleenex packs. I wanted to cry, but my eyes were glued dry. What was wrong with me? My stomach quivered in answer. A lady fainted. The deacons sprang into action, turning her body into an X with a deacon for each leg and arm as they carried her out quickly.

The preacher stepped to the podium and took off his dark glasses. He was a self-appointed community rep from right outside of Chicago. In the week since the shooting, he'd been on television talking for the family about Little Petey and blasting the police and the violence going on. The center of his forehead shone like a glob of Vaseline. His hair was wild. It stood straight up into a gray-and-white flaming tower on top of his head. He wore a black preacher's robe; a fancier version of the black robes the choir members behind him had on. Soon as Mama and Nana Mae had seen him on the news, they nicknamed him the Reverend Don King after some old guy I'd never heard of. Apparently, that guy used to be famous for something to do with boxing. They showed me a video of a thick man with his hair standing up like gray flames. The preacher did seem like maybe he was copying the look.

The Reverend Don King took the time to wipe his tinted glasses slowly with a white handkerchief, then he swept it across his glistening forehead. Still, he didn't speak. He put the dark glasses back on. It was a wonder he could see out of them. The hum and rustling rose again. But he just rested there, frowning out at us like he was trying to figure out a crossword puzzle.

"You know, folks love to take out little teasers from the scriptures. They got favorites like, 'The Lord giveth and the Lord taketh away,'" he began as if he was having a casual chat with one person and the rest of us were eavesdropping.

The hum and rustle paused.

"Somebody sitting in here right now said so when they heard this young boy had been struck down before he had hardly begun his life. But I'm here to tell you, the Lord didn't take this child."

He thumped his fist right on the gigantic black Bible on the podium.

"Did anybody hear me now? I say the Lord ain't took nothing. But somebody did. That somebody who pulled the trigger took him. But you know who else guilty? You." He pointed a fat finger with a thick gold ring at us. "And me." He struck himself right in the chest with the same finger.

The hum and rustle resumed. I sneak-peeked at the faces in the packed middle aisle. Some looked like they wanted to run out of there as badly as I did. Others were defiant and rolled their eyes like *not me*. But more people nodded and waved him on.

"Tell the truth, Preacher."

"Preach."

"Uh-huh, yes, sir, yes, sir."

The Reverend Don King moved from behind the podium with the mike in one hand and his white handkerchief in the other. The three pulpit steps creaked in complaint. Out from behind the podium, he was huge. He stopped where the family sat on the first bench in the center, right in front of Big Pete and Shayla. The hum and rustle quieted again.

"Our children don't value life. Don't even care about they own lives. How it get that way? We done got so corrupt and bankrupt in our souls, we raising children who don't know they got a soul. Uh-huh. Say they ain't got jobs, the school system broke, they don't got no hope so the street get him, uh-huh."

Shayla tilted a bit toward the preacher, transfixed, clutching Kleenex. Reverend Don King moved in front of the casket, blocking it from view, but not Little Petey grinning out at us from the poster-size picture. The preacher waved his handkerchief at us. The greasy sweat on his forehead shone brighter as he preached in a sing song voice.

"But I remember a tiiiiiiime, I say, I remember the time, we didn't have no jobs, we worked sunup and sundown but didn't get no pay. A mama couldn't read a bedtime story to her child. Papa couldn't even read a word in the Bible to the family. They catch you with a book or trying to learn one little word, they might beat you or cut your hands off. I remember the tiiiiiime, we couldn't even name ourselves, couldn't even count on raising our own children."

The deaconess in scrubs, standing by in case someone fainted or needed more fanning, turned on like a battery-operated doll. I'd seen people at church get happy in the Lord all my life, dancing in place and waving their arms in the air, but it was strange that it was going on at Little Petey's funeral as if it was a regular Sunday church service. Reverend Don King rested a big hand on one hip as if the preaching brought on pain and waved the white handkerchief in the other. He stooped at the waist, back stiff as if a lash was about to whip down, then straightened suddenly and tiptoed down the aisle, turned abruptly, and high-stepped to the front of the coffin. Normally, this would have been entertaining. Soon as the spirit got somebody whipped up and showing out like the Reverend Don King was, Dontay and I would get to winking at each other and holding in laughter, with Miracle Ruth trying hard to stay serious and faltering with a reluctant smile or giggle.

Reverend Don King was hyped and went on preaching. "We lived day in and day out with the lash at our backs, uh-huh . . . but in the meantime, we kept on praying, kept right on believing, and kept on hoping . . . I said, in the meantiiiiiime, we kept right on sooooomehow . . . loving each other and trying to live. In the meantiiiime, we went right on trusting the Lord . . . we come out of hell right on into Jim Crow, uh-huh. And still, we kept on trying to live, and stiiiiill . . ."

The preacher's voice grew raspy. He lifted his heavy arm and brought it down on the coffin and wiped at the river of dripping sweat with the handkerchief. "We raised some life-loving children. Children who hoped, who dreamed, who marched us to some better times . . . They say things is worse now, children got so much mess around 'em, guns and drugs on every corner, and the video games, the TV and the internet doing the raising instead of Mama and Daddy, uh-huh, but I do believe, I want you to hear me now . . . I do believe, uh-huh, we done forgot some things. Ain't never been no time, since the first African was kidnapped and brought to this place, ain't never been *no time*—in case you don't know—between the lash and the lynch rope, the Black man and woman, and the little Black boy and girl, *ain't* lived in violent times. Still we kept goin' and loved one another, stilllll we hung on. Is there a witness in here today? Anybody in here know how we fought for life, how we wanted our babies to live and discover a better way?"

His questions hit me hard right then, and that old

gospel song line popped into my mind again. *This too shall pass.* The Reverend Don King wasn't through with us yet, though I wished he was. He turned his back to us and crumpled to his knees slightly, leaning toward the casket. He looked like a huge fallen bear. The church blew up like firecrackers. A sea of black hats rocked together from side to side, and white-gloved hands waved. Others sent up fist-pump praises to the ceiling. The deacons hopscotched in place, and the choir stood and took turns humming and singing "Jesus" over and over in unison. I really wanted to cry again. Somebody's shouting sounded like gibberish to me, but at church they called it speaking in tongues. I translated this to mean it was a language no one but I guess God understood. Another deaconess caught the spirit and swayed past the flower-girl pew and back down the center aisle, hands on her hips, head thrown back, shouting the whole time.

"My Lord, my Lord!" another woman chanted.

My belly churned and twisted into knots. I closed my eyes and concentrated. *Breathe, breathe.*

I was living the fourth worst day of my life. The first was the day I found out my father was gone forever. The second was the day at the cemetery when we left Daddy waiting to be covered by dirt. The third was the day Little Petey died, when I stood over him, his eyes boring into mine as he lay there dead on the sidewalk.

The preaching was finally done. It was time for the

burying, a too-sorry end for Little Petey. He deserved to be alive. Instead he was smiling from his five-year-old birth-day photo and trapped lifeless inside a gray box.

My stomach lurched.

Mama took me home after the funeral. No cemetery for us. "That's enough for you and me today," she said.

I was thankful. I did not want to see the tiny box with the mound of dirt beside it and hear the preacher, his voice like the slow heavy bell on top of the church: *Ashes to ashes and dust to dust, we commit his soul.* I just wanted to find out why we had come to burying him.

As-salamu alaykum.

Dear Alima,

It's really interesting that you live close to Bethlehem. That is a place I've heard about my whole life. Ms Lexie made us research our pen pal's country, where it is on the map, holidays, agriculture, languages, weather information like that. Al-Khader (الخضر) is a very small town as far as population, but the land seems vast. Train is considered small as far as cities go, too (population 50,000).

Thank you for giving me the picture of the olive trees. Nana Mae and my mother cook with olive oil and it's like a sacred oil at church. After the preacher is done with his sermon on Sundays, he does an altar call. People go up and stand in line until it's their turn, and the preacher does a special prayer for them. Sometimes people whisper their issue in his ear. The pastor takes a dab of olive oil, lays the oil on each person's forehead, then prays with his hand still there until he finishes. Sounds strange to me describing it in writing.

I've only been in that line once, after my father died, and the pastor wanted to pray for me, Mama, and my grandmother. There was a clump of oil on my forehead afterward. I could feel it and wanted to wipe it, but couldn't with everyone looking at us.

Favorite memory? I have too many I think, but there are some that came to me first. My father reciting his favorite Langston Hughes poetry to Mama and me when the electricity went out during a storm one time. We snuggled up together in candlelight while he made us laugh at how he said the poems. Another one is all the times we moon watched. I haven't thought about this in a super long time. If there was an awesome moon at night, one of those big yellow ones that looks like it's so low you could touch it, or a perfect crescent moon, or a rare blue or red moon, my father would wake me up so I wouldn't miss it or drive a few blocks from our house to find the best view for us.

My mother's thing is watching sunsets. I notice both.

Peace,

Nia

CHAPTER

5

"Now my momma, she used to give us the B.B. beating," Ms. Torrence claimed as Mama tucked her under the dryer.

"B.B. beating?" Nana Mae asked as she took her place in Mama's swivel chair.

Ms. Torrence tilted her head to one side and leaned slightly from up under the hood. "Yes, ma'am, B.B. beating. You know you was in trouble if she sent you to get one of them tree switches or a belt and put that B. B. King on, may he rest in peace."

Mama laughed. "Girl, you know you oughta stop it."

"I'm serious. Just as sure as you Black, my mama got her whip on to B. B. King. That B.B. gave me and my sister all kind of blues. She'd put on that 'Why I Sing the Blues,' and baby, she'd whip you right along with the song. You ain't got your butt beat till you getting timed to B. B. That was some long whipping."

Mama and Nana Mae fell out laughing. It was funny, but I couldn't work up to it. Little Petey was on my mind. Deciding to solve his murder was one thing. Doing it was another. Another week had almost gone by like that, and we had no solid clue. My major activity had been in the shop sweeping hair and listening to Mama and her clients talking about some of everything.

Diva's had been a house once, then became the neighborhood convenience store for some years before becoming Mama's beauty shop. It was a one-stop-for-everything sort of place: hair, gossip, even shopping. The purse-and-shoe man came around at least once a week. But it was a Thursday, and he didn't come until Friday and break up the normal boring flow. One of the noisy hair dryers was setting Ms. Torrence's hair and the radio was set low on the Grown Folks station. When I wasn't sweeping hair, I sat on a stool at the front desk, tending to the phone as needed and flipping through a hairstyle magazine I'd already looked at least ten times as I waited for enough hair to collect on the floor. Back in the day when I was deep into the Nancy Drew books and was still working my way through the series, I'd sit there reading so lost in whatever crime Nancy was into, I'd miss Mama calling my name until she'd be standing over me, telling me to get me head out the book long enough to sweep the floor or grab more towels or whatever she'd asked me to do.

Mama was pressing the curly edges of Nana Mae's hair with a hot flat iron. With her other hand, she gently guided my grandmother's head to the right, left, up, and down with a hand push to keep Nana Mae's scalp just one nod ahead of the sizzle. Nana Mae's neck stretched around like *The Incredibles* mom every time she got the hand press, scared her ears or forehead was gonna get in the way of the flat iron. She hated the process and didn't suffer through it often, but the choir had some special singing event.

Sometimes I'd ask Mama to straighten my hair, and once in a while she'd agree, so I'd sit there dodging the flat iron, too. She wouldn't let me get a perm because my hair was just like it needed to be she said, natural and plenty beautiful already, but when she did do my hair in a straight style, she was relentless with kinks. I believed she was willing to sacrifice an ear or a forehead to reach bone-straight, though she never burned anybody.

"Y'all know the devil is busy around here."

Okay, now whenever Ms. Torrence said this, you knew she was about to talk about something serious and was through reminiscing and filling in everybody about who was getting divorced and complaining how milk and gas were sky high. She dropped into that for-grown-folks-only voice, the kind designed to signal it wasn't a PG minute and not for children's listening, to lessen the chances of us running off at the mouth about it at some future inappropriate time. The lightweight stuff was over, time for the heavy-weight news.

A couple of years ago when Nana Mae would do this, I was still in the young kid zone to my mother, so she would find something for me to do. *Go in the back room and organize those supplies or run home and bring back some baking soda.* At home such moments meant a sure *Don't you hear grown folks talking? Take yourself on outside somewhere and play.*

Things were different now. I was "half-grown," as Mama put it, except when I was working her nerves for not tending to business fast enough to her liking. After the Little Petey situation, Mama wasn't too inclined to send me off anywhere. She was still thinking, without saying it out loud, that I could have been the one killed.

I pretended to be engrossed in the magazine and glued my eyes to a page.

"You know they sayin' somebody know something about who killed that precious love. Bless his soul," Ms. Torrence said. "I just continue to look to the hills from whence cometh my help."

Miracle Ruth got it honestly. Ms. Torrence knew every scripture in the Bible and liked to show it off. She couldn't resist throwing them into the mix no matter what the talk was about.

"Well, that's the right thing to do," Nana Mae said. "Better not to speak too much about some stuff." Nana Mae did not go in for a lot of gossip.

Ms. Torrence conveniently ignored her and thankfully got right back to it. "Well, the Lord know, I hate even thinkin' about it, let alone talkin' about it. They sayin' it's some mess out of Chicago got that baby killed."

Our town—population 55,265 and exactly 110 miles east of Chicago—was, as Mama put it, no place in between someplace.

"Chi-town, hmph—Chi-raq they call it now. But no surprise there. That mess there been making its way here for a while now. Getting worse and worse, too." That from Mama. She didn't miss a beat on the flat ironing.

"Uh-huh, dragging our young people down in the streets right with 'em. I'm tellin' you, these kids need Jesus and some good BB on they backside," Ms. Torrence said. "I'm just glad the Lord see *everything.* They can run, but they can't hide from Him."

Nana Mae sat up cardboard-straight as Mama pressed the tiny strands around her edges. "Well, it's not likely anybody's gonna go down there to the police station and start talking."

"You know that's right. Don't matter who know what," Mama said.

"Well." Ms. Torrence bent her roller-set head so she was only halfway under the dryer. She was a good one for pause and effect. "That's why it pay to be careful who you fool with. Bad enough the daddy of that precious lamb a devil and Shayla's cousin run with him. Trouble all around."

Mama grunted and shook her head, the usual response to any mention of Big Pete.

Ms. Torrence ignored that and went right along. "Khalifah, I believe is his name. They sayin' he and that baby's daddy gon' take care of whoever it was soon enough."

I turned the page of the magazine but started taking notes in my head. Just like Nancy Drew, I was ready to pick up clues just by listening and paying attention.

"Lord help us. It's a sin and a shame. All this killing, and for what?" Nana Mae said into a sheet of hair hanging over her forehead.

"Now, somebody know who hurt that baby," Ms. Torrence shouted over the dryer hum.

"And if Khal-ee-fa and Big Pete know, they not trying to tell the right somebody, sitting up there hanging their heads at the funeral."

Mama's left eyebrow sharpened into an upside-down U. "I don't know about our people. Seem like folks 'round here rather let everybody get killed. Long as they don't snitch," Mama added. "But you almost can't get too mad at 'em. Try to do right, and you might end up in the grave, too."

"Like I said, the devil is busy. We gotta stay prayed up 'cause if the Lord ain't our help, nothin' is." Ms. Torrence wasn't one to let anybody but her have the last word.

I forgot to keep turning pages and pretending igno-rance. Mama gave Ms. Torrence the look. Ms. Torrence shut up momentarily, then got back to complaining about gas prices. It didn't matter though. I added Khalifah to my mental list as a witness right across from the first suspect, the bald-headed funeral crasher in black.

CHAPTER

6

When Mama finished Nana Mae's hair, we left the shop, leaving Mama to finish up her last two customers for the day. It had been a good four days since I'd seen Miracle Ruth and Dontay, but instead of getting with them to talk about my newly gathered clue like I wanted, Nana Mae determined my hair needed some tightening up, too, so we sat on the porch and she went to work taking down my frizzy braids and plaiting my hair back. She pulled the strands of my hair into an underhand cornrow and patted my head lightly when she needed me to lean or twist my head to accommodate her.

"You all right, baby? I know things seem pretty dark right now."

"Yes, ma'am, I'm all right."

"Hmmph. We all thinking about losing that baby and the rest of this craziness going on out here."

I didn't say anything. Nobody lost him. Somebody had blown him away from us.

Nana Mae was the only grown-up who talked to me like she recognized I was somewhere between childhood and adulthood—almost grown, not just a kid who didn't know anything. She had this way of telling somebody something with two or three meanings, then was kind enough not to try to make you understand it all in one sitting. Nana Mae kept it real, too, about the good and the ugly as she called it.

On top of that, her stories were the best and not stupid fairy tale stuff about Cinderellas and Sleeping Beauties. When I was younger, she'd tell me a lot of her stories while she braided my hair or sat with me at bedtime when Mama and Daddy were working late. Some were stories about herself when she was growing up and family from down South that lived long before I was born, and others were what Nana Mae said were somewhere between real and made-up. The best one was about Nzinga, an enslaved girl whose African mother named her after a real African queen who lived hundreds of years ago. The way Nana Mae told it made the story and the girl seem for real. When I was younger, I couldn't get enough of the story. Nana Mae always told it the same way. Sitting there with Nana Mae braiding my hair, massaging my scalp a bit with her fingertips in between just as I liked, was comforting.

"Nana Mae," I said, surprising myself, "will you tell me about Nzinga?"

Nana Mae's fingers paused. "So, you didn't forget that story, huh? Thought you was too grown around here for my stories." She laughed, pleased.

"No, ma'am, I wouldn't forget that one," I answered.

"What got that on your mind all of a sudden?"

I couldn't say exactly. Maybe the girl running in my dream. Maybe because things were simpler then, when Nana Mae used to tell me stories. My father was alive and I lived for him and loved that story.

"I don't know . . . I just always remember that story," I offered.

She accepted my weak reason and started the story as if no time had passed, just as she used to do.

"One day, Nzinga gets sent to collect flowers for the mistress," Nana Mae began. She paused to explain, "Now that's what the white lady call herself, presuming to own Nzinga and the other Black folk on the plantation. Anyhoo, so the mistress got this big company coming to the Big House."

The first time she told me the story, I had interrupted her at this point. "What's the Big House?" I had asked back then.

This time Nana Mae teased me a bit. "You remember me telling you that the Big House was sometimes a mansion or not depending on how poor or rich the slave owner was, and it tended to be white. The white folks lived there. Some of the Black folk they call themselves owning—the house slaves—might sleep on the floor somewhere nearby so they could come running anytime the mistress or master got a mind for them to do something. The rest of the Black people didn't live in nothing like that big house. They stayed in shacks, usually poor excuses for shelter not fit for human beings to live decent."

I nodded my yes. I hadn't forgotten at all, and I had seen pictures of plantations in social studies class since then.

Nana Mae massaged the back of my head and went on. "Now this mistress liked baskets of pretty wildflowers all around the house. Make the house smell sweet and look pretty. She was known to have the best flowers on display. Now this was something this young girl about your age, Nzinga, loved to do."

Nana Mae skipped quizzing me as she had during her first telling of the story when I was probably seven. ("You know why Nzinga loved being sent to gather flowers?") At first I didn't know but guessed that she loved flowers. Of course, I had been wrong.

"'Cause she liked being able to run around for that little while, feeling free and alone in that beautiful spot," Nana Mae had explained, "out there in this little forest area where the flowers grew so pretty on each side of a running stream. See, Nzinga had lived on that one plantation all her young life. That's all she ever got to see—that

Big House and the fields where the other Black folk worked from sunup till the sun went down. Every day was about what the white folks made them do, day in and day out. Nzinga ran around all hours for the mistress and the Black women who had to do the cooking and cleaning and so on. When she went to the field, Nzinga always stayed on the one side just like instructed. But that day, the flowers there just weren't good enough for that picky mistress of hers, let alone her company. She noticed the beautiful flowers across the way, on the other side of that running stream. I mean, they just seemed to call to her. It was like a parade of colors dressing up that other side. For the first time, she noticed how the bushes sitting a little bit farther back grew the kind of purple-and-white flowers that smelled like a sweet perfume. They were Mam Sue's favorite, and the white lady's, too."

Mam Sue. When I'd first heard Nana Mae say it, I had laughed thinking it was a funny name for somebody's mother. Then Nana Mae explained that as well, giving me my first lesson about slavery. Like a lot of children born in slavery, Nzinga had been separated from her parents. Mam Sue was at the plantation when she was born, and after her African mother was sold away, Mam Sue took care of Nzinga. So Mam Sue came to be the only mama she ever knew. I had answered her then by shutting up and curling into her side.

Nana Mae pulled two pieces of my hair together and

pressed close to my scalp to begin another perfect braid. "So now Nzinga looks down, and she see how slow the stream was moving, how the sun rays from the sky glitter on the surface of the water. She sees her own face staring back at her. The water wasn't that deep, and it was so clear, she could see the dirt and the rocks. She sees something else, too; she hadn't paid no mind to before, this tangled mess of skinny tree branches from each side reaching across and meeting over the stream. Well, now, next thing you know, she reaches out and grabs hold of a tangle of branches. It's a little high, so she kind of hops up there and catches hold with both hands real tight. The water's not deep, but she scared of falling in. She tiptoes in. It's so cold—you know how it is when you jump in a pool and don't know it's gonna be ice cold? It surprised those bare feet of hers." Nana Mae's voice fell quieter.

"The water soaked the bottom of her old throwaway dress the mistress had given her, but that wet dress would get her a sure whipping, so she went on across the stream, still hanging on to the tangle of branches until there was an opening. Nzinga got really scared, standing there near the forbidden side of the stream, nothing to hold onto. Then she remembers the basket sitting on the other side. She had done all that work of getting to the good flowers, so she wades on, puts one foot in front of the other and keeps crossing that stream until she gets close enough to grab a tree branch hanging within reach. A few steps later,

she's where she never been in her life—on the other side.
Once she's there, first thing that catches her eyes isn't the
flowers—no, instead she sees this parting in the flowery
bushes off to one side. She goes toward it, then stops, trying
to make out what it is. It's a path, lined with trees and that
pretty purple-and-white flower. She recalls hearing the
older folks on the plantation say there was a path to freedom across the water, only nobody that they knew so far
had been able to take it all the way to freedom. They'd
been brought back. Nzinga had never known *what* water,
never even occurred to her maybe the stream where the
pretty flowers grew was the water. The path is narrow, but
she's small—a slip of a thing, her mistress said."

Nana Mae paused and massaged a spot on my scalp
that I was hoping she'd get to. It felt so good.

"Nzinga thought of Mam Sue, who was, as you know,
not just the only mama Nzinga had known but also the
master's favorite slave. Mam Sue took care of Nzinga
and every sick body on the plantation, including the
master and mistress, and every child with no parents like
Nzinga. Mam Sue had been allowed to name her Nzinga,
even though mistress said it sounded like a witch name.
Nzinga's mama had whispered the name to Mam Sue the
morning she'd been sold away from her baby girl. Now
Nzinga didn't want to leave Mam Sue. But the old woman
was sick. The white doctor had come and said there was
nothing to be done, and the other enslaved folks on the

plantation whispered how Mam Sue's time was coming soon. Nzinga didn't want to think about life or the plantation without Mam Sue. She walked a little closer to the tiny opening of the path and just stood there, thinking. She recalled something Mam Sue had said to her not long ago as Nzinga spooned water down her throat. 'If I had it to do again,' she whispered in a weak voice to Nzinga, 'I'd run on down that path. Oh yes, Jesus, just run on down that path.' So Nzinga did. She moved a little in the day but mostly at night, hiding in the bushes and trees, getting her skin scratched and bruised, and her feet blistered up. Every second, she was terrified the mistress and master had somebody after her, so she kept going."

I still couldn't imagine this, alone in the dark woods all by herself at night, nobody taking care of her and bad guys and dogs looking for runaways—a fact that we'd gotten during a brief section on slavery in another social studies class.

"Nana Mae, did Nzinga make it?"

She laughed, tickled at my usual old question, and answered, "Well, think about it like this. That day the flowers didn't satisfy on the side she was supposed to stay on, the one she always stayed on. Now, ain't no coincidence those beautiful flowers on the other side commanded her attention on this one day and she stepped across that water and sees that path, *the path*. That's not happenstance. That's the universe calling, baby, and when you answer yes when the universe calls, you step on into your destiny. Everybody's got one, too. In my story, Nzinga follows hers and nobody catches her. And in real life, I believe—I know," she corrected herself, "plenty more made it in real life." She finished another braid and parted my hair to begin one more.

Nana Mae's words made me feel a little better. I couldn't tell her about me being late getting to Little Petey that morning and how I felt things would have turned out differently if I had been. I definitely couldn't tell her about our plan to find out who murdered him though I was used to sharing things with her. My father was Nana Mae's only child. She called Mama the daughter she and my grandfather never had. And me, I knew she loved me deep in this way I could always feel. Nana Mae gave us the house after Granddaddy died. She said it was too big for her, even though it wasn't all that big—just three bedrooms. After Daddy died, she moved back in to be with us.

"I suspect you thinking about your daddy, too. I know I am. Always."

This was Nana Mae. She talked to you like you got some sense, and sometimes she seemed to be able to read your mind.

"Yes, ma'am . . ." Tears threatened out of nowhere and my throat caught. "I think about him a lot. I dream about him, too."

"He visits my dreams, too, thank the Lord. You know,

baby, sometimes we can't do nothing but ride the time out. Sometimes during it, we figure some stuff out." She nudged me around so she could finish the last braid. "And then there's things no amount of thinking and figuring can make right."

"Nana Mae, you think everything happens for a reason?"

Adults had been saying that my whole life, but secretly I didn't think it was true. *Everything happens for a reason*, they'd say, but never gave the reason and settled for tossing it on the Lord. *The Lord know*, Ms. Torrence's saying.

"Hmmph, I tell you what, I don't believe everything that happens got reason *in* it," she answered.

She examined my head, making sure each braid was tight enough to survive any running and restless nights but not so tight to cause a headache. She pulled a couple suspect braids for confirmation, finding one unworthy. She undid the braid just as Dontay's purple hat jogged into view. His camera hung from around his neck, and a yellow shoelace spilled out of a white tennis shoe as he came up to the porch. He bent and tied it quick. His legs peeked from under long black jersey shorts.

"Hey, Ms. Nana Mae." He gulped, making his Adam's apple bobble.

"I see you still heying folk." Nana Mae smiled at him.

He aimed his camera at us, then adjusted a setting and settled the lens back on us. "May I?" he asked.

Nana Mae nodded her approval, and I shrugged okay. If he had his camera, which was a lot, Dontay had to record something or snap photos. He seemed to like capturing the most ordinary moments, like Nana Mae doing my hair, instead of ones you posed for. He filmed Nana Mae fixing the braid, then gathering all of them into a ponytail before she stood up.

"The end," Nana Mae teased Dontay, then bowed like the porch was the stage before going in the house.

"What you up to?" he asked me.

"Nothing," I said. "But we gotta talk, you know, about the thing."

"Okay, you want to go to Miracle Ruth's?"

"Nana Mae, I'll be back," I yelled toward the screen door.

She came back to the door, peering at us over the top of the glasses on her nose.

"We're going to Miracle Ruth's. Um, is it all right?" I asked like some fourth grader.

It wasn't something I'd usually have to ask. I'd just say, "I'm going down to Miracle Ruth's," or "I'll be at Dontay's." No big deal, going just up the street to their houses or with them to the store we'd been shopping at since we had moved there. But not lately.

Nana Mae let out a breath. "Suppose so. Just to Miracle Ruth's and back here before the lights come on, clear?"

"Yes, ma'am." And we headed out.

Dontay and I met before we were in first grade together, before Daddy, Mama, and I moved into Nana Mae and Granddaddy's house. His dad and mine were friends from way back when they were in high school together, and Mama became good friends with Dontay's mom. Sometimes when we visited Nana Mae and Granddaddy, I'd be sitting on the porch or in the driveway riding my bike around in circles, and Dontay would come by with his dad and mom. While our parents talked away, Dontay snuck looks at me and fidgeted. I would grin at him. His daddy or mama invited him to play with me, but he was so shy, for a long time he wouldn't. I remembered the first time we did. Nana Mae and my grandfather surprised me with a little trampoline with a net around it in the backyard—something special for playing at their house. Dontay watched me bouncing up and down and falling, then laughing until I almost cried. Daddy didn't have to invite him *that* time— we jumped up and down, competing to see who could jump the highest and the fastest and fall the best for hours.

A few weeks into first grade at my old school, my grandfather had a heart attack, though. He died, even though he wasn't old. We moved in the house over the Christmas break. Nana Mae said she needed to "ease her soul" and went down south, and that January I started going to the same school as Dontay. One day in the spring some boys raced at recess. I joined in, the only girl that did. I'd always liked running. Mama said I tried it in the womb, then skipped crawling and learning to walk and went straight to running. I never stopped moving fast. I beat all the boys, including the fastest one who was a whole year older. Me and Dontay became best friends. And Fernando, then Miracle Ruth. It was the four of us until Fernando moved to the other side of town at the end of third grade, the same year Dontay's mom died from a disease called lupus.

We walked slowly, knowing without saying anything aloud that we were both dreading passing the intersection of MLK and Abernathy, where Little Petey's house was. We passed Mr. Carter's house next door to mine. The blue trim was fading into gray. A FOR SALE sign sat in his yard. Mr. Carter was the old high school janitor. He'd left about a year ago when the school laid people off. We passed another empty house that had a red-and-white sign in the front yard that read FOR SALE with a picture of a smiling blonde white lady above the number.

I hated empty houses. Foreclosures—people fussed about them a lot. This one had a wooden board in place of a window. It had been empty over three years, since a few months before my father died. The board had been added by my father and Dontay's dad after somebody tried to break in one night. Daddy said nobody was going to turn our neighborhood into some kind of haven for violence. Daddy, Dontay's dad, and one or two others kept the house safe and the grass cut. Dontay's dad still did that with Ahmad's and Dontay's help. The lady who used to live there had kept a garden in the backyard. She used to give us fresh greens and okra—ugh. Okra is one of my most hated vegetables.

"So you come up with any of them big Nancy Drew ideas about how we supposed to find out who did it?" Dontay asked, half-teasing and half-serious.

"For your information, yeah. I mean, I got an idea or two. I got our first clue, too."

"For real? What you got?"

"I'll tell you when we get to Miracle Ruth's."

He didn't protest. We turned at the King–Abernathy intersection. Too soon, we were opposite Little Petey's. Neither of us looked at the spot where he died. We kept our heads down while our feet sped up in agreement. We knew there'd been a yellow tape with black block words encircling the spot. Dontay had glimpsed it going down the street in the car with his dad, and Miracle Ruth had reported this to me the day after it happened. She also reported that there'd been a white chalk shadow etched on top of the concrete. My stomach twisted at the thought. I wondered if there was blood still there, or worse, maybe no sign of Little Petey or what had happened there.

We rounded the corner and saw Miracle Ruth's hot-pink ponytail scarf and a flash of her white shirt and hot-pink capri pants. She wore something pink every single day. If her pants, shirt, or dress wasn't pink, then her watch or a belt, purse, shoes, or even her Bible was sure to be. There had to be some pink.

Miracle Ruth was carrying dishes to her grandmother's car. Up close, her T-shirt looked bleached-white clean, like the dress at the funeral, despite loading the car up with food. I guess it wasn't surprising a girl named Miracle Ruth would be that way. Ms. Torrence was headed to help set up the reception after the funeral of a young man whose mama worked with her at the hospital. She was an unofficial funeral planner for church people in their time of need and the bonus was that she was as famous for cooking the best sweet potato pies and casseroles for holidays and funeral receptions as she was for rescuing flowers after funerals.

"I left some of this casserole on the stove so you all can eat if you want." She was in the car and belted in, without one Bible quote, to our surprise. "Wash them hands. Cleanliness is next to godliness," she called out the window and hit the gas.

We followed Miracle Ruth through the living room, decorated with pictures of her and Mary, Miracle Ruth's mama. She had Mary's eyes and color, and according to Ms. Torrence, Mary loved pink, too. Miracle Ruth never brought her up. After high school, Mary had attended a community college about twenty minutes out of town. She'd wanted to go away to Spelman College in Atlanta, but Ms. Torrence wouldn't go for it—too far away. But then Mary had started going down the wrong path with the wrong guy and doing drugs. When she'd gotten pregnant with Miracle Ruth, she straightened herself out, got back into church, and started taking classes again. Ms. Torrence said the Lord worked in mysterious ways, and the baby was a blessing in the disguise of sin.

She and Mary almost fell out when the baby was born. Mary had wanted to name her baby girl Miracle. That did not agree with Ms. Torrence. She'd wanted her first and only grandchild to have a name from the Bible, as she'd done with Mary. She'd wanted Ruth, to be exact. Mary had compromised by going with Miracle Ruth.

Of course, whenever Ms. Torrence told the story, she left out the part about twisting Mary's arm to get her way. The mix was kind of funny, but I think Miracle Ruth's mama got it right. The thing was, though, by the time Miracle Ruth had turned two, Mary was lost out there in the streets again. One day she'd left Miracle Ruth with Ms. Torrence and said she'd return before night, but she never came back.

Every so often when Ms. Torrence visited us, she worried aloud about her daughter to Nana Mae and Mama, asking them to keep Mary in their prayers. "How I'm ever gonna rest easy with my own child out there in the world and don't even know if she dead or alive or what. The Bible say, 'Raise up a child in the way he should go, and when he gets older, he won't depart from it.' Look like hard as I tried, just wasn't good enough."

I felt kind of sorry for her then.

My bedroom was a shoebox compared to Miracle Ruth's. Two pictures hung on one wall of her room, one of a boy and a girl kneeling in prayer, the other with praying hands on a plaque engraved with a scripture about honoring your parents so you'd live long. The room hadn't changed from the first time I'd seen it when we were seven, except for the Spelman College poster Ms. Torrence had recently bought Miracle Ruth. That was on the wall over the desk. Miracle Ruth was set on going to Spelman for college, and unlike with her mother's dream, Ms. Torrence was showing love for Miracle Ruth's plan to go there.

I loved her pretty canopy bed and the whole wall of books. But the dolls of every kind and color that Miracle Ruth had gotten over the years, from Barbies to little girl dolls that wet, cried, and ate if you put in new batteries—ugh, really? I had never taken to dolls, even when I was a lot younger. Still, Miracle Ruth had her own television and a newish computer while I had to settle for an outdated desktop in Mama's room and a television in the living room and Nana Mae's room. Mama did not believe in televisions in the bedroom unless you had the flu or were contagious-like sick.

Soon as Miracle Ruth shut the door, I launched into my rundown of the short suspect and witness lists we had, starting with the funeral crasher dude.

"You saw the way Big Pete got, right? He upset quick when he saw this guy," I began.

"But for real, if the man who killed his son came up to him at the funeral, you think anybody could've held him back?" Dontay countered.

He had a point. "Probably not," I conceded reluctantly. "But something real foul is between them, so he's still a suspect for now." The problem was Big Pete had to have a lot of people like that.

Miracle Ruth had her own shocker for us before I could move on to Khalifah. "Okay, so I found a report online," she explained, pointing to the laptop on her desk. There was nothing on the screen except her screen saver, a field of pink flowers.

"Come on, girl. What kind of report?" Dontay and I huddled over her back, trying to see.

She moved the mouse over the pad. "'Patience is a virtue.' It's a report the medical office does, you know. After people pass—are deceased," she corrected herself.

I got it, but didn't want to say. I didn't like the word *autopsy*.

Miracle Ruth clicked, and there it was. Boxes with Little Petey's name, birthday, address, and one for the date he died and the place. There was a diagram, too, of a body without any face with the hands and legs spread out like a gingerbread man, an outline meant to be his little boy body. Farther down there were different categories with notes, some handwritten. Manner of death, *homicide.* Internal Examination—

Miracle Ruth scrolled down the page.

"Slow down. You going too fast," Dontay fussed.

I stepped back. I wanted to see but didn't want to at the same time. Little Petey was a diagram on a piece of paper. That was it.

A jolt went through my body. Somewhere out in virtual nowhere, there was probably a report with my father's name, the day he was born, and the date he died. And with *homicide* written in a diagram and an arrow pointing to where the bullet went into his head and killed him.

Miracle Ruth was looking at me. "You okay?"

Dontay scrolled to the handwriting about the circumstances of the death.

"Yeah," I said and leaned back over her shoulder. "Maybe there's a clue where it talks about what happened."

We read, Dontay half-aloud and Miracle Ruth frowning at the screen and taking little notes on the pink pad by her computer. I read how several gunshots were fired and one struck the victim. That's how it referred to Little Petey—the victim. My stomach rumbled. I squelched the sick feeling down.

"I've got something else to show you guys, too. Look at this." Miracle Ruth clicked away from the autopsy report and clicked again. Another report.

"The police report? How you get that?" Dontay asked, awed.

Miracle Ruth smiled. "Everything's online. If you know how to look and you're patient."

You had to give it her. The girl had mad skills on the computer.

The police report was different. More boxes were blacked out. We scanned every word that wasn't. On one page, a Sergeant Somebody—whose name was of course hidden so we couldn't make it out—talked about being dispatched to the intersection of MLK and Abernathy. Upon arrival, they immediately tried to revive a male child, a gunshot victim, who was lying on the ground unresponsive. CPR was performed. But it was already too late before the paramedics arrived. The cops supposedly interviewed a few people. A joke. No one claimed to have witnessed the shooting. An unnamed somebody mentioned seeing a tan Cadillac.

Miracle Ruth bookmarked the page.

"A possible car is better than nothing," I said. "But somebody that knows is a whole lot better." That was my segue to the beauty shop chatter about Khalifah.

"Awww, man, see? This is what I mean," Dontay said after I'd explained. "You get in people's business, you don't know who you might be messing with." Dontay frowned and shook his head

"You know Khalifah?" I asked him.

"We all know him."

"Say what?" Miracle Ruth and I asked in unison.

"Lightning. That's Khalifah," Dontay explained.

"The guy that be with Big Pete?" I asked dumbly as the image of a skinny reddish guy with a bandana came to mind.

Dontay went on with his Wikipedia report, "He used to run with this other crew. Now he run with Big Pete. You know Ahmad and Big Pete was tight from kindergarten till middle school."

I did not know this. How my former secret future husband, Ahmad, Dontay's big brother, could ever be close friends with Big Pete was beyond me. They might as well have been from different planets, they were so different.

"Big Pete started getting in all kinds of trouble and slanging and that was it. My dad put that hammer down. No more hanging with Big Pete. Ahmad know Lightning, too, says he used to be a nice dude before he got out there."

He meant the streets. At home and at church, we got the sermon constantly. The streets lay in wait for us to misstep and lose ourselves like so many in our town before us. The streets were the doorway to hell. We had glimpsed this for ourselves. They were scary and mysterious, gobbling up Black and brown boys and girls as they had Miracle Ruth's mama. They landed them either strung out, in jail, in early pregnancy, or in an early grave.

"And he's family to Shayla?" I asked.

"Cousin. On her daddy's side."

The only thing I recalled of Shayla's father was that he'd been killed when we were little, right after Mary took off and Miracle Ruth's grandmother was already raising Miracle Ruth.

"Him and Big Pete tight," Dontay went on. "He was at the cemetery."

Miracle Ruth nodded in agreement. "He was. He left with Big Pete."

"Okay, so they could already know who it was," I said.

"You think so?" Miracle Ruth asked.

Dontay leaned in and clicked the mouse. The tab with the terrible police report closed. "I don't know about that. If they do, we probably would've heard."

We understood. He'd be dead already, and the word would be all over the Black neighborhood network— whispers at church, barber shop, and the street.

"Or maybe," Dontay concluded, "they just ain't moved yet. But you can bet Big Pete will."

If it was a Nancy Drew book, Nancy would already be talking to her suspect and putting the clues together to get him arrested. But we weren't in a book. Tomorrow there was a candlelight vigil for Little Petey. We'd have to see what more we could find out after that.

CHAPTER

7

I'd seen TV news clips of candlelight vigils given for victims on the news but never gone to any. There had been a vigil inspired by Daddy for all the murder victims that year. It was held at city hall a few days after the funeral. Mama and I stayed home, curled up together in their bed. Nana Mae went with Ms. Torrence, Miracle Ruth, Dontay, and his dad.

The vigil for Little Petey was at Ronnie Shields Park. The far side of the park was the dividing point between where the east side ended in one direction and the west side officially began. Ronnie Shields was a lady who started an orphanage and took in a lot of children. She had helped get my former elementary school built. When I was little, my father and mama would take me to play in the park.

Nana Mae came with us sometimes, too. On summer holidays, Daddy grilled, and we'd set up a picnic table and then play on my favorite thing at the park, the merry-go-round. I used to get so dizzy when Daddy spun me around, I could barely stand after. I loved climbing the mound and going down the monster slide, too.

The merry-go-round was long gone, the swings old and rusty, and the slide seemed smaller every year. Mama and Daddy stopped letting me go when I still liked going. Too much riffraff hanging around that far side, Mama said, and kids with too much time on their hands and too little supervision starting trouble and fighting one another over whose side this or that was when neither owned any of it or anything else in our town.

Dontay and I rode slowly to the vigil on our bikes with Nana Mae tagging right behind us on foot, along with some people headed the same way. Mama was at Diva's since she had a rare late-evening appointment set for one of her regular customers. Miracle Ruth was already there with Ms. Torrence.

We got there just as the sun dipped lower, blazing like an orange moon sitting on the earth, the way I loved it best, before it dropped out of sight. The heat was still going strong, so we were in for another warm night. My skin already felt sticky.

Dontay immediately got busy with his camera, recording snippets and snapping photos. He walked his bike over to a boy from school who was talking to two girls new to our neighborhood. They both ran around in tight crop tops, and like right then, they were usually laughing breasts-first into some boy's face. Boob Crew candidates for sure. They turned their full attention to Dontay. He seemed fine with it and aimed his camera at them while they posed and giggled, acting like Dontay was about to make them YouTube famous or something.

Boob Crew was mine and Miracle Ruth's name for these girls at school and around neighborhood who specialized in showing off super-size boobs. Their tacky uniform of choice was tiny T-shirts they threatened to burst out of with some dumb picture or words stretched into distortion right across it. The shirt was as low-necked as they could get away with and their jeans or tiny shorts were so tight they had to be choking off air in the area Nana Mae said needed to breathe. Sometimes, the principal's office sent them home to change. The Boob Crew entertained themselves and the whole school with their favorite pastime, swishing their butts and sticking their chests out past boys, while talking loudly and pretending to ignore the nasty boys grabbing at their own crotches. Those boys would woof and congratulate one another like they'd just done something great.

"What you looking at?" Head Big Boobs cut her eyes at Head Nasty Boy.

Uh, duh.

Head Nasty Boy grabbed his crotch harder and said something worse. The Boob Crew girls killed themselves giggling while poking their behinds out more and trying to take cute selfies. Mama couldn't stand them. Whenever she picked me up or dropped me off at school and saw the Boob Crew hanging out in front, straining in those T-shirts and second-skin jeans, she shook her head and gripped the steering wheel with both hands.

"Mmph, hot ass girls. Looking and acting like they here to slide down a pole instead of focusing on their education," she muttered under her breath, but loud enough so I heard every time and got the message. My mother was still on the young side but straight up old school. I believed that she would follow me around school and sentence me to life in the house and Diva's until I was eighteen if I ever attempted to behave like them.

She had no need to worry. A) I didn't want to be anything like the fake Boob Crew girls with their stank attitudes. B) I would have to double stuff a padded bra to wear their uniform. I was the most underdeveloped of our class, which followed me being the last girl to start her period, at thirteen, when everybody I knew, including Miracle Ruth, started a good year or two earlier than me.

The WEKV Channel 4 truck arrived and pulled up near the curb close to us. A Black lady with shoulder-length, bone-straight hair from the nightly news got out. Shandra Bell wore a yellow pantsuit and looked as perfectly pretty as she did on television. Her hair wouldn't dare frizz no matter how hot or humid the weather got. A camera guy followed her as she came right up to us with her mike in hand.

Then the strangest thing happened. Instead of sticking the mike in Nana Mae's face for a comment, Shandra Bell actually hugged Nana Mae.

"Shandra, good to see you," Nana Mae greeted the newswoman. "I mean off TV."

I stood there thunderstruck as Nana Mae moved on after a few more seconds of chatting and joined Ms. Torrence and some other women from church. They were standing in semicircle around a stranger, a tall, dark guy with a beard. He wore jeans and a black short-sleeved T-shirt. The guy's muscles bulged through the shirt. The church crew laughed and fawned over him and shifted their hips from side to side.

"Hello." Shandra Bell flashed a big smile at a starstruck woman nearby, who stared in awe at Shandra's chalk-white teeth and TV smile. She extended her mike to the woman and asked, "How do you feel about what's happening here tonight?"

The lady blushed and smiled at Shandra Bell with only her lips. "It's bad out here, you know? Kids is being killed. I don't know, seem like everywhere you look, there's trouble."

I busied myself trying to check out everybody coming

and going. There were some kids I knew from middle school and our neighborhood, and police officers scattered about mingling with one another, eyes darting around as they talked.

"Did you know the little boy?" Shandra Bell caught me off guard, sticking her microphone in my face. Her camera guy aimed right at me. The light was so bright, it kind of blinded me.

I answered without thinking, "I babysat him."

Before Shandra could follow up, the cameraman called to her as he hurried toward the front. Reverend Don King from the funeral had arrived with Shayla and her family. Ms. Shandra Bell turned off the mike and leaned toward me.

"You're Les's daughter," she said, catching me off guard.

"Yes, ma'am," I said.

She smiled. Her teeth really were super white. "You're almost all grown up. Looks like you got your dad's height and his smile."

The camera guy called to her again and she turned to go. "Your father was one of the real good ones," she said over her shoulder. Then she was gone and racing over to her camera-man.

The vigil started. Dontay left his admirers and rejoined me. A man opened with a prayer and called for a moment of silence. Reverend Don King took over after that.

"We are not here to shake our heads and go on home till next time, am I right?" he boomed through the mike, getting everybody's attention.

"Got that right."

"Amen."

"We don't want a next time," he continued. "We here to demand, I didn't say ask—"

"Yes, sir. Yes, sir."

"We here to *demand* justice for this little boy and all the victims of senseless killing in our communities."

Fists pumped into the air, and people nodded in agreement.

"We want the police to stop policing the innocent and start protecting us. Serve our neighborhoods like they charged to do and our taxes pay them to do. If they did this better, we might not be here holding candles and pictures of this child." He was getting revved up to preach but pulled himself back.

"Now, can't nobody speak to the pain of this more than the mama. Shayla, come on up here." Shayla stepped up to the platform and took the mike the preacher held out.

She looked very young still with her hair pulled back into a ponytail again and no makeup covering her freckles.

"My baby . . . Petey, he never did a bad thing, but he's gone." Her voice broke on the last word. I was afraid she was about to cry or fall out, but she was a trouper.

"I want justice for my son. The person who did this

need to be in jail. I pray God don't let him rest. If anybody know who did this, please tell. This gotta stop. Killing all the time, it don't make no sense. My baby . . . ain't 'posed to be in no grave. Just stop, stop," she cried out.

Reverend Don King hugged her in a bear arm and took the mike. It was on the verge of getting dark. People with candles lit them. Others flickered their lighters and flashed their phone lights. Someone on the platform led the crowd in singing a song.

Dontay leaned over his bike and nudged me, whispering, "There he go."

Lightning, aka Khalifah, was wearing his usual white bandanna around his plaited head, a red T-shirt, and pants that hung down his waist, revealing black shorts underneath. He stepped up on the side of the platform near Shayla, who was encircled by other people comforting her. There was no sign of Big Pete. Dontay had heard he was going to stay away, was asked to actually, maybe by Shayla, in order to keep down the possibility of trouble.

It didn't seem to make a difference that Lightning was Shayla's cousin. Two women I'd never seen before got all up in his face in a flash. Whatever was being said wasn't going his way. He was talking—or was trying to—but the women seemed to be getting in the most words. They both flicked their hands at him as if shooing away a flea and cut their eyes at him. Lightning gave up quick and threw his tattooed arms up in defeat. He turned from them and made his way fast off the stage through a patch of people right past us. He passed close enough for me to see a tattoo that looked like a sword or maybe a bolt of lightning starting right below his ear and continuing down his neck where it disappeared into the red shirt. He took a cell phone out of a pocket, spoke a few words, then moved closer to the street.

A bumblebee-yellow Hummer cruised slowly down Ralph Abernathy toward us, pulling up across from the park. The tires on it were huge. The silver rims sparkled. The windows were too dark to see anybody inside clearly. It didn't matter. Everybody knew Big Pete's ride.

Lightning crossed the street as it pulled to a stop. Just as he was about to get in on the driver's side, a brown Cadillac with jacked-up spinning tires crept toward us from the other direction, then slowed and paused by the curb where we were standing, directly across from Big Pete's Hummer. More police appeared out of nowhere with their hands grazing the guns on their hips. Three of them flowed to the edge of the crowd a few feet from us, not far from the Cadillac idling curbside. The bearded guy with Nana Mae unfolded his arms from across his chest, his hand going to his side, too. I saw then that he was also armed.

Lightning glared from across the street, threw up his fingers, and got in the Hummer. Suddenly, the back-seat window of the Cadillac on the passenger side facing us rolled halfway down, and white teeth grinned out, but it was the face that I wouldn't forget. I stood straight up off my bike. Dontay nudged me, captivated by the sight of him, too. The man's light brown bald head was the only unmarked skin above the neck that I could see. A quilt of dollar-sign tattoos covered his entire face. There was even one right in the middle of his forehead between his eyebrows. The vehicles seemed to exhale together, then crept slowly away, Big Pete and Lightning going one way and the Cadillac with the scary-face guy and whoever was driving inching away in the opposite direction.

Dontay looked at me. I glanced around for Nana Mae. She was a few yards farther away with her back to us. Ms. Torrence and Miracle Ruth were part of the semicircle around her. The guy with the beard was gone. Miracle Ruth looked over her shoulder at me and Dontay, frowning.

Now, Nana Mae had given us very clear instructions: Stay near her and stay together. Mama had done the whole worst-case scenario thing capped off with one of her I-mean-business eyebrow arches. "Just stay close to your grandmother. First hint of any kind of trouble, come straight home. Clear?"

"Yes, ma'am," I had answered dutifully. My mind was on information we hadn't gotten yet to solve Little Petey's murder.

The brown Cadillac crept patiently toward the end of the street. Dontay and I glanced at each other, then back at Miracle Ruth, who bit her lip nervously, watching us. We took off after the Cadillac.

I half-regretted our move as soon as we started pedaling but not enough to turn back. The Cadillac was still easing farther to the intersection we'd crossed a half hour ago. Dontay was ahead of me, riding smooth and fast. The Cadillac turned the corner in slow motion. Dontay made the corner a few seconds later. I was seconds behind him, pedaling while ducking as if Mama was everywhere and might spot me at any minute.

Another intersection was ahead, and the car turned. Dontay paused mid-pedal for a second and twisted to look back at me. I was fading. I couldn't go fast enough on my old bike, but the car was still moving slowly enough for Dontay to keep it in sight. He pedaled off, faster than before, until he was a blur in the receding light. I stopped in the middle of the block, wondering what to do.

A) For one thing, it was getting toward really dark, proof of which were the streetlights sneaking on.
B) For another, I was supposed to be in Nana Mae's sight. I imagined her frantically noticing we were gone and running around talking to the cops, looking for us until Miracle Ruth finally couldn't stand breaking the "Thou shall not lie" commandment and confessed what she'd seen—me and Dontay following the brown Cadillac.

C) And last, Dontay was off somewhere chasing some serious guys and hadn't he been saying all along we were asking for trouble?

I didn't know what to do. Go back to the park and deal with Nana Mae, who might already be gone looking for me at home anyway, or just head there first? I chose the shorter trip, home, thinking up a plan of defense against Mama's wrath as I rode.

I had barely gotten my bike inside and gotten into my T-shirt and shorts when I heard Mama charging through the front door. I turned the light out and hurried into bed, pulling the top sheet up over me just in time.

"Nia? Nia?"

"Yes, ma'am," I called back, trying to sound weak but be loud enough for her to hear me.

She opened bedroom door and turned on the light.

"She here, uh-huh, I don't know, but you can bet I'm about to find out." She was on her cell talking to Nana Mae.

She came around the side of the bed.

"Ms. Lady, you better explain yourself. I know you got better sense than to leave the park without your grandmother. What were you thinking?"

There it was. I could A) tell her everything, take my butt whipping, and get ready to be confined to the house forever (or at least until I was eighteen); B) lie (which might add to every other sin and land me right in hell for sure); or C) go with a combination of both and pray neither A nor B happened. I liked to keep to the commandments as much as Miracle Ruth, but I had to protect our case and my behind.

"I didn't. I felt sick." This was true now because my stomach was roiling. "Dontay rode with me. I think he told Nana Mae. Maybe she didn't hear him . . ."

"You think he told her? You guess she didn't hear? You don't *think*, Nia, you supposed to *know*. Your grandmother didn't hear anything about what no Dontay said, young lady. You know you're the one that's gotta get your grandmother's permission, not nobody else."

"Yes, ma'am. I just didn't feel good."

She laid her hand on my forehead. "What kind? Where? You don't seem to have a fever." She softened and patted my forehead and cheek.

"My stomach. Feels like it did at the funeral."

"Oh. Well, let me get out of these clothes, and I'll get some seltzer or something."

She stood up and turned to the door. "Absolutely no going anywhere unless we know about it. Understand?"

"Yes, ma'am."

I heard Nana Mae come in downstairs, then the muffled sound of her and Mama talking and both their footsteps on the stairs.

Mama brought in the nasty cup of seltzer, and I downed it, holding my breath against the taste.

She rested her hand on my forehead again. "Probably just a little stomach upset. Get some sleep. I am tired, too. Been on my feet all day." She flipped the light switch off and shut the door.

Lord, forgive me for lying and please don't let anything bad happen to Dontay, I prayed hard as I could, and must have prayed myself to sleep.

I'm riding Daddy's back. I tilt backward. I'm flying . . . Daddy holds tight to my knees. I'm not afraid. We laugh and laugh . . . He disappears. My mouth opens. I'm calling him without words. Little Petey smiles and fades, red spreads . . . A girl running . . . "See you in the morning, Bright Eyes." My father's face smiling . . . His lips move. "Bright Eyes . . ."

Tapping. The sound grew louder and faster. I twisted out of the tangled bedsheet, fighting the fog. Was I still dreaming? The knocking came again. It was at the window. The only light was a soft glimmer under the bedroom door from the night light in the hallway.

"Nia . . . Hey, wake up. Nia?"

I hustled up, pausing at first to make sure neither Mama nor Nana Mae had stirred. I tiptoed quick to the window and pulled back the curtain. "Dontay?"

"Who else gon' be out here?" He was hoisted up on his bike as if it was a ladder, which leaned against the house, and gripped the window ledge.

I raised the window.

"You know how long I been knocking? And you know

I couldn't be but so loud—they asleep?" he whispered, climbing into the room.

I was so happy to see him, and looking all right, too, I ignored the fussing. I squinted at the clock sitting on my desk by the bed. It glowed red—10:30 P.M. "I guess I fell asleep. What happened? What you doing here?" I asked.

Dontay's dad did not play, his brother either.

"Pops is working an extra hour, and Ahmad's on his way back from Chicago. I don't got a lot of time. You want me to tell you what happened or not?" He covered the room with one stride and sat on the edge of my bed.

"Duh, yeah," I whispered. Last thing we needed was Mama or Nana Mae hearing.

"I followed that brown Caddy, right, and, man, every block I'm saying if they don't stop now, that's it. They keep going right to the west side, and you know where they go?" His Adam's apple dodged up and down. "Jackson Street. That's Hell Town."

"Hell Town?"

Some of everything had been happening on the west side for a long time, especially the neighborhood there designated as Hell Town. My father had been killed on another street over on the west side. Hell Town stayed on the news. The police were raiding some house or somebody got robbed. Or there was a drive-by shooting and another funeral because of it.

"Yeah, yeah, they pull up in front of this white house with this raggedy porch and the dude with all them dollar signs on his face and two more get out. They looked whacked, too. So they get out and these other guys are out there on the porch, three or four of 'em, looking almost wild as dude with the dollar signs. I mean *scary*."

"What happened next?" I asked impatiently.

"Let me finish, all right? Now they go in, and I just kind of wait across the street and pretend like I'm just checking tire pressure. Then I get on the bike, right, and I'm riding around in circles close to the Caddy."

"Okay?"

"But I know I gotta get up outta there 'cause you know that street over there in Hell Town is too wild. Dogs is barking, it's getting late. Something might be about to pop off with those guys 'cause I'm thinking a summit going on in there. And you know Pops, he gon' get me if I'm not home when he get in."

"That's all?" I asked, anxious for him to get to a clue.

"That's all? Girl, I followed those dudes and spied on 'em much as I could. It's not like I could be out there taking pictures. And if Pops or Ahmad find out I was anywhere near that spot, I'm done. But that's not all. Some grown dude came down the street on this tiny bike looking like the ones in the house. He comes straight up to me. I thought he was 'bout to do something to me. And then he says, 'Man, I seen you before.' I'm like, 'No, sir.' He goes, 'Yo, you Ahmad's little brother, right?' I didn't know whether it was good to say yes or no."

"What did you say?"

"Nothing. Just nodded yeah. And he was like, 'Yeah, your brother did some music for me. What you doing over here?' I told him I was lost. Dude gave me directions. Then I hauled up outta there. Hat almost fell, I was moving so fast. Then I came here and now I'm going home. Is that cool?" He got up and went over to the window, but getting out that way would be harder than getting in. I stood up.

"Yeah, sorry," I said, remembering how worried I'd been and how glad I was he was okay.

"We know where dude with the dollar signs hangs, and we know some bad blood between his crew and Big Pete and Lightning."

The hairs on my neck tingled. I cracked open the bedroom door and looked up and down the hallway. No light was coming from either Mama's or Nana Mae's bedroom door, and the bathroom door was open with the nightlight barely filtering out. I motioned to Dontay. We hurried downstairs on tiptoe to the kitchen back door. Before he slipped through the door, Dontay turned, smiling and too pleased with himself. "I noticed something about that brown Cadillac. I don't think it's always been that color. Until real recent."

Before I could react, he was through the door and grabbing his bike like the guys he'd followed to Hell Town or his dad and Ahmad were chasing him.

Wa alaykum as—salam.

Dear Nia, my friend,

Thank you for sharing your story about your father.

   I was near when my mother and sister died. My father covered me as everything exploded around us. When we awoke and crawled out of the rubble, my mother and sister had not survived, only we four—my father, brother, grandmother, and me.

   I did see when the soldiers arrested my brother a year ago. I was coming to tell him that our father wanted to speak with him, but soldiers were surrounding him. One of his friends lay badly beaten.

   Every two months for forty—five minutes we are allowed to go and see him behind the glass. My father goes every time by himself. The first time I went and so did Grandmother. It was very hard for us to see him and for him to see us. He told Father it was best if he came alone to visit. We have hope that perhaps he will be released before the two—year sentence ends.

Alima

عَالِمَة

CHAPTER

8

My pen pal, Alima, was eight when her mother and sister died during an explosion. A lot of other people were hurt that day, too, and some lost their lives. She had a brother, too, Jibreel. A little over a year ago soldiers took him away to a detention camp for throwing rocks at the soldiers when they were building a wall around Alima's community. They get to see him every couple of months or so for a few minutes, and sometimes not even then. It doesn't matter that he's a kid my age. Miracle Ruth and I looked it up online. Basically, it's a prison. He's been there over a year. Alima's dad doesn't think he's ever coming home, but her grandmother believes he will and so does Alima.

That's not the only bad stuff that happened to her

family, either. An uncle of hers stepped on a land mine and some of her cousins died fighting in a war. Before what happened to my father, her life would've seemed unbelievable to me, more like a movie than real. We had more in common than I ever thought people living across the world from each other would have.

The night after the vigil, I was in my room with my notebook organizing the little information me and Dontay and Miracle Ruth had so far. It wasn't much:

- Funeral intruder in black who was still a big question mark.
- A brown car that an anonymous witness in the neighborhood might have seen.
- Another enemy of Big Pete and Lightning, who might be the one—Scary Face, tag name, dollar sign tattoo man in the brown Cadillac that maybe was painted.
- Scary Face hangout, house on the west side.

We had a puzzle with pieces that didn't fit for sure yet. An idea occurred to me. Whenever Nancy Drew had a mystery to solve, there was one stop that was always necessary: returning to the scene of the crime. I'd been avoiding the spot in front of Little Petey's grandmother's house where he died. I was going to have to get past that and go back.

A soft knock on the bedroom door interrupted my note-gathering. Mama stuck her head in. "You feel like walking?"

I tucked the notes under my pillow and grabbed my tennis shoes. I liked going to the track with Mama. She jogged, then speed-walked for a few minutes, slowed down, then did this again for several laps. I did it with her, then she'd sit on the bleachers and time me to see how quickly I could complete a lap. I welcomed the challenge. Like I said, I love running. The wind hits my face and shocks me in that good way. My heart pounds against my chest like it's going to burst. The only sounds are wind and the slap of my feet. Just when it feels as if my body will split open from the pressure, the finish line is in front of me. I'd hear Mama clapping and yelling, "Go, go, baby. You got it, Nia."

Our track outings had started one Saturday afternoon in April, eight months after my father's death. I was reading a Nancy Drew book from the box Mr. Carter had given me when Mama knocked on my bedroom door.

Mama opened the door. "Come on." She motioned to me. "We're going to the track."

I got up, surprised, but followed right along. Mama had on her white gym shoes, a long T-shirt with DIVA's in gold letters, and some yoga leggings. I put on my black running shoes. I already had on sweatpants and a T-shirt. We drove without speaking. That was normal for us. Mama and I didn't do a lot of talking when it was just the two of us. She was the quiet one in our family. Daddy had had the big voice. He loved to laugh and make other people laugh same as my grandfather, who he was named after. Daddy could even make Mama giggle until she cried, which wasn't a given. She didn't let go so easily. When she did, it was something to see. Her whole face lit up.

We'd gone to the track at Carver G., my middle school where I was in the sixth grade. Me and Daddy's spot to run was the track at my future high school or every now and again this peaceful park out in North Bay, the rich part of town I secretly nicknamed Perfectville 'cause of the huge houses and green lawns.

On the track, the first thing Mama had said was "Well, if you're going to do track team this year, you need to stay fast." I didn't say aloud that I was thinking about not running. Maybe I wouldn't be on the team. In elementary school, I had been the fastest girl and was still faster than some of the boys I knew. I liked winning, and I loved running. Running took the place of screaming as loud as you wanted or saying exactly what you thought in a room full of people when you're not supposed to.

But I hadn't been looking forward to joining any track team. My father wouldn't be there to see me, so what was the point? We'd had it all planned. I would run track in middle school, then high school, earn academic and track scholarships to college, and maybe try out for the Olympics.

And then that worst day happened right before sixth grade began. I still ran, but alone, not as part of a team. Mama had been on a mission to end my self-exile—it was what my father would have wanted.

As it turned out, our first excursion to the track together was about more than running or exercise that afternoon. I found this out at the end of our third lap around when Mama stopped us.

"I was talking to your grandmother, and we were thinking, you know, we've been through a lot. What do you think about maybe going to talk to somebody about everything?"

I had no idea what she meant. "Somebody like who?"

"A counselor."

"Why?" I was getting the idea and wasn't having it.

She eased into her fast walk. "Because when a terrible thing happens like what happened to us, you gotta make sure you're dealing with it, not keeping it your head."

"I'll do better," I promised.

"No, baby, it's not anything you're doing or not doing. I gotta make sure you're all right now and will be in the future. That's all." She slowed. Mama wasn't in the habit of talking about him like that. "Our lives got turned upside down, and I want to make sure we're okay."

"You're going, too?"

She didn't answer until we crossed the mile mark.

"Yeah. We'll both go. Nana Mae maybe, too. Okay?"

"Deal."

"Now, I need to get in a little more exercise. I put on a few too many around here lately." She pointed to her waist.

I didn't know what she was talking about. My mother's figure was as perfect as always, just like her face. If anything, I thought she had lost a little weight since Daddy had passed. I've known my mother was beautiful since I was little. She's named after Dorothy Dandridge, this movie star the grandmother I never got to meet loved. I looked her up on the internet, and a bunch of pictures came up, most from a movie called *Carmen Jones*. She was definitely very pretty, but Mama was that pretty and then some—like her mother, from the few pictures of her Mama had. When we walked down the street or were in a store, wherever, people took a second look at Mama and a third. Especially men—they stared at her after we passed. Sometimes they acted like the boys at school and whistled, which really made me mad. Most times, they just went out of their way to speak to her and if she was carrying groceries or anything, they offered to help her whether it was heavy or not.

Mama could've been a model or a movie star. She's got these hazel brown eyes. Mine are brown, too, but Mama's eyes glow. She has flawless Hershey-brown skin and beautiful locks that flow down her back. I've begged her to let me grow locks, too, but she says I need to wait until I'm older and can make a conscious decision, whatever that means. Mama didn't need makeup and wore very little. Everything fit just right. People agreed on three things about my mother: A) She was a good person, B) she was a good mother, and C) she was very good-looking. My father was the one who thought I was truly Mama- and Dorothy Dandridge-like beautiful. I was his "Bright Eyes" or "pretty baby girl" always.

I have his nose, which looked fine on him, but in my opinion hadn't turned out as perfect on me. When we were together, people would say, "All you gotta do is look in the mirror, you the spitting image of your daddy." Now people had begun to say how I was getting to look more like my mother, which was a lie to me. But even though I wasn't pretty like her or the actress she was named after, sometimes when I looked in the mirror, my face made sense. It fit me, unlike my chest. Anyway, that was how the track thing with me and Mama got started. Sometimes we'd go two or three times a week. Other times just once. We'd even go in the winter if there wasn't snow. But as the second year without Daddy came in, we went way less.

This time at the track, my mother didn't waste any time getting to what was on her mind. She wanted to discuss Little Petey, and it only took half a lap before she brought it up.

"Nia, what happened to Little Petey breaks my heart." She paused. That was an invitation for me to say something.

"Yes, ma'am." I didn't want to talk about Little Petey with her.

"It's been rough on you. I want to know what's going on with you, really, on the inside."

"I'm all right, Mama."

We crossed over the mile mark.

Mama sighed. "You shouldn't have seen that. It shouldn't ever happen anywhere." She sounded so sad. "I think there's a lot going on in your head right now, baby. Anything you want to tell your mama?"

"Uh, no." I could tell by the way she slowed and shook her head, it was not what she wanted to hear. She looked at me sideways, hard.

I followed her lead, bending and stretching. I figured I needed to say something else or she'd be watching me like a hawk even more.

I took a deep breath. "I had a dream about Daddy. It— it wasn't bad, though," I lied. Probably no matter what I said, she was going to worry and drag me to the doctor.

Mama put her hand underneath my chin, lifting my face so I was forced to look directly into her eyes. I was not expecting this. It was like staring into a pool of brown light, and that made me feel kind of funny, like crying. She hugged me to her hard. She seemed shorter standing there with my head lying against her, reaching up to right under her chin. She rocked me a little.

She had grabbed me the same way when I was on the floor in the bathroom after seeing Little Petey on the ground. We didn't hug every day or anything, Mama and me. It was something me and Daddy and me and Nana Mae tended to do way more. Not that I didn't love Mama or she didn't love me. I knew she did. Daddy was the hugger. Mama was the one who touched my head or stomach just right if I was sick or made medicine taste better than it really did so I would take it without a fuss.

When she did hug me, it didn't matter that we didn't go around doing it that much. There were a thousand hugs in that one. I wanted her to keep holding me that way, and I didn't at the same time. I was sorry that I couldn't tell her everything.

She pulled away. "Hey, you recall that doctor? The one we went to see for a while? I'm thinking you should go see her, you know, talk about what happened."

"Uh, yeah, I mean . . . yes, I remember her." That was the last thing I wanted to do. I just wanted to find out who had killed Little Petey. I swallowed and looked at her as serious as I could. "Could we maybe wait, maybe until school starts and see how everything's going? Unless I really need to. I'm okay right now, really."

She nodded. "All right, I think you've had plenty rest. Let me see how fast you can get yourself around this track."

I showed her, too. I shaved a half second off my mile run, and Mama promised me a strawberry shake as a reward.

Things went off in a different direction when we walked up the sidewalk to the house a little bit later. Nana Mae was on the front porch, talking and laughing with a strange man. He was a tall guy wearing some paint-splattered pants and a black T-shirt with more white paint spots on it. The man turned around as we walked up. Dark-skinned, beard, and muscles. Lots of muscles. It was the man the church ladies had acted all extra with that night at the vigil. He wasn't expecting to see us, especially Mama. I could tell by the way his eyes stay glued on her while he introduced himself. He stared right in her face.

"I'm Jay. Like Jay-Z. Only without the bling and Beyoncé. Just Jay. Jay Dele."

Nana Mae laughed as if he'd made a great joke, and Mama kind of half nodded. Good. He pulled himself away from looking at her for a second and looked at me.

"Wow, three lovely new neighbors," he said.

I looked at Mama. She was still not looking at him. She kept turning her head like the sun was in her eyes, though it wasn't, and a hint of teeth flashed. Was she smiling or trying not to? I instantly could not stand Mr. Jay-as-in-Jay-Z Dele. He grinned at me with his movie star mouth. Braces work, probably. No way they were naturally straight and white like that.

But there was that mat of hair framing the mouth and covering the lower part of his cheeks and chin. Once Daddy had experimented with growing a mustache. Mama fussed and fussed, said she never liked no man with hair on his face. She hated mustaches and beards. When Daddy went to kiss her, she pushed him away and gave him that eye.

"Don't even think about coming near me with that fuzz mess on your lip. Next thing you know, you be nuzzling me with a beard. No thank you," she'd said with that eyebrow arched up on him.

The next morning, Daddy didn't have so much as a whisker on his face. The mustache was history.

Mr. Jay Dele had a beard. That was a deal breaker, no matter what.

"Mr. Dele bought Mr. Carter's house. He's a police officer," Nana Mae volunteered like he was the real answer to world peace. "Sure makes my day knowing we got him around here now."

"Welcome to the neighborhood, Mr. Dele. I better get on in the house and get cleaned up," Mama said. She was already opening the screen door by the time he recovered and called out "Nice to meet you" to her back.

I did my best to look and sound just as unenthused with my "Bye" as I passed him and followed Mama on into the house. Mr. Jay-as-in-Jay-Z Dele was definitely not welcome. Not only had he stared at Mama, but he'd also taken Mr. Carter's house. I had held on to hoping that Mr. Carter would come back. Every Saturday morning at about nine or ten, unless it was raining, he'd wash his car—a classic, according to Daddy, a gray 1970s Buick something or other. Mr. Carter washed that Buick for hours until the gray became silver, and all the while he'd be playing these really old love songs. Saturday mornings, the neighborhood would wake up to "Float, float, on." Warrior, Mr. Carter's big German shepherd, would be on the front porch, out of the way of the sun and Mr. Carter's water hose. Warrior wasn't asleep, though. Soon as he heard anybody getting close to Mr. Carter's place, he'd raise his head. If he didn't know you, he'd stand up and come on down the stairs until you passed or Mr. Carter gave the okay by greeting the person. If he knew you, and you were okay by his standards, Warrior would come to the sidewalk, wagging his tail to greet you himself. But if he didn't care about you and you were familiar but safe, he'd just raise his head up and look but never stand or come one down the stairs. Warrior liked me.

I had never given Mr. Carter the big thank-you I should have for the Nancy Drew books and being the good neighbor that he'd been. Now Jay-as-in-not-Jay-Z was living in his house.

CHAPTER
9

We finally staked out our neighborhood on the last Friday in June. The intersection of MLK and Ralph Abernathy was our beginning and end point. Our mission was to find out who was coming and going and at home on Friday mornings and then discover the witness who saw the car. Or maybe the witnesses who weren't admitting they were.

It was no easy trick getting to do it either. Since Little Petey's murder, Mama and Nana Mae teamed up to have eyes on me more than usual. Most days, I was holed up in the shop or at home not far from Nana Mae. Sometimes we walked down to the Y pool or to a matinee movie. Mostly, I hung out by myself puzzling over the riddle of Little Petey's death and trying not to think of how I'd seen him that day.

Luckily, Mama got to feeling a little sorry about the way the summer was going for me. She and Nana Mae agreed we had to relax a little and get on back to normal, as much as that was possible and whatever that was. This meant I could go back to hanging out with Miracle Ruth and Dontay without a big fuss or some long pause, followed by a list of cautious dos and don'ts just to go down the street. We took our bikes and rode up and down Ralph Abernathy, stopping way before Miracle Ruth's house, which was on the opposite side and farther down from where Little Petey had lived.

I still didn't like to look at the quiet gray-and-white house. When I glanced there, I could see him, grinning, with ketchup or peanut butter on his face, and sitting on his bike or in the bit of yard with his head thrown back, screeching and laughing hard as he stumbled and fell trying to kick the soccer ball to our goal—the stone rock circle around the tree in the middle of their grass.

I wondered if Dontay and Miracle Ruth thought about him as much as I did. Neither of them saw him that day on the ground dying, with blood drenching the Batman on his shirt. He had not stared into their eyes and accused them. By the time Dontay fought his way through the scene, the crowd was being pushed back for the paramedics rushing out of the ambulance.

We started at 8:45 in the morning. Some folks worked the same hours every day. You knew them better by their job instead of by name. There was the guy who drove for UPS who wore brown pants and a jacket in winter and shorts in the summer, and his wife who worked in a bakery. Two ladies on the same side of the street as Miracle Ruth were nurses. A couple more had jobs at plants way across town in the industrial park area. By 8:45 A.M., they were long gone.

There were one or two people who had lived in the neighborhood forever. You saw them on Sundays at church or sometimes in late evening before dark sitting out on the porch watching the cars and people move by. They hid inside from the summer heat. Big air conditioners sat on the outside of their windows, humming and rattling along all day into the night.

There didn't seem to be that much to notice as we circled up and down awhile. I was keeping in mind a lesson learned from Nancy Drew and TV crime shows: Pay attention to the smallest detail. A lot of times, these led to the biggest clues, which solved the crime.

"Man, how long we stayin' out here?" Dontay asked forty minutes later.

We paused and parked on the sidewalk by the street signs, too close for me to where Little Petey had died.

Dontay rested on his handlebars, his eyes squinting under the sun. "For real, how long we staying out here? It's getting hot."

He was getting on my nerves.

"It's summer," Dontay whined on. "Man, we supposed to be sleeping late. I already gotta work with Pops at the shop two mornings a week and got basketball I gotta be up early for on Saturday."

He was right about one thing. It was hot already. I was starting to get a little damp under my armpits and in the center of my chest. I didn't have on a hat either. Or sunscreen like Mama was always telling me to put on.

"Let's just give it another few minutes, okay?" I said. Really though, the stakeout wasn't near as interesting as it'd sounded beforehand, though I wasn't about to say so.

Miracle Ruth took her cell phone out of the pink pouch strapped across one shoulder. She was prepared, as usual, and we weren't even in school. She almost looked like it wasn't hot compared to me and Dontay, except the damp hair around the edges of her face curling up. She'd been sipping on a water bottle in the holder on her bike the whole time, unlike me. I had forgotten all about water.

"The people we saw left for work by nine, and there hasn't been much going on," Miracle Ruth pointed out. "Except the air conditioner at that blue house two doors from Little Petey's that came on right around nine A.M."

It was a noisy contraption, rattling and hissing so much that we thought it would immediately putter out and go back to resting. This older man who'd moved in a couple of years before lived there. He stayed to himself, no other family that I could tell. I never saw anyone else except him sometimes, cutting some flowers on his lawn. When I was with Little Petey or when I passed on the other side of the street on my way to Miracle Ruth's, sometimes he'd be walking, wearing a straw hat and looking straight ahead, on the way to the bus stop I guessed.

"We also got the lady right at the corner in the green house," I offered.

"Yeah," Dontay said, smirking. "Whew, when she came out and bent over, and got that paper . . ."

"We shouldn't be talking about her," Miracle Ruth tried to say with a straight face, "That's Mrs.—Mrs. James."

We fell out laughing, picturing the morning's main show.

Mrs. James had come out, all right. White scarf wrapped around her head and a polka-dotted red robe with a hole under one arm and what looked like a big bleach spot right where her butt poked out. She'd given a full view of the bleach spot when she tried to reach the newspaper that had fallen short of the mark. She had to come all the way off the porch and turn to get it. When she noticed us, she grabbed her paper and rushed back in the house fast. Miracle Ruth said she knew Mrs. James's name because Ms. Torrence knew the lady. I'd only seen her before out in the yard or coming and going. Miracle Ruth said the woman barely spoke unless she was passing time with her grandmother.

"She definitely might've seen something. People are creatures of habit," I said, echoing some detective I'd heard on TV. "She probably gets that paper about the same time every single morning."

"Uh-huh," Miracle Ruth said. "I don't think we'll ever find out about everybody that might've seen something. Who knows who was looking out a window or something?"

"Why anybody gonna tell us? They sure ain't telling the police, and they not going to talk to some kids," said Dontay.

"I got an idea about that," I said.

"Can we hear about it out this sun? I need to get something else to eat." It didn't matter that he'd eaten breakfast not even an hour before.

"Okay, okay." I wanted to continue because Mama would be dropping by home around lunch, she'd said. There was no telling if I'd be able to get away for a while again that day. Most Friday afternoons, Nana Mae enjoyed a long lunch with one of her friends or a book club meeting, but not so much since the shooting. She might hang around the house noting my activities.

"Wait, don't turn," Miracle Ruth whispered.

"What?" Dontay demanded, twisting around anyway. "Why you whispering?"

Our bikes stood next to each other, our backs to the street but facing Miracle Ruth.

"Don't," Miracle Ruth whispered. "Act like you're not

looking. A car's coming." Her hands gripped the handle-bars. She raised up on the seat just slightly, clearly looking past us.

"So? That is a street," Dontay said.

"Miracle Ruth," I said, looking at her hard and willing myself not to turn to the car. "Is it—"

"Yeah."

"The brown Caddy?" Dontay's voice rose.

"Shhh, yeah," Miracle Ruth shushed him as if who-ever was in the car could hear. "It's about three houses down now. Is it the one you followed from the vigil?"

I shifted on my bike, squinted, and wiped my face like I was trying to block out the sun. I made a half-circle so I was at a slight angle. I could just see the car out of the corner of my eye just as it got about even with the intersec-tion and Little Petey's house.

"I think so. Looks like it." My heart thumped in my chest, I was so excited. Then something occurred to me. If it was the car from the day Little Petey got killed, then it was probably the killer or killers driving right then. Maybe they were back looking to do more shooting. The sun felt suddenly hotter.

"What's happening?" Dontay whispered now, too. Sweat dripped down his forehead and both sides of his face.

"Nothing. It turned around," Miracle Ruth answered. None of us spoke.

"It's gone." Miracle Ruth let out a breath and sat down on her bicycle

"Man, what was it doing here?" Dontay lifted his hat and wiped the sweat off his face with one arm.

"Maybe returning to the scene of the crime. Criminals do that sometimes." That was something that happened on the television police shows a lot. Detectives got some of their biggest breaks when the guilty guy returned to the crime scene to retrieve something he dropped or hid, and sometimes the star detective with supernatural smarts solved the whole thing and outlined the crime just how it happened.

I didn't have supernatural smarts. Neither did Miracle Ruth or Dontay. We hadn't even narrowed down yet if it was Scary Face from the vigil and what his real name was or if it was one of his boys or the unwelcome intruder from the funeral or someone else.

"Too bad we didn't get a photo or video. Something," I said.

"Yeah," Miracle Ruth said. They were reading my mind. Both of them had their cell phones, but they could hardly have whipped them out and started taking pictures of the car.

"I'm going home and eat," Dontay declared.

"When aren't you hungry?" Miracle Ruth chided.

I didn't argue with him. I was glad the car had only turned around instead of something worse.

CHAPTER

10

Fourth of July weekend meant putting major clue hunting on hold and I hated it, but the Friday before the number one summer holiday, people didn't want to be bothered. They were kicking off a long holiday weekend, getting ready for barbecues, parties, and travel. Mama worked late into Thursday night and early Friday morning in a marathon day making clients look good for their holiday plans, then shut Diva's down by the afternoon for the holiday weekend instead of working herself until she was dead tired. I was thrilled not to be spending all of Friday or Saturday sweeping up the overflow of hair and running here and there fetching items as Mama or any of her customers demanded.

I was parked in my favorite reading spot other than my

bedroom, Daddy's big reclining chair downstairs, my feet anchored on Pepto Bismol, the big stuffed animal Daddy had won at the carnival our last day together. I had pulled out *The Clue in the Crossword Cypher*, one of the old Nancy Drew books from the box. *The Clue in the Crossword Cypher* was one of the first few Nancy Drew books that I'd read. Nancy was off in South America with her friends investigating a case. I wished it was possible to go somewhere exciting and far away like that with Miracle Ruth, Dontay, and Alima, too, chasing a mystery that wasn't life or death.

Back in the day, by the time I got to where Nancy was about to break the case, nothing could pull me away from reading until I got through the last chapter. Now I slogged through a few pages and got to the point where Nancy was revealing her theory about how the clues fit together. But I couldn't get lost in it like I used to when I was eleven, reading book after book. I already knew how things would turn out. It was almost too simple in the end when Nancy Drew solved the case and showed up the police and even her dad.

I read several chapters, but then I drifted back to wondering what would have happened if I'd just been on time. Would Little Petey have gotten shot? Would we have been huddled in the kitchen with Shayla during the shooting? I shut my eyes against the thought. Then I turned my focus back to the words on the page. Minutes later, I was still on the same page.

"My Lord," Nana Mae said suddenly. "Turn it up, baby."

I looked at the television. *Breaking News* rolled across the screen in white letters while the anchor with the silver hair on Channel 3 talked. I joined Mama and Nana Mae on the couch.

"We are still gathering details for you. What we do know right now is that sometime between eleven twenty and eleven thirty, a gunman entered the Bright Future daycare in Muncie, Minnesota, and fired multiple shots. There are casualties." The newsman was gray, not his normal pinkish self.

"Lord, have mercy," Mama said, and pressed the remote several times. The report was on every channel.

We sat there staring at the reports, listening to minute-by-minute updates as the late afternoon drifted into the early evening. The reporters were pale, even the Black journalists with their usually perfectly made-up skin like Shandra Bell. Their hair and clothes were uncharacteristically a bit messy, as if they'd been sleeping and somebody yelled "Fire!" so they'd run out minus careful makeup and hairspray.

Mama got her fill of watching first. "I'm going in the room and lay down for a little while. What do you want to do about dinner?" Her voice was heavy.

"Don't you worry about it. I'll put a little something together in a bit," Nana Mae answered.

The doorbell ringing startled us. Nana Mae muted the volume and went to answer. Seconds later, she came back carrying a pan covered with foil with Jay Dele following close behind.

"Well, Jay, you must be psychic. We just spoke about dinner and here you come with dessert."

"I recall somebody saying peach cobbler was a favorite over here and, uh, I sure don't need it all to myself." He took in me and Mama still reading the closed-captioned words across the silent television screen set on CNN. More breaking news in bold white ran across the bottom. Thirteen little kids and two teachers were dead.

"Lord have mercy." Nana Mae swayed from side to side holding the pan. No one spoke for a long second.

Jay Dele cleared his throat. "It's a terrible day."

Mama nodded and stood up. "Yes, it is," she said, shaking her head. "Thank you for the pie. Peach cobbler is a favorite around here, right, Nia?"

I couldn't believe how she'd put me on the spot. Lying was out of the question. So was agreeing.

"I don't want any," I blurted out.

Mama's eyebrow arched up. Jay Dele stood there shifting his feet. I backtracked.

"I'm not hungry, my stomach—" I cut right between them and past Nana Mae to escape up the few stairs. It was true. My stomach had started spinning and gurgling as soon as that first breaking news flashed across the screen. Thirteen little kids were dead. Just like Little Petey, they were gone like *that*.

The bubbles reached toward my chest. I couldn't have

eaten anything right then, not even peach cobbler, and certainly not his. I lingered at the top of the stairs.

"It's been a terrible day . . . terrible the last few weeks . . ." Nana Mae trailed off.

"No need to explain. This is difficult for adults to handle, let alone the kids."

He was about to go on duty and had to leave. Good. Mama called him Mr. Dele. "Be safe out there," she said politely. I heard the door close and the deadbolt slide into the lock.

The phone rang. I was right outside Mama's room. On the third ring, I went in and picked it up.

"Hello."

"You hear?" Dontay asked.

"Yeah, we watching."

"Everybody is." His deep voice surprised me. We didn't talk much by phone.

We hung on for a few seconds more, knowing each other was still there but not speaking.

"You okay?" he asked finally.

"Yeah." That was a lie, of course. "You?"

"Yeah, it is what it is," he said without conviction. He sounded like his brother. "They talking about canceling the fireworks this weekend."

"Really? I doubt Mama's feeling like going now anyway. Maybe Monday on the Fourth," I said.

"Yeah, tomorrow. I gotta go, okay—"

"Night," I said to the air. He'd gotten a call. Maybe from one of the grownish girls from the park again. I set the phone down and powered on the computer. I tapped and clicked, then entered my password. Besides advertisements for store sales in my email, there was a new message from Miracle Ruth: *Can you believe this?* There was a link she'd inserted beneath her words. I typed *No* and sent it, then clicked the link. A caption on a popular news site came up: *God's Angels*. Thirteen little faces smiled and posed cutely with names like Ashley, Tommy, Miranda . . . white versions of Little Petey, each one alive and happy. Except now none of them were.

I left Mama's room and paused at the top of the stairway. I could hear Mama and Nana Mae at the bottom of the stairs.

"I swear I feel like taking my child and going off somewhere."

"Going off to where, baby?"

"I don't know, some place safer." Mama sounded very tired.

"Hmph, safe? There ain't really no such place. I know you already know that. If there's not one kind of danger, there's another, and people will do wrong and bring it anywhere." I could tell from her tone that Nana Mae did not take any pleasure in saying it.

"I know, Mae, I know. Should be, though, should be some damn place."

I went to my room and stayed there watching the evening light fade to dark. When my stomach settled down, hunger stabs set in. I got out of bed and eased down the hall and the stairs, hoping the quiet meant Mama and Nana Mae were tucked away for the night. Neither of them was in the kitchen or the living room. I opened the refrigerator, got out the lemonade, and grabbed the turkey sandwich with the brown edges cut off the bread that Nana Mae had left for me. I ignored Jay Dele's peach cobbler on the stove. I ate and drank fast and resisted the urge to turn on the television.

Back in bed, I couldn't fall out like I wanted to. Little Petey's face mixed into the row of those thirteen faces from online and the breaking news ran through my mind all night and drove me to the bathroom it seemed like every hour.

We saw no fireworks that weekend except on television. The city dedicated the Fourth of July celebration the Monday after to the children and teachers in Muncie.

Wa alaykum as–salam.

Dear Nia, my friend,

When I was very little, the wall seemed far from me. Mornings, the sun would rise on the olive trees. My father would be early tending the trees and our vineyard. I would always want to help even when too small so I could eat the grapes and be with him.

I loved the trees. They seemed to be forever. Now my father makes bricks and sells them.

Do you know the story of Zarqa al Yamama? She could see all things and so know of the things to come. If I were her, I would have saved our trees. I would have told of the explosions from the sky that day. And the walls that would be built around us and the soldiers who wouldn't see us as we are, people like them.

I would have told of these things long, long before the coming.

Alima
عَالِمَة

CHAPTER

11

The whole world seemed paused and glued to one reality—what happened at the daycare in Muncie. At the beauty shop where Mama kept me busy, the talk and the television stayed on the news. I began to get really anxious as the days passed. I needed Little Petey's murder solved. The local news had all but moved on, occasionally mentioning him at the end of coverage on the other children, more often not at all. When he was, sometimes he wasn't even referenced by name, just mentioned like a minor note as the little boy who'd been shot on the east side a few weeks ago.

For an unheard of seven days, I couldn't reach Miracle Ruth on her phone. When I'd called the house, if Ms. Torrence was yapping on the other line, she'd snap, "Nia,

Miracle Ruth got her own phone," or she'd say she was sleeping. Miracle Ruth was online a lot and could usually be counted on to answer a message quickly, but not anymore. I'd made my way to Miracle Ruth's house twice when I was pretty sure she was there by herself, but I'd been left on the porch ringing the doorbell and knocking.

Dontay had no better luck texting, calling, or emailing her. Three days of no word from her, let alone a week, was a record and enough for both of us. We finally went over together, determined to see her face-to-face. I was hoping we could make some progress with continuing our mission to find out who had killed Little Petey, so I had the notebook in hand that I had begun jotting down my thoughts and notes in about the shooting we were trying to solve.

Soon as we stepped in the house, Ms. Torrence kept right on blabbing on the phone and waved us off to Miracle Ruth's room with a hand. We tapped on the cracked bedroom door, and I entered just ahead of Dontay. Miracle Ruth began talking fast to us without getting up from her desk or looking at us, as if she'd seen us just yesterday. She tapped away on her laptop, fixated, eyes barely blinking. Her words tumbled out, leaving no space for breath.

"You know how many children from babies to our age that died from guns between here and Chicago so far this year? Guess, go on." She didn't wait for us to answer. "I'm starting a petition. Something has to be done. We gotta, we gotta—"

"Miracle Ruth—"

"You believe this? You don't know, do you? Forty-six. FORTY-SIX. That's right, forty-six. Did you know that?" she rushed right on.

Dontay glanced at me and swallowed. "Uh . . . uh . . ."

"Miracle Ruth," I started to say again, but she charged toward us with a notebook of pink paper crumpled in her hand.

"Listen to this. Last year it was MORE THAN THAT by this time in the summer." She flipped the notebook page. "I can't believe this! You know there was this nine-month-old baby KILLED in his dad's arms. You hear me? How was that being in the wrong place at the wrong time, huh? Here's another one . . ." She frowned down at her notes. Her braided ponytail had gone the way of my hair at the end of most days, hair strands sticking out on the sides or top no matter how carefully and tightly Mama or Nana Mae braided it.

"Children are getting killed EVERYWHERE, drive-bys or bombs or some pervert is strangling them. You want to know how many worldwide this year so far, huh? How many have been murdered in a DECADE?" She said this really slowly in case she was talking to two dummies who didn't comprehend what she was saying. "It's just an estimate. It's thousands. Maybe a million. It's too many to count, okay? Guess how many homicides they got in Chicago alone this year?"

I did know that number, actually. It had been on the news, since all the talk was about violence and guns. We took in her pinkish-red eyes, her chest rising and falling fast as if she was sprinting.

"Like four hundred. More, they say," Dontay offered, studying the floor.

Miracle Ruth looked at Dontay like he was missing good sense or something. "Four hundred thirty two. That's four hundred and thirty-two funerals. And it's just July! People are out there taking lives, killing, and it don't matter who." This was surely something Ms. Torrence probably said but this was the first time Miracle Ruth's actual voice sounded like her grandmother's. She was a runaway train right then and showing no signs of pulling in for a stop.

"MIRACLE RUTH," I said too loud. "Miracle Ruth, you right, it's messed up. You right. We all know it."

"Nia, Little Petey . . . he's dead, he's really gone." She looked from me to Dontay, then swayed like she might trip. And then the faucets turned on. Tears streaked down her cheeks. "Nobody cares either."

"That ain't true. You know it's not. *We care*." Dontay hugged her. For a couple of seconds, she let herself cave into his chest, but then she pushed away from him.

I recognized that pain she was feeling. There was no day that I ever forgot my father had been murdered. There were short periods when the fact was in a corner of my head so I could live without my heart burning all the time.

But the truth was the same every day I woke and went to bed. Daddy was in the grave, and so was Little Petey and the children at the daycare. Every day there were more people killed with no reason in the killings, leaving the rest behind to do the missing and puzzling over the nonsense of it. I felt tears trying to gather in my own eyes and that sensation of trying to swallow rocks, but I willed them back.

Miracle Ruth dropped her hands. The notebook floated to the floor. I knew that scared, lost look. The first time I'd really paid attention to Miracle Ruth in life, it was during recess. She'd had that same look. It was like I was the girl in the book who felt everybody's pain. I sensed her emotions.

Miracle Ruth had transferred into our class in the third grade when she and Ms. Torrence moved into the neighborhood. Our school was okay except for the kids who liked to pick on one another and strangers. She was alone, mostly, and quiet. Even back then, every day some part of her outfit was sure to have a shade of pink. I'd seen her at church helping her grandmother cook her famous coconut cakes and sweet potato pies for the anniversaries and funerals. She'd be in the kitchen, the only kid among a sea of white-dressed, bustling, hip-bumping ladies all talking at once to one another, while the rest of us kids were busy running around until some deaconess or our mothers got at us for playing too much. At school, the teachers clearly liked this new girl who was always wearing something pink and acted perfectly polite and well-behaved. Our home-room teacher even let her stay inside on the computer sometimes during recess.

The bully at our school was a girl who was big for her age, even bigger than all the big kids in her class a grade higher than us. She ruled over several other girls, and she loved to mess with Miracle Ruth about her name and wear-ing pink so much. That day, I was playing with Dontay, Fernando, and a couple of others. Nearby, the big girl laughed loudly, pointing at Miracle Ruth, who ignored her and kept swinging.

"Hey pink girl, you hear me?" the big girl yelled, approaching the swings. "You hear me, girl? Hey, M-I-R-A-C-L-E? You ain't no M-I-R-A-C-L-E. Your mama was a crackhead, and everybody know it, too."

The clones the girl ruled over giggled.

Miracle Ruth stopped swinging and stood up. "The Lord don't like ugly," she said very distinctly.

This hint of a fight on the horizon caught the atten-tion of the playground, so children gravitated toward the swings—me and my circle, too.

The girl in pink wasn't through. "My name is Miracle Ruth. MIRACLE RUTH. If you can't say it right, then don't you say my name."

I was almost as shocked as the big girl. Her crew

cackled—this time at her, not at Miracle Ruth. For a quick second, the girl considered her target. Most of us had never heard Miracle Ruth speak, outside of giving teachers the shortest possible right answers when called upon in class.

Then the girl charged Miracle Ruth. Time slowed.

Miracle Ruth stood up straighter and her lips moved. *The Lord is my shepherd, I shall not want . . .* She glanced around at our faces. She and I tagged eyes, and there it was. She was brave and terrified.

As the big girl rushed to get in Miracle Ruth's face, I stepped forward without thinking and stuck my leg out. The big girl toppled inches from Miracle Ruth's feet.

"Girl, watch where you going," I said, a hand on each hip.

Dontay grinned at Miracle Ruth. "Miracle and Ruth, like in the Bible, right?"

The good Lord really did work in mysterious ways.

"Yes. Like in the Bible," Miracle Ruth answered, smiling so shyly we caught only a hint of teeth.

From that day on, we were our own crew—me, Dontay, Miracle Ruth, and Fernando until he moved away.

"Miracle Ruth, let's try to do what we said for Little Petey, okay? Get justice like you said, don't you think?"

I hoped I was getting through. It would be easy for us

to go off the rails. I felt as sick as she did. So did Dontay. I could tell by the way he hardly said anything and how low his voice sounded that night on the phone after news of the daycare murders broke. Now he was looking helplessly at Miracle Ruth as she went off. My stomach bubbled up furiously every time I thought about what had happened to the children and teachers at the daycare, and then always, my mind went back to Little Petey and my father. They haunted my dreams at night, and in the daytime I walked around with a digital photo frame of images flip-flopping in my head—Little Petey sitting on his blue bike grinning up at me, still cute and goofy with that missing tooth, and the picture that sat by my bed of my father and me hugging and laughing outside of the amusement park after a day of rides.

Those numbers Miracle Ruth quoted—forty-six, thousands, a million—were unbelievable. In one of her letters, Alima wrote that she'd known how unsafe the world was since she was born, practically. *The many dead*, her grandmother said. Why it was like this, I didn't understand. And the worst thing was, I didn't have a single idea about how to solve it, or if anybody, from the president to the police, was going to stop it someday or if they even wanted to as badly as I wanted to find out who had taken Little Petey from the world.

"Yeah, Miracle Ruth." Dontay stepped up to her and put a hand on each of her shoulders. "I know this stuff is wild. But we need to focus right now, all right? You and Nia talked me into this, now I'm in. For Little Petey, like you said. Now what do you want to do?"

Miracle Ruth finally looked up at him. She blinked, shook her head, then looked at me. I did not drop my eyes from hers.

"Okay," she said.

All three of us exhaled.

CHAPTER

12

We left a calmer Miracle Ruth and walked back up the street to Dontay's. Our feet automatically slowed in agreement as Shayla's grandmother's house came into view. Mama had claimed my body for a couple of hours for some Diva's cleanup early evening, so there was nothing to do but chill until then and consider where we were. We sacked out on the couch half-watching Dontay's favorite channel, SportsTV, not saying much. Everything that was going on and the scene with Miracle Ruth on top of that was a lot.

The inside layout of Dontay's house was different from mine. It was a ranch-style house with all the rooms on one floor. The comfy extra-large sofa we sat on was in the center of the family room with its back to the dining room and the kitchen. The look was pretty much the same as how Dontay's mom had kept it, except for the messy order that Dontay's father, Ahmad, and Dontay had created over the years. The sheer bronze polyester curtains on the windows were the same ones Dontay's mother had picked out and hung when she and Dontay Sr. moved into this, their first house. Dontay had fingerprinted them with a few permanent jelly stains from wrapping the curtains around the length of his body as a little boy, playing hide-and-seek with his mother, who Dontay Sr. liked to recall, stayed on a one-woman mission to preserve her elegant curtains.

Since her death, one corner of the family room had gained a tall stack of old records topped by headphones that belonged to Ahmad. Dontay Sr.'s archive of auto mechanics magazines and Sunday *New York Times* littered the living room table. Dontay had a corner, too, where his basketball sat underneath a camera tripod. Over the small fireplace, pictures competed for space, most of Dontay's pretty mother alone or smiling and hugging their father and cuddling her boys, and others a montage of the four together, dressed up for the picture, starting from when the boys were infants, toddlers, then bigger boys, to the last photograph of Dontay's family before his mom got sick and died. There was a picture of my father somewhere in back of the crowded shelf of family pictures, too.

While Dontay watched TV, I stared at the fragments of notes in my notebook and tried to piece together a whole puzzle from the floating bits we had about our secret mission. Suddenly, there was a *BAM, BAM* from the back door in the kitchen followed by weaker tapping. It startled us. Usually a knock on that door was one you were expecting. Dontay looked at me and shrugged as he went to answer it.

"Who is it?" Dontay called out, then gasped as he opened the door. "AHMAD!" he yelled, running past the living room to the hallway, "Ahmad, come quick, man."

I got up and followed him as he dashed back to the kitchen.

Big Pete was half slumped on the counter by the door. Things sort of ticked into slow motion mode. Ahmad and Dontay rushing over, hoisting the big man up on either side. Big Pete grunted and talked while they struggled to half-drag him to a chair in the dining room.

"Got shot . . . damn, you b'lieve that?" Big Pete kept saying, like it would make sense if he said it a few times.

Ahmad tore the big man's white T-shirt. A dark red splotch was growing over his left shoulder. My heart drummed hard and fast in my chest. My stomach tightened and bunched up into a fist then burst open. *Please, please, please, God, please* . . . I couldn't even fill in the word missing in the prayer. I saw Little Petey, lifeless, blood drowning Batman, turning his baby blue shirt into a dark red lake. *Breathe, breathe*, I warned myself, and willed my insides to stay in my stomach instead of spilling out right there on the kitchen floor.

"Aw, man, damn. Look like the bullet went straight through, though," Ahmad said, sounding a little relieved. "You might not be dying today."

Big Pete half-laughed and grunted. "I told you, I told you, went right through. Hurt like a motha— Damn, easy, bruh. Clean shot. Guess I'm lucky like that—"

Lucky? Blessed. That's what Miracle Ruth and Mrs. Torrance would say, Nana Mae too. *The Lord look out for the fool, too*, she'd say.

Ahmad ripped more of the T-shirt. And there it was, literally a quarter-size hole rimmed in maroon that was trying its best to overflow. I swayed.

"You okay?" Dontay asked reaching for my arm. His fingers steadied me.

Big Pete blinked and looked at me. "Little Babysitter," he grunted, just realizing I was there. Ahmad pressed the hole with the torn T-shirt piece. "You watched my son good. He adored you, yeah, think he mighta been baby crushin' on you." He half-chuckled, wincing. "I remember your pops, too . . . He was good people . . . And your moms? She not like the rest neither, naw. They look at me like I got two horns . . ." His breath caught and held a second. "Like two horns is on top of my head for real. But your mama, she look a nigga eye to eye. She ain't approve of what you do, but . . . but she go right at you eye to eye, yeah . . ."

I looked him in the eye for the first time in my life. He wasn't wearing the dark shades he usually wore, no matter where he was, at his own son's funeral or leaned back in in the driver seat of his big yellow Hummer. I could see now the long eyelashes, the deep brown of his eyes even with the redness in them. Petey's eyes. I took in the rest of his face—the nose, yes, that was Petey's nose. But the lips and the skin color were different. Those Little Petey got from Shayla.

Little Petey asked me about his dad once. I was halfway reading, halfway paying attention to him.

"Grandma says Daddy's gangsta."

I didn't say anything. He kept rolling his yellow race car on the floor.

He looked up at me and stopped racing the car. "My daddy bad?"

I didn't know what to say and really wasn't inclined to say anything. But he was a little kid and he was asking *me*.

"Uh, well . . ." Oh Lord, what to say? "Your dad's your dad. You love him, right?"

He nodded.

"And he loves you. You ready for a snack? Some cookies?"

He seemed satisfied, or maybe it was the cookies. He beat me into the kitchen.

Strange that I was there in another kitchen with Little Petey's father feeling dizzy as he was on replay in my head. I took in Big Pete's face. His forehead was wet and oily. Drops of sweat rolled down his face like steam, dropping off the long eyelashes, same as his son's. Dontay's fingers clutching at mine kept me up.

"Damn, Mad, easy now—shit hurts," Big Pete groaned again.

"Tay, man, get that hydrogen peroxide out the bathroom, quick," Ahmad directed.

Dontay squeezed my fingers hard once and rushed off.

"And some clean towels, Tay," Ahmad yelled.

The pieces of bloodied T-shirt collected on the floor. Big Pete sat with his eyes closed now, grimacing, steeling his muscles as Ahmad pressed on his wound.

Big Pete growled, "Tell 'im to grab that Grey Goose Pops keep around here for the holidays, too."

Ahmad almost grinned. "Yeah, right, I got you, it's some ibuprofen in the bathroom."

"I'll get it," I volunteered, and rescued myself from that bloody hole and Big Pete's face.

Ahmad got Big Pete patched up the best he could. He gave him a quadruple dose of ibuprofen, no Grey Goose though. Big Pete was already a little out of it. He was going to need to be totally sharp head-wise, Ahmad told him. The white cloth bandages covered up the wound, and

Ahmad's improvising with black duct tape seemed to be holding it in place.

Big Pete sipped the glasses of juice and water Ahmad and Dontay plied him with. We formed a half-chorus in front of him, Ahmad sitting on the same side of the table with him, me and Dontay a step behind Ahmad's chair. We watched Big Pete sit there, naked from the waist up, save for the bandage and the elaborate tattoo scene covering his chest. A pirate, in red and yellow, complete with hat and an eye patch, reached menacingly toward another pirate, cowering with a black sword.

Big Pete clenched his teeth and breathed in as if hard at work. Sometimes he'd close his eyes, this weird smile on his face. It felt like a long time, though it was only minutes.

The big questions were on our minds. What had happened? Who had shot him? Big Pete made us wait until he was good and ready.

"Mad, I ain't shoot nobody. If I had, you know this the last place I'd run to."

Ahmad nodded.

"I just got my ass shot is all." Big Pete grinned. "Now, that wasn't 'posed to happen, but the best laid plans, right?"

"What went down today have anything to do with your son?" Ahmad asked slowly.

They regarded each other, communicating without either dropping his eyes from the other.

"Everything got to do with my son. Everything."

"You think you know for sure, right? Blade?" Ahmad interrogated.

Big Pete howled, then groaned in penance as his wound's pain grabbed him. "Blade? Man—"

"Everybody saw how he busted up in the church. You was this close to getting at it right there."

So that was our bald-headed funeral crasher in the black. Blade. My eyes were still glued on Big Pete and the clumsy bandage covering his wound, but my brain got busy at the mention of our first suspect.

Big Pete's face turned into a mask and he sat back. "Wasn't him. Wish it was. You know what that's about already."

Big Pete's gaze held Ahmad's, no flinching, not even a blink. "Shayla."

The bandaged wound lost my attention. Dontay and I glanced at each other, then back at the big man.

"Fool still can't get over Shayla getting with me. He think this opportunity. That nigga guilty"—Big Pete winced as he shifted in the chair—"of being a fool, but his punk ass ain't killed nobody."

And just like that, the mysterious bald-headed funeral crasher was off our barely there list of suspects.

"Okay." Ahmad nodded. "You could've died today, you know that, right?"

Big Pete actually laughed, then quickly grunted and

caressed his bandaged shoulder with a huge, callused hand. "Errrbody," he emphasized jokingly, and grimaced. "Everybody I know almost dying most days."

"What went down, BP? You made a move, right, and it didn't go right?" Ahmad asked.

"Hold on, wait, Mad, damn. Less you know the better." His eyes darted to me and Dontay. He gestured with his good arm and winced again.

He and Ahmad exchanged a coded look, then Ahmad looked at Dontay and me. We got the message loud and clear.

We waited in Dontay's room, me occupying myself with staring at the pictures that I'd seen a million times on the walls, and Dontay lying on his bed zooming the lens in and out on his camera. When Ahmad called us back to the kitchen, Big Pete was on his feet but leaning on the same counter by the door where it had all begun, only now he wore Dontay Sr.'s black sweatshirt. Since their dad was taller than Big Pete and almost as big, it just about fit him. Suddenly, there was a timid tap on the kitchen door. We all froze, Big Pete included, who straightened, placed one hand over the bandaged wound and raised a finger on the other to his lips, demanding our silence. He didn't have to though. None of us moved or dared to breathe loud. The knocking came again in a sequence. Three single knocks followed by two precise taps. Big Pete nodded and slouched on the counter again.

Ahmad went to the door peeked out and opened it. Lightning slid through the crack, exchanging a quick nod with Ahmad and glanced at me and Dontay. The tattoo on his neck did look like a bolt of lightning up close, inked in black marker against his skin. The open neck of his shirt revealed a bunch of other tattoos on his chest. He and Big Pete tapped with single fists and an elbow, though the movement obviously caused Big Pete pain. They didn't exchange any words aloud.

"'Tay, Nia, I won't be gone long, all right?" Ahmad spoke while he tied closed a black plastic garbage bag with the bloody T-shirt and the towels inside. He studied us. "I cleaned up, but—"

"I got it, Ahmad," Dontay said, sounding older than I'd ever heard him. "We got this," he added, speaking for both of us.

I nodded like a question had been asked of me that Dontay hadn't already answered. Lightning and Ahmad got on either side of Big Pete and helped lift the arm on the opposite side from the bullet wound around Lightning's neck, then slowly navigated through the door. As soon as the door closed behind them, Dontay and me knew what to do: Make sure nothing, not one shred of Big Pete's T-shirt or drop of blood, had been left anywhere. We did, too. We even wiped down the hydrogen peroxide and ibuprofen bottles before setting them back in the medicine cabinet exactly where they were before.

We understood very well the last part of what we had to do, the most important of all: Keep our mouths shut.

After triple checking Ahmad's and our cleaning, we set out for Diva's. The clock was ticking. I had to be on time, so we walked fast. I was not trying to be late since it wasn't like I could explain to Mama what happened. We had barely turned the corner onto MLK when unwanted company caught up with us. Jay-as-in-not-Jay-Z Dele pulled up alongside the curb in his police car. He saluted Dontay and motioned to me. I didn't go all the way to the window, staying on the curb just close enough to hear.

"How you getting along, Nia? Headed home, huh?" I caught the strong scent of coffee. He was holding a McDonald's cup. He took a sip and looked straight at me.

"To the shop. I'm fine." I glanced away.

He nodded.

I stood there. No way was I helping him out.

"You know I was born here? Yeah. Lived just past the park. We moved when I was in the eighth grade. But to me, this has always been home. Still got cousins and an aunt here."

I looked at him but kept my face as blank as I could.

"A whole lot of violence is going on out here. I know that's something you kids see too much in your lives."

He wasn't just talking about Little Petey. I felt like maybe he was referencing Daddy, too.

"I moved back here a few months ago and waited to buy a house. When that happened to the little boy—"

"Petey," I interrupted. "Little Petey."

He nodded apologetically, looking straight ahead. "When Little Petey was killed, I finally decided where I wanted to move. This was always a good neighborhood. It should stay that way." Then he turned back to me. "I'm here to look out for *all* the kids around here—young ladies, too." He smiled at me. "And your families, all right?"

I felt he meant Mama in particular, which ticked me off, but I nodded and stepped back.

He saluted Dontay, who gave him a half nod from the sidewalk. He restarted the car and eased off the brake but then stopped before the car quite had a chance to move.

"Nia—that's a good name. Means purpose, right?"

Purpose. I nodded yes. I didn't think about this that much. Mama discovered the Kwanzaa principles when she was pregnant and she fell in love with Nia, the fifth principle, because it meant purpose, and it was the name of one of her favorite actresses, who was quite pretty, too, so Mama followed my grandmother's example in naming me after an actress—as she was for an actress her mother loved, Dorothy Dandridge. To me, Nia was just my name, one that too many other girls shared. I was not even helped by a cool middle name since I hadn't been given one.

I wished Mr. Jay-as-in-not-Jay-Z Dele had moved back to the west side on that street he'd grown up on. He was irritating. He seemed determined to make me work hard to hate him. I wanted him to be a bad guy so it would be very easy not to stand him, like I couldn't stand those Big Boob girls with the attitudes at school. Jay Dele wasn't cooperating and was starting to seem like he might be just a nice guy. He was just the wrong nice guy to have as a neighbor.

"What'd he say?" Dontay wanted to know.

"Nothing," I answered. And it was true except for the part about my name.

Down at the shop, the ladies were buzzing about the gunfire on the west side. Everybody weighed in on what they'd heard rather than what anybody knew. I kept my mouth shut—no one was going to know from me that Big Pete was involved and had been shot. I figured he'd gotten his punishment since he'd ended up getting hurt and could have died. Mama turned on the small television up in the corner where I sat at the front register. When a newsbreak report came on, Shandra Bell reporting from her desk in a bright red top got the ladies stirred up more. But the police didn't have any suspects and believed rival gangs had been fighting. *Miraculously*—that's the word the reporter at the scene stressed to Shandra—no known injuries had been reported. A lie. I kept my head down and committed to being busy, answering the phone when it rang, sweeping up hair before Mama asked, and listening just in case somebody let something slip that could help us with our quest to find whoever had shot and killed Little Petey.

After I made it back from Diva's with Nana Mae later that evening, I went straight to the computer in Mama's room to research my name. I typed in *Nia*. A bunch of hits came up right away, especially as a Kwanzaa principle, which I already knew. We'd never done too much of anything to celebrate at home except to light the red, green, and black candles. At school, it was barely mentioned unless some teacher referenced it as part of a holiday lesson. When we had started the pen pal assignment in class, the meaning of our names or the story behind how we came to be named was on the list of suggested topics that we might write about with our new pen pals.

But now, for the first time, my name seemed like a sign to me. It meant purpose. Me, Dontay, and Miracle Ruth had a serious purpose. We didn't want Little Petey's murder to be an unsolved case the police marked "cold case" and forgot about over time. I needed to know why it had happened.

Unfortunately, we had one maybe-suspect and no evidence. Nothing we had pointed to the reason or who for sure. With every crime, whether in the Nancy Drew books or the crime shows on TV, there was always a motive. Somebody was after money or revenge or wanted to hide a bad secret. A murder mystery was one-two-three and solved like a puzzle. Real life was messier and scarier than fiction.

CHAPTER

13

I was determined to keep our mission moving, so I came up with what I thought was a pretty genius plan, or at least I hoped so. Make a film, a pretend movie, and interview everybody and anybody in our neighborhood who would allow us, especially those living right around Little Petey's grandmother, and anybody else who was willing.

Nobody was going to have any real talk with the police, and they weren't going to be in the mood to be chatty with us either. Everybody agreed it was a terrible shame what happened to Little Petey, but silence was expected and a safer bet than the police.

But if they thought it was only some children's film, a project we were doing as kind of a tribute to another child, a dead child at that, to say "stop the violence," then that wouldn't be threatening. "Stop the violence" was constantly said in the media and at vigils and funerals for victims. I figured people would be more likely to talk, and the next thing you knew, we might have a clue. A lot of people wanted to be a star or at least get two minutes of fame from being on TV or in a film.

Before we got to everybody else, there was one person we had to speak to first to make the film plan look legit: Shayla. It wouldn't be too much of a pretend film without her, and Shayla's grandmother, too, if she agreed. I had not seen them since the vigil. Shayla and her grandmother had gone to visit with her mother in California right after the funeral. According to Ms. Torrence and Nana Mae, Shayla's grandmother was distraught over what had happened. Shayla had returned home alone without her grandmother, who was still in California with her daughter, Shayla's mother.

I was nervous when I called Shayla to ask her. Part of me hoped she'd say yes and the other half was scared she hated me and might cuss me out and say no. But she didn't. She was happy about the film and told us to come down to her grandmother's the next day.

Getting out of the house to go hang out beyond an hour or two still took a little work. Mama went all FBI on me sometimes. Her eyes were on me, worrying when she thought I wasn't paying attention. Other days she was less so, but she might hesitate a couple of beats when I'd go down the street, as if she was in battle. Then she'd let out a breath or the eyebrow would arch up into that U, then she'd say "All right" and tell me to call when I got there and be back by such and such time. Before, her normal warning had just been, "Be back here before the streetlights hit you, now." But now she had specific expectations.

It was too late to treat me as if I wasn't old enough to go down the street by myself. I'd been doing it for years now. That was the trouble with being in between. I wasn't too young for that, but not nearly grown enough to go off as I chose—or drive. But we also couldn't act like we didn't know what I could find just going down the street. The real problem was, I wasn't bulletproof.

Not to mention I didn't even have a cell phone yet, though the rest of the world did, including my two best friends. That fact meant zero to my mother.

"Mama, you could keep track of me better if I had a phone," I pleaded.

"You'll get one when I *feel* it's time for you to get one and not a day before. Teenagers been survivin' for years and years without these cell phones and parents been keeping up with children before anybody thought up one. Spending all day texting and posting mess, no, ma'am, not you. Don't you worry about what somebody else got. I'm certainly not worried about what nobody else's parent let they child have. I'm your mama. *Period.*"

Lucky me, I was smart enough to think and not say.

Mama approved of us making the film and even more me going over to speak to Shayla. The next day, our feet got slower as we neared the house. We passed right by the spot on the curb. I wondered if Dontay and Miracle Ruth were doing like I still did, avoiding looking where I'd seen Little Petey with the blood spreading across his chest. I dragged my feet as we went up to the front door. Miracle Ruth reached up to ring the doorbell, but her hand hovered. There, right over the doorbell, was a bullet hole. A clean, perfect circle. The door opened. Shayla grabbed me and held me tight me for a few long seconds. Then we were following her down the short hallway, Dontay with his camera and tripod.

"Girl, how you doin'?" she asked.

I was super nervous. My arms hardly moved.

"Hey," I mumbled, and kept my eyes from hers.

We sat in the kitchen, the same place where I used to give Little Petey apple juice and cookies or his favorite peanut butter and jelly if it was lunch. I'd sit and read until he finished. I took the time to study Shayla while Dontay got the camera set up on the tripod, then worked on getting the lens on Shayla in focus, Miracle Ruth assisting him as he directed her.

Shayla wasn't the zombie she'd been at the funeral, but she was definitely a changed girl, no fake eyelashes and her hair pulled back again into a ponytail. The dyed-blonde color was grown out, leaving her natural sandy hair color at the roots. Some of the freckles around her nose showed through a light layer of powder. The finger-nails she loved to rock, long pointy ones that almost curled over, sometimes with designs in banana yellow or black, were history, too. She had on some snug jeans and a baby-blue T-shirt, same color as the Batman one Little Petey had worn that day. Her shirt was loose, though, not Boob Crew tight like normal. Shayla didn't need it anyway. She had never been a flat-chested girl like me. Usually, her tees had some kind of words like QUEEN B, which would get Mama raising that eyebrow. But the picture across the chest of this one was Little Petey, tooth missing and smiling.

The bubbles kicked up in the middle of my stomach.

Dontay stayed hidden behind the camera. Miracle Ruth sat right beside me, but it was me Shayla looked at when she spoke. I could barely meet her eyes. My throat got dry the way it was when a cold was coming on. I told myself to say, *I'm sorry. I was late, and I'm sorry.* The words sounded stupid and small even in my own head. Instead, I swallowed, fighting the rocks building in my throat.

"You guys want something to drink? There's some Kool-Aid in the fridge? I tried to make some of Grandmama's biscuits, but they didn't turn out too good . . ." she apologized.

"How's your grandmother doing?" I asked, mostly because it was the safest thing I could think of to say. Two minutes in the house, and usually her grandmother would be offering some food or lemonade.

"She fine. Just staying in California longer," Shayla said sadly.

We all kind of redirected our eyes to the floor and the corners of the room.

"But she glad about the film. It's hard for her, you know, but I like being here now. Petey feel close." She smiled and looked around the kitchen though her mouth trembled. "Nia, I know you said to just talk about my baby. What kind of stuff you want me to say?"

Miracle Ruth, thank God, helped me out.

"Um, anything you want to say that lets people know him a little bit." She paused. "And, um, whatever you want to say about what happened since, um, we kind of want to get people thinking about things."

"And maybe doing something about it, too," I said. "So, you know, whatever you want to say is okay."

Once she got started, Shayla shared a lot. About how he was so cute as a baby and you knew he was gonna be a heartbreaker when he grew up, and what he said first, how he was so smart and good, and smiled at everybody all the time.

"When I got pregnant, people looked at me like I didn't have no sense. I know what they was saying. I was young, and Pete, he was already out there running the streets. Maybe I shoulda waited. But I had my baby. I ain't sorry neither." Her eyes pleaded with me to get it. "I ain't perfect, but I loved him. I was a good mama. I was. He shouldn't be gone. Shouldn't no babies be getting killed nowhere. No matter who the mama or the daddy is. You know what Petey asked me and my grandmama?

"He said, 'Mommy, why people die? Where they go?' Five years old, asking that. I wasn't smart like that. But my baby, he was gonna be something great though."

She turned her head, and for a second there was that faraway eyes thing like at the funeral. "You think it's possible to run out of tears, you know what I mean? You think you can't cry anymore 'cause you all out. Then they start again outta nowhere."

I'd rather she cry than sit there looking back and forth at me and Miracle Ruth, dry-eyed, waiting for a reply that none of us could give.

"Sometimes that morning play in my head like it's stuck on repeat," Shayla went on.

Dontay swallowed hard. Miracle Ruth mouthed a prayer. My insides seesawed in waves.

I willed my focus back to what we had to do. "Um, so you remember everything about that morning?"

"He had Froot Loops. You know he loved them things. I was running around getting ready for my job interview, then I went to the kitchen to straighten up. Petey begged me to go outside. You know how he do. I said he could go but stay in front on the bike, wait till he see you."

Wait till he saw me. My stomach boiled.

"You know somebody been bringing money over here leaving it right at the back door." Shayla brightened. "I'm starting a group, an organization. Mamas Against Violence, and I'm using that money and some of my pay, too." She said this proudly.

The stranger leaving money part got my full attention.

"That sounds good. So you don't know who been leaving money?" I nudged.

"Nope. Can you believe it? It be like a couple hundred at a time, right in the back door, no name or nothing."

"Uh, Shayla, how many times it happen so far?" Dontay asked, ducking from behind the camera.

"Three times so far since Grandma been gone to California," she said. "They come when I'm not here 'cause it's not here before I leave for work. It's there when I get back."

The killer? That didn't sound right, though. Miracle Ruth and Dontay both telegraphed the same idea in quick glances at me.

"I don't know who it is," Shayla explained like she'd heard our silent asking. "It sure ain't who killed him. They just take and don't be sorry one bit," she said in a flash of anger. "Sorry," she added.

This was a bonafide Nancy Drew–like moment. We needed to take full advantage.

"Um, Shayla, did the money come the same week?" I asked like a CSI agent, trying to sound nonchalant.

"Naw, uh-uh, it was like over a few weeks but not back-to-back," she answered.

"Oh." It was going the way of not being a great clue. "Well, um, was it on the same days?" I asked, willing it to be a yes.

Her freckled nose crinkled. "It's been Friday, yeah. Normally, I gotta be at cosmetology school at nine in the morning 'cept Fridays, my short day. I go at noon, and I leave by eleven 'cause they don't play about being late. I get off at two thirty and go straight to the bank before I come home. The money was here when I got back."

"Last thing, Shayla, when was the last time you got the money?" I tried not to sound overly interested.

"Not last week. Maybe the week before that," she answered.

Friday was payday for a lot of people, so that made sense. There had not been a visit last week. So maybe every other Friday? Today was Wednesday. Concentrating on this eased the busy bubbles percolating while Shayla talked, the photo of Little Petey on her shirt staring out at us.

At the door, Shayla gave us T-shirts like the one she was wearing. She stepped out onto the porch with me. Dontay and Miracle Ruth waited in the driveway. On the last step, I turned back to her, my stomach bubbling over.

"I'm sorry." The words tumbled out of my mouth. I heard how stupid and small the words sounded. That morning Shayla had let Little Petey go outside and wait because I was supposed to arrive. He was looking out for me because he was happy I was coming to watch him. Only I hadn't come on time. I'd been too busy in the mirror, sweating over what I didn't have up top.

Shayla reached out and hugged me. "For what?" Our cheeks brushed. Hers was wet.

In my mind I said, "For being late that morning," but I couldn't follow through with the words aloud. "Sorry, um, this happened," I said instead.

"What you guys think? Somebody leaving money in secret like that?" Dontay asked as soon as we hit the sidewalk, contemplating who to target next for our film.

"I don't know," I answered. "Like Shayla said, it sounds kind of whack thinking whoever that is was the one that did it."

"Hmm, I don't know. People can sin and feel bad for real. Like the murderer on the cross beside Jesus. Jesus forgave him, too," Miracle Ruth preached.

We ultimately agreed it could be anybody feeling sorry about what happened or who knew something, or maybe, slim chance, the killer. Then we spent two more hours ringing doorbells, asking the same questions if people came to the door. Did they know Little Petey? What did they remember about him and how did they feel about the violence that was going on? A couple of people did nothing but cut up for the camera.

Our next to last stop was the house two doors down from Little Petey's grandmother, the old man with the loud air conditioner. We waited until there was a sign of life. The curtains on the window facing the street moved ever so slightly. Miracle Ruth rang the doorbell twice and we waited, taking in the neat porch with its little swing on one end and the light gray floor panels that looked freshly painted. Another minute went by, then several more.

"We know he's in there. The curtains definitely moved," Dontay said, and rang a third time.

"Could've been air from a vent with that, though, or maybe it takes him a little longer to get to the door," Miracle Ruth offered.

I had the feeling the man had already seen us coming up his walk and might be checking us out through the peep hole on the door that very second. Just as I started to take my turn with the doorbell, the door opened so slightly that the safety chain stayed curled into a U-shape.

He was shorter up close and older perhaps than I'd thought, judging by his watery eyes and gray-speckled hair.

"Hello, sir." I raised the funeral program photo of Little Petey as I'd done all afternoon. "We—"

"I don't want no trouble," he said, shaking his head, then shut the door in our faces.

"Oh-kaaay," Miracle Ruth said. "Uh, should we ring again?"

"Won't do no good," Dontay said. "The man not talking to us no matter what we say." He picked up the camera bag, slung it across his shoulder, and went on down the porch steps.

Much as I hated to admit it, he was right, which was too bad. I was convinced the man had probably seen or heard something important.

Our last target was the lady with the holey robe, but she didn't answer her door, and there was no sign she was home. We resolved to return and headed to Diva's instead. Several of Mama's clients and the purse man embraced being on camera and said things about Little Petey, like how full of energy he was. Each said something about needing to stop the violence, including Mama.

After we left, we got lucky with Mrs. James, the lady in the holey bathrobe. We watched her drive up to the house in a dark green car and pull into her garage. Before she lowered the door and got the chance to go in the house, we stood there almost right under the garage door.

"Not today." She waved us off before we hardly got our hellos out. "I'm not interested in nothing nobody selling."

"No, ma'am, we're not selling anything. We're making this documentary—a film. About Little Petey, you know the little boy—"

"'Course I know. That baby lived right across from here. Everybody know. You doing a movie, huh?" She reluctantly let us follow her inside.

"So, you knew Little Petey, ma'am? I mean, Mrs. James?" I asked. Miracle Ruth and I sat beside each other on a sofa wrapped in thick plastic. She had her pink pad and a pen in hand ready for notes. Dontay stood off to the side, adjusting the camera on his tripod. He zoomed in on the lady, who sat across from us on a matching plastic-covered armchair.

"Uh-huh, been knowing his grandmama for years. Know both your grandmamas," she said to me and Miracle Ruth. "Know some of your people, too, young man." She smiled hard at the camera.

"Yes, ma'am," we said just a beat out of pace with each other.

"Now the little boy's mama Sheila—"

"Shayla," I corrected her.

"Uh-huh, yeah, now that girl was hot as a firecracker when she wasn't no older than y'all." She squinted over her eyeglasses at me and Miracle Ruth, checking to see if we were, too. I swear she studied our chests, Miracle Ruth's promising mounds and my flatness. Miracle Ruth blushed. I concentrated on keeping my face blank and innocent like I didn't even know what she meant.

"Sure enough, she had a baby. *Early*, too early. Look like she was trying to get herself together around here lately, for a minute anyway. Taking classes down there at the community college, her grandmama said. Now if she just had had the good sense to keep away from that baby daddy of hers, maybe—" She stopped and adjusted the purple dress again, though it didn't need it.

That put me on guard. What did she mean by "if she had had the good sense to stay away" from him? Shayla was through with him. That was why for the past year she'd been at her grandmother's house. That was why I had gotten to be Little Petey's sometime babysitter when his grandmother was away, like that morning. But Big Pete was still his dad. Every now and again, that yellow Hummer would be pulled up out on the street in front of Shayla's grandmother's house, the engine running, music playing just loud enough so you could hear it if you passed by. Shayla wouldn't come out, but she'd be standing inside the screen as Little Petey ran giggling outside to his father.

"Your daddy," Mrs. James said, looking straight at me, "helped my nephew move something off the moving truck for me the day I moved in here. Nice man, your daddy. Another shame what happened to him."

My stomach balled into a fist and felt about ready to explode into bubbles.

Mrs. James went on. "Didn't make no sense what happened to that child. It's just a mess, that's what it is." She patted at her shiny, curly black wig. In her purple-flowered dress, brown lipstick, and wig, she looked a lot different than she had that day in the raggedy robe and the scarf. "Go ahead, child. Ask your questions."

"What kind of stuff do you remember about him?" I shifted my legs. The skin under my thighs stuck to the plastic, but I had chill bumps on top of my legs and my arms.

She had the air blasting. Miracle Ruth sat there unfazed in her lightweight pink sweat suit, perfectly still except for her hands.

"Young man, you sure you getting me from the right side?" She patted the wig again on the left side and wiped the purple-flowered dress.

Dontay ducked his head from behind the camera and nodded at her.

"Mrs. James?" I urged.

"Uh-huh, I heard you. What I remember? That child was his grandmama's heart, I can tell you that. Precious lamb . . . He used to run around the yard over there, riding that little bike of his, you know. Almost ran out in front of my car one day. You got to keep your eye on these kids, you know?" She squinted at me. "You kept him for his mama sometimes." It sounded like an indictment.

Yes, I knew. I wasn't trying to think about that right then. I made myself not go to the question I wanted to ask. It wasn't quite the right second yet.

"How do you feel about what's going on right now, with the guns and all the violence?"

She shook her head from side to side. "It's bad out here now. A disgrace is what it is. That's why I stay before the Lord." She stopped looking at the camera and forgot to sit straight and smile. "I don't know how things got so bad, they killing babies in school and killing 'em right in my backyard." She wasn't so much talking to us—she was thinking aloud things that she'd been thinking a while.

"Ma'am, you remember that Friday?"

She looked up at me and frowned. "'Course, who can forget a day like that? Lord knows, I won't anytime soon. Sad day for this neighborhood. Sad day period."

"Well, maybe the police will be able to do something," Miracle Ruth said. Dontay and I exchanged quick glances.

"The police? They'll do what they usually do. Nothing. That's about all you can count on." She sat back in the chair.

"The police say the suspect may have been driving a brown-colored car," I added. Of course, I didn't say it was from the bootleg police report we read online.

Miracle Ruth tensed beside me.

"Brown? Somebody don't know they colors, or they lying. That car wasn't no more brown than the blue sky out there. They got any sense, they best be looking for that gold Cadillac."

I could feel Dontay and Miracle Ruth holding their breaths with me.

"Um, maybe it just looked gold from a distance?" I said.

"Honey, listen, it was gold. 1975 or 76, I'd say, but messed up with them dark windows and some kind of made-up words on the back like they do these days, hmph. And them weird tires, too."

"Were they spinning?" Dontay piped in and peeped at her over the camera.

Mrs. James shook her head. "Spinning? Guess that is what they was doing. They was big tires for a car." Her forehead crinkled, then she remembered she was being filmed. She broke out in a fake wide smile that stretched her lips across her face. "Now you got your film done? I gotta be getting my dinner on," she said, and shooed us out the door.

CHAPTER

14

We left Mrs. James pretty pleased. *The car was gold with spinning wheels.*

Dontay started talking the second we stepped off the porch.

"It wasn't dark brown like that Cadillac either. Too bad she didn't get a license plate number," Miracle Ruth said.

"Remember what I told you about the car that night?" Dontay asked, grinning.

How could I forget? "You said you thought it was painted."

"Yeah, right. Now what I didn't say was the reason I said that. It looked like a bad paint job, rushed."

He would definitely see something like that. His dad could do anything that had to do with cars.

"How you know it was rushed, though? Was it smudged or something?" Miracle Ruth asked

"When a car gets painted right, it's a process. You gotta take that old paint off, scrape all that, then put the primer on, then you do a coat, and it's gotta dry, then do more coats—"

"So?" All that about car paint was going over my head.

"I mean, it might take like twelve coats to get it right or more."

"Dontay," I said. I was right on the verge of hurting his feelings

"Anyway, the car has a couple of spots," he said like didn't we get it.

"So?" Miracle Ruth asked him impatiently.

My heartbeat stepped up. "Gold?"

"Could be. I don't know, couldn't see what it was. All I did was kind of circle around close to it, and I had to play it off. Wasn't like I could get up on the car with a magnifying glass. And it was too dark."

"We'd have to get a close look at that car to be sure, then," I responded.

I wanted us to go to Dontay's house to think aloud about this some more and review the footage, especially the interview with Mrs. James. Unfortunately, my mother and Mrs. Torrance had signed me and Miracle Ruth up for some kind of girls' summer group that met at the middle school. Dontay headed home with the camera equipment slung over his shoulder, and we went off in the other direction, past Ronnie Shields Park to the school.

Supposedly, the group was going to help us navigate the teen years without getting caught up in the streets and keep us on the path to college. This was the second session after an initial information meeting that had taken place before summer started. Mama and Mrs. Torrence came with us to that first meeting. There were eight other girls with their mothers, grandmothers, or guardians—several girls we knew, and a few we didn't. One of them was named Nia, too. That made three girls I knew with my name, two from middle school, and now a girl in the summer club. I wished again my name was something unique. Nzinga. Alima. Even Miracle Ruth's weird name stood out. Nobody had a name like hers. I had to accept that mine was popular.

At the first meeting, all we'd done was listen to the school counselor and a teacher give information about the club and introduce ourselves. I was not interested in going after that, but we had no choice. This time, we were supposed to come without parents or guardians, which was good since Mama was busy with back-to-back heads at Diva's. Nana Mae had her volunteer day at the homeless shelter, and Ms. Torrence was leading afternoon prayer service at the church. We were to text on Miracle Ruth's cell phone when we got there.

Finding out who killed Little Petey was more important than sitting around gabbing about nothing. I had a feeling we were close to making some real progress now that Mrs. James had talked about the Cadillac.

Miracle Ruth sent the required text to Ms. Torrence and my mother soon as we approached the cafeteria where the meeting was taking place. We gathered in a circle around the same counselor and teacher from the first session, but a college girl was there with them. They introduced her as the guest leading the session.

"Hi, ladies, so I'm Trixie, and I'm happy to be your facilitator today. I know what you're thinking—what kind of name is Trixie?" She gave us a dimpled smile, showing perfect teeth.

She was right. Me and Miracle Ruth glanced at each other, thinking the same thing: *Really?* There was a girl in a mystery book series with that name that I hadn't gotten into like I had the Nancy Drew books. The name was ridiculous, whether for a super sleuth in a book series or a young person like the college girl introducing herself. But then again, a pretty girl with her breasts and smarts could have such a name and be read as unique instead of just dumb.

The other girls giggled. Trixie went right on laughing with them. "I won't say any names, but let's just say somebody at my house liked Trix cereal a lot and had a good sense of humor. This afternoon we thought we'd discuss something that young girls and women spend a lot of time thinking about—our bodies. By that, I'm talking about body image, and that includes what we think and believe about how we look, and the pressure we get from other people or the media that makes us feel some kind of way about how we look."

Instead of the club meeting being as boring as I feared, it was worse. I didn't like the topic for several reasons. A) Anything that directed my attention back to my flat chest was off limits, and B) it was a reminder of how I had been distracted from doing my job babysitting and Little Petey had paid that morning with his life. Lastly, C) the only subject that interested me at the moment was our quest to find Little Petey's killer. The group was a serious time.waster.

Trixie and the counselor asked us a bunch of questions anyway. What did we think about how women and girls were portrayed in television, films, and videos? Were we comfortable in our skin? Of course, it just made me more aware of my very too-small chest. Every girl in there was at least bigger on top than me, including Miracle Ruth and the other Nia, who looked like she was already seventeen.

Everybody said something after some coaxing from Trixie, mostly parroting what the one who spoke right before said.

"I think looking at celebrities too much is a big problem. You can't watch anything on the net, TV, or anywhere without getting the idea about what they consider pretty," Miracle Ruth offered.

"Uh-huh, true," the other Nia joined in. "I mean, too many people think it's about looking like some kind of super model or J-Lo and Beyoncé with light skin and long hair."

I half-listened, one side of my brain going back to the case and the other on guard, watching for Trixie and company to call me out. When she did, after every other girl had offered some brief comment, I was still caught by surprise. "Nia? Nia Barnes, right? Anything you want to say?" Trixie begged with her dimpled smile.

I smiled right back and shook my head.

Trixie wasn't having it. "Don't be shy, we're sharing the same load. What do you think?"

She wasn't going to get off my case until I offered up something. "I think we do a lot of judging on looks. Nobody wants to be judged by them, but we do it anyway. Of course, pretty much everybody cares about looks in some way. It's just we don't do so good with other things just as important or more important, like how people act and treat other people."

Trixie nodded and beamed at me like a satisfied Sunday school teacher, and soon happily declared the second club meeting dismissed. I was satisfied, too, because it freed me to devote my attention to something I'd been turning around in my head figuring out.

As-salamu alaykum.

Dear Alima,

I hope you're fine, and the sun is shining wherever you are right now. I haven't gotten a letter from you in a long time, and I put in your city when I was online a few times to see if any major news comes up. I was glad when nothing bad did. But other times it seems like in the media here, bad news is all around, about people fighting and killing each other for nothing or the police (or soldiers). Some lives are treated like they're lesser and others more than other lives. STOP it already, right? Life matters.

I was thinking about that woman Zarqa, who could see ahead. That's like an Avenger superhero skill. Nana Mae used to tell me a story about Nzinga, a girl who was enslaved but then ran away. It's not an old myth or a folktale like Zarqa. It's a story Nana Mae made up for me, but she did name the girl in her story after a woman who really lived. Nzinga was an African warrior queen who helped her people fight against being conquered. It's kind of long, so one day when we get to be twenty-first-century teenagers and each have cell phones, I'll tell you the whole story.

Peace,

Nia

PS: How do you feel about wearing a hijab?

CHAPTER
15

The next day, I rode my bike over to see Mrs. James again. In between dozing in snatches during the night, my mind raced, but my resolve was less shaky by morning. Other innocent people could end up dead in the whole mess or somebody like Big Pete and Lightning might kill someone in Little Petey's name. Little Petey, who thought ants were cool and begged you not to step on them.

When I couldn't sleep, I went alphabetical order down the tidbits we'd collected, which brought me back to the car and Mrs. James. I figured going back to her was the place to start.

How I was going to get anything else out of her, if there was anything, I didn't know. I had no reason, but my gut sense—one of Nana Mae's sayings—was telling me that if there was some piece, Mrs. James was the key. She was the one person we knew who was admitting to seeing the car from that morning, and she swore it was definitely gold. After I talked to her, I was signed up for another long afternoon and evening sweeping up hair and answering the phone at Diva's.

Mrs. James cut her eyes at me when she opened the door and saw me on the other side of the screen.

"Child, why you knocking on people doors this time of the morning? I know you got better sense than that."

"Yes, ma'am." That's what came out of my mouth. I didn't want to dispute her on the morning thing. "Uh, I was . . . We still working on the film and I'm just following up on stuff, making sure we got it right."

"Where them other ones and the camera?" she asked me without a sign she was going to let me in.

"Well, we, uh, have different things to do now. Dontay, he's doing the editing and Miracle Ruth's helping. I'm the narrator so I gotta make sure I introduce you right and everything before we see you talking in the film."

She opened the screen. "Oh . . . well, come on, then. Guess I can spare a few minutes. You got me in there, I sure want you to get it right."

The TV was blasting when I stepped inside. Two angry female voices competed to see who could be the loudest. Mrs. James led me past the plastic furniture room and down a hall to another room. The television sat on the floor against the wall across from a small couch with some kind of flowery blanket over it. She almost left me, she was moving so fast to get to the remote on the couch. She didn't want me to see what she was busy at. She clicked off this talk show just as a woman with a long blonde weave reached over the white guy in the middle and grabbed the purple hair of the girl sitting on the man's other side.

Mrs. James motioned me to sit down. "They got too much foolishness on TV." She sat on the other end and crossed her ankles.

"Yes, ma'am," I said, then babbled something about wanting to make sure we got her full name right and how long she'd lived in the neighborhood. She answered my questions as if she was reporting them to the police or a real reporter. I took my notebook and a pen out of my book bag and scribbled as she talked. I skimped on the details and wrote a few fragments of what she said.

"That what you need?" she asked, shaking her feet. I could feel her being anxious about getting back to the baby daddy drama on the talk show.

"Uh, yeah, just about." I was nervous. What if I couldn't get what I'd come for? "It's just—"

"What? Speak up now. I don't have all day."

"It's not really for the film or anything. It's just, Mrs. James, you ever think about why it happened though? I mean, nothing like this should ever happen to a child ever, right . . . and right here in our neighborhood." I said the truth and spoke as if it were Nana Mae I was talking to.

"Hmmph, well, you got that right." She uncrossed her legs and turned a little bit toward me instead of sitting forward as if the television was still on. "Only the Lord know why some things happen. We can't comprehend the Lord's ways."

If she was going to stick with being church lady about it like Ms. Torrence and the rest, I could hang it up. All I'd be getting was more scriptures.

"But sometimes these kids is hard-headed. They learn the hard way or no way." She couldn't mean Little Petey. "Take that baby's mama. She run around with the wrong kind, *that one*, and look what happened to that baby?"

I tried my best to arch my eyebrow up and aim an eye at her as good as my mother could. She made me mad, blaming Shayla again. Shayla, whom I'd seen crushed that day and a zombie at the funeral. "But she couldn't do anything about who Little Petey's dad was now, right, or what he does wrong? At least she did break up with him."

Mrs. James laughed and waved her hand at me. "Broke up with who? She mighta broke up with him, but she sure was still laying up there with him. That girl's grandmama didn't hardly make it out the driveway that evening going to the convention when *that one* come walking real fast down the street and up the front steps. The sun was going down, and there he was, thinking he slick, walking. Know he got that yellow gas guzzler and you sure don't see him walking slow or fast nowhere. Oh, she was waiting on him, too. He didn't have time to hardly ring the doorbell before that screen door was open. He went right on in. Don't know who you talking about broke up."

"Maybe he was coming to see his son," I offered.

"Uh-uh, if he was, it was an overnight visit or a late, late night one 'cause he sure didn't come out of there that early. I saw him out there on the phone, there in the yard, then go right on back inside like it was his house. 'Bout eleven o'clock, uh-huh. That's when I went to bed. I always check my doors before I lay down, that's when I saw him last."

I was having a hard time processing what she'd said. Big Pete was at Shayla's the night before his son was shot? No way he was in the house the next morning when Little Petey was lying on the ground and Shayla howling like a wounded hound dog.

She nodded, then frowned. "Hmph . . ."

"What?" I said, forgetting she was grown a minute. "I mean, yes, you remember something else?"

Her forehead wrinkles gathered. "Naw . . . well, a lot people came out after the shooting stopped, but I don't know . . . there was somebody out there in the yard earlier that morning though. A man. I forgot to bring my sprinklers in the night before."

Another person was over there? Where was he when the shooting went down? Already gone?

I couldn't hardly contain myself. "What'd he look like?"

Mrs. James shook her head. "Lord, girl, look like one of them thugs, no shirt whatsoever on, shorts sagging. Couldn't tell what he look like—stuff on his head, tattoos . . . Look like the rest of 'em running around here. It wasn't *that one*. Him, I know when I see him. Now, I don't have no more time for interviewing. Got a lot to do today."

Since I was dismissed, I thanked Mrs. James and followed her down the hallway to the front door.

Outside, before my feet and mind got on the same page, I was holding the handlebars and looking down on the sidewalk where Little Petey had looked up at me with big eyes and died. Somebody had scrubbed the cement blocks where he'd lain. They were a darker gray than the rest with a hint of sparkle under the sun. No chalk remained, no tape, but there were a couple of faded stain drops with no color, so you couldn't be sure whether it'd been blood there soaking into the pavement.

But I knew it had been blood. I closed my eyes. I could almost hear him calling my name. But there was nothing there of him, not in the wind or on the ground, to tell you he'd ever been there alive or dying. Only a red ribbon tied to the street sign pole and under it a splintering photo of him—the one on Shayla's T-shirts—secured with tape.

Tears gathered. I shook them away, then pedaled off.

CHAPTER

16

"**S**o," Miracle Ruth responded to my new information from Mrs. James. "What you thinking?" She was at home on self-imposed hibernation thanks to cramps, curled up on the bed with a heating pad. Her grandmother had the air blasting as usual. A couple of times when I had come over there Ms. Torrence had been stripped to the waist save for a support bra, muttering something about the change and hot flashes.

Dontay piped in from video on Miracle Ruth's phone. "More than likely, they was after Big Pete."

That was the truth we had assumed from the very beginning.

"Yeah, they thought he was in the house. And he was, the night before, but not when the shooting happened.

People were running there too quick right after. No way
he was outta there without nobody seeing him," I added.

"And," Miracle Ruth said, almost like she was asking,
"no way he wouldn't be right there, trying to save his little
boy."

"Right, he probably would've chased the car down,"
Dontay answered. "Oh, gotta go—talk later." Click.

We were cut off before we got our *bye* out. We rolled our
eyes as if on cue at the same time. Sometimes we were on
the same exact page with our thoughts.

"Ugh, bet it was one of those girls always grinning in
his face like he a superstar," Miracle Ruth said.

I didn't like thinking about that.

"Could've been his dad or one of his boys," I offered
without any faith. Of course, it wasn't. "Forget about that
though, we need to figure out what these clues mean."

It wasn't as if any of it was concrete proof about anything. This had me stressing. Time was racing, taking the
summer along with it. Every year the Fourth of July seemed
like the peak of summer, after which the rest of the days
grew hotter and sped by in a hurry. I hated that. August
didn't even count as summer break anymore since school
started so early.

And August meant the day of the year that would
bring the sad quiet that had come to sit around our house
the last few years. The anniversary of my father's murder
submerged all sound—TV, dishes clattering, Mama's usual

hurried footsteps across the floor, and any laughter over something Nana Mae said about somebody acting up down at the church or the shop or some mess on the news. Even the phone seemed to know and rarely rang. If it forgot, our quiet answered.

I squashed thinking about it. The day wasn't here yet.

"Miracle Ruth," I said. "Come take a walk with me."

"Huh?"

"It's Friday," I said.

"Girl, that don't mean the money's gonna come today," she argued, but dragged herself up and rummaged through her drawer.

"Come on, Miracle Ruth. It seems like he's coming every other week. He didn't last week. Shayla goes in later on Fridays, eleven, and and gets off about two thirty then to the bank she said. That's not a big window of time."

"You know I got cramps."

"Scale of one to ten?" I interrogated her, knowing the meds and heat had her past the worst. "Plus, moving around might help."

After talking her out of her fuchsia sweatpants, which would be too noticeable, and into some black ones and matching T-shirt with a pink emblem, she followed me out the door. She didn't appreciate too much having to cut through Shayla's neighbor's lawn to get to a side view that would let us see the backyard of the house. We shimmied ourselves in the middle of the thickly tangled high bushes bordering the yard until we were belly-flat down on the ground. My legs got scratched up. A red welt formed on my left arm.

I was thinking maybe I'd thought too big of myself for having us out there in such a silly position. Miracle Ruth went into a mini-fit. A bumblebee liked the same spot and kept dashing too near her face, but she about kissed dirt, shooing it away with one hand when it zoomed in.

"It won't be that long," I said just above a whisper.

Miracle Ruth cut her eyes at me like she'd caught a sinner committing the crime of lying. "Really?" she groaned.

Fifteen minutes later that faith she talked about so much came through. A figure moved stealthily across the backyard and quick-timed to the door. The bee fluttered into Miracle Ruth's face at the same time and she jerked. The bush shook. We froze. The guy's back was to us at the door. He was medium height and not thick or skinny, but that was about all we could tell. It was the end of July and already headed to eighty-five degrees, but he wore a gray hoodie and some blue jeans.

Miracle Ruth grabbed my hand and squeezed too hard. I turned, raised up slightly on an elbow, and followed her gaze to some brush on the other side of her.

She mouthed a scream, "OH MY GOD. GUN."

Sure enough, there was a gun. A layer of shrubbery right next to us cradled a black gun, as real looking as any I'd ever seen on my TV crime shows. We froze at the same time with an identical thought—would he be coming for his gun? But then the guy was moving across the yard in the same direction he'd come, without so much as a glimpse our way. I ignored the stinging welts on my arms, grabbed Miracle Ruth's hand, and mouthed back, "Slow." We crawled backward, flat on our stomachs still like two turtles, with all eyes on the gun. Once we cleared the bushes, I tore across the grass, yanking Miracle Ruth along by the arm.

I knew exactly where to go.

"Ouch, what're you doing?" Miracle Ruth complained as I steered us through the yard we'd trespassed on the way to hide. "What about the—the gun—"

"Just come on," I said.

We zigzagged onto a homemade path through the grass and came out on a narrow side alley on the backside of the neighborhood.

"Okay, okay—there's a gun—in the bushes and this guy and—and what should we do? Nia, you listening?"

I hurried us down the side street. It was so tight that cars could only go through in one direction and didn't really park. But there was one defying the space, a black SUV.

"Just act normal. Talk regular," I said, though nobody was in sight.

"What?"

"Just do it," I hissed.

Give Miracle Ruth credit, she did as I asked and babbled along, just above a whisper. She looked at me sideways. We drew near to the SUV from the back.

When we eased up closer, I noticed the back door was just slightly ajar. A sign, maybe? It had to be the mysterious donor's ride. He hadn't come from wherever he was from on foot.

Little Petey, sitting on his blue bike grinning, his tongue pushing against the hole in the front teeth, flashed in my mind. The person who shot my father was just a shadow, always hanging out in the back of my head. I had no name, no face. Sometimes I passed a random guy on the street and thought, *Was it him?* Or I'd be standing in line at the store when I went grocery shopping with Mama or Nana Mae and wonder if the man in back of us or in front or in the lane next to us was the guy, or if maybe he knew anything about the one who did kill my father.

It wasn't right. I knew this. They were just buying cereal and milk like we were and minding their own business. But that was the thing with never knowing. Mama still called the police every month and asked about updates. There never was.

I couldn't let that happen for Little Petey.

I took the chance. Before Miracle Ruth could stop me with a word or a scripture, I was easing the back door of the SUV open a couple inches more, holding on so it wouldn't swing up high. I climbed in, flattening my body, and wriggled over the far back seat, which was slightly tilted downward. Then I crouched onto the floor of the second row on the passenger side and curled up like a ball. A beach-size towel and a pile of clothes lay next to some tennis shoes that smelled as bad as the garbage cans on the street. I pulled it all over me and made myself into a small snail. *Crawl back out, stupid girl.* But the voice of reason was a second too late. It was okay for Nancy Drew to do such a thing because that was fiction. She was always going to get out of every tough spot she was in no matter what.

But I wasn't Nancy Drew in a book who couldn't be killed off. My heart raced faster than when I was on the track, and the bubbles in my stomach got going again.

A door slammed. Too late to get out. I imagined Miracle Ruth on the sidewalk, paralyzed in shock or falling to her knees right there on the concrete to pray for me.

CHAPTER

17

An item I couldn't identify plopped down out of nowhere near me. The SUV pulled off slowly, then crested to a steady speed. *Please, please don't go far*, I prayed. I squinted one-eyed through the sliver in my stinky hiding place. A gray blur plopped out of nowhere onto the space on the floor of the seat right next to where I was crammed in. The car stopped, then there were two voices, and the passenger door opened and slammed shut.

"¡Mano! Let's slide by Juanita's. I gotta drop off some bills for little man. Him and his mama must think I'm made of money." The passenger laughed. "Tonight, I gotta make a run. You down?"

I didn't like his voice, and it seemed too close me. His laugh was hard, no fun in it. The driver didn't reply that I could hear.

"Damn, what's up? No funerals today, son. Not today."
The passenger laughed by himself.

"Headache," the other answered quietly. Definitely the
driver, the guy who'd left the money. His voice was softer
and more distant.

"Headache?" The first guy laughed. "Want some of
this? This'll make you forget 'headaches' and all kinds
of shit."

If the other guy replied, I didn't hear it. My own heartbeat was loud in my ears and my armpits seemed to be
dripping rivers. The car stopped and started several times
within seconds. Lights for sure, but how many? After what
seemed like three, I lost count. The turns, maybe left, then
a right or the other way around, rocked me forward slightly.
The twisting and tightening in my gut worsened.

"E, you remember the water your pops took us to see
that one night in Puerto Rico? The bay?" the softer one
asked.

"Acho meng . . . the bay," the other scoffed.

"Yeah," the driver continued. "I know we was little,
but I never forget those blue lights, looked like fireflies in
water. Your pops kept sticking the paddle and his hands
in, moving the water, laughing. I thought it was magic for
real." He chuckled lightly.

"Drunk ass, taking two five-year-olds out there in the
middle of the night. That was some tricked-out water.
We sitting out there in that tiny ass boat, Pops drinking. I
'member being scared some monsters was gonna come up

out of them blue-light things." This from the scarier voice nearest me.

"Organisms," the first guy filled in.

"Organisms, whatever, shit was scary."

The car started forward again.

"Your pops, man, he was happy. Like he was witnessing gold being made."

"Yeah, yeah," the passenger side grunted. "Then he was magic and disappeared. Poof. Maybe he went to them blue lights." His voice trailed off. "What's with the memory lane trip, huh? We a long ways from Puerto Rico. And I ain't talkin' just miles." He went on, "How long we go back? How long? Me and you, we the first to come up on this side. We go back to the cradle. Family, right? We seen a lot, been through a lot of shit together."

"Yo sé," the other one replied. "Not all bad, though." His voice lightened a little. "I remember being in the ocean."

"Sí, el océano. Now, that's what you need. Sun and sand. I keep saying, we gotta make that move to Miami. All this cold and no water is no good for us. We Puerto Rican. We got connections out there, man."

"You know I can't leave," the somber softer voice replied. "Maybe one day I'll get back to Puerto Rico on La Noche de San Juan for my parents."

"There you go. Forget La Noche de San Juan. It'll only make you think of one thing—"

"The last night." There seemed to be the longest pause.

"No good luck, that's for damn sure. Let it go, bro," the rider said, sounding irritated.

"Let it go?"

"This about what went down? Some shit you can't change? It's finished. La Noche de San Juan, too. No good thinking about none of it," the other one insisted.

The softer guy's voice rose for the first time. "You think I ever forget about Mami or Papi and that night? Or Ceiba? The things that happened there, the trouble we got into together?" His voice dropped back into the sad softness. "We was always trying to take care of family, E, of each other—spilling no blood. I can't get with little kids getting hurt."

Little kids? My stomach churned faster.

"War has casualties," the voice from in front of my hiding spot explained. "Every war. Plans don't work out sometimes. Los caseríos taught me that. You think I wake up and go, let me shit, eat, and take somebody out today? Nah . . . We all got family. Sometimes they get caught in it. That's real. You and me, we know this better than most. How many he put in the grave, brother? Plenty of us. Don't forget that. How old was Mannie? Fourteen, right? How many kids we know gone? Too many. Sins of the father—"

"Sins of the father? That's what happened to Papi and Mami?" he asked.

It took a few seconds before he got an answer. "Not

them," he said without any bite. "That was . . . the universe getting it twisted, ending up on the wrong people instead of somebody like my father."

"Least he gave us the lights," his friend offered.

I choked down a cough. The funk from the shoes and the heat under the blanket mixed with fear had my stomach doing the familiar bubble-hopping and flip-flops. I was too scared to peek out from under the blanket and take a quick breath. The SUV stopped again.

"What you want?" the passenger asked. "You know he lookin' right now. Maybe he'll get me before we get him. You not with me?"

"You saying that serious?" his friend answered.

Neither said anything for what seemed a long minute.

"Los niños at the school," the guy driving went on. "That's messed up. What if that'd been your little man?"

"¿Mi hijo? I blow his head off. What you think?"

The promise in his statement made me feel my agitated bladder. I had to pee bad.

"There's gotta be better life than this," the driver said. "Who wanna be old doing the same shit?"

"No worries," the scary one returned. "Ain't no more old men. La vida es una sola. No ifs, no regrets. It is what it is, mi amigo."

The talk ended. Music bumped suddenly. *My cousin Juju, barely a juve' lost it and turned on the oven. He wasn't playin', blew out the flame . . .*

We traveled the length of the song and another began. A man rapped in Spanish at a pulsing speed. *La vida es una sola* ... The same words the scary voice on my side had spoken.

My left foot buzzed inside and the right was numb. I needed to stretch out. I sincerely hoped Miracle Ruth was praying hard for me right then.

The car finally pulled to a stop that lasted more than a minute. My knees and elbows tingled. I tried to wriggle my toes, but they were too stiff inside my socks and tennis shoes. Doors opened, then slammed shut, one after the other. I heard the rear door pop and some rummaging. I held my breath. What if I wasn't covered up completely and they saw me? Lord, what if they were headed to the very side I was hiding in to get something out? My insides swirled faster and my heart pounded so hard I was afraid they would hear it.

The back door banged closed. I heard talking but couldn't make out any words. Their voices faded out. I waited an extra few seconds, then eased the pile covering me with my fingers a tiny bit and peeked out. A gray hoodie lay next to me behind the driver seat. I raised up a hair more and looked through the tinted window across from me. The driver, the one who had left the money, was in the same dark jeans and just a T-shirt. I still couldn't see his face since his back was to me, but he had close-cut dark brown or black hair. The passenger, though, stood facing him so I could see his face. He was THE GUY with the money signs patterning the whole of his head, Scary Face from the Cadillac the night of the vigil. He grinned and said something into the phone he held. He gestured to his friend, and they walked down the sidewalk.

I pushed the pile off me, still crunched up, as I scanned outside the window. No one else that I could see was standing outside the car. I willed my rubbery, aching legs to move and crawled out over the seat, staying on the same side I had crouched in for the ride and the one farthest from where the two had walked away. I wriggled my legs against stiffness while trying remain flat as a pancake, then felt around with one hand for the inside lock. I found it and clicked. Thank God I was on the skinny side. I turned sideways and landed on the concrete, crouching on wobbly legs. I had to escape before they returned. I stayed low until I cleared the back of the SUV, and then I did not look back. I ran faster than when Mama watched me at the track or in any race I'd ever run. The houses and cars parked on the street were just a blur. I forgot I ever felt the need to pee. The thought of Scary Face chasing me down was enough to help me try for a new mile record.

Dontay. I just needed to get to Dontay's in one piece.

As-salamu alaykum.

Dear Alima,

No one's ever asked me why I like to run. I get this feeling, kind of like flying. When I'm running, my mind clears. My body is stretched to the max. I feel strong, fast, like nothing can catch me. I'm not thinking about all the stuff going on in my life and the world or how I look. I'm racing against myself, trying to push further and see how I far and fast I can move. I block everything out and focus on controlling my breathing and form. If I'm racing somebody, I have to be aware of that also. My father said that I'm poetry in motion when I'm running, and poetry is in everything just like math is in everything. I know, he sounds slightly corny, but he was the best.

Anyway, it's funny how we both want to have careers in criminal justice. Miracle Ruth, too—a forensic scientist. We all have something that happened to us, and we don't know why or who. I hope you're safe and you get to see your brother soon.

Peace,

Nia

CHAPTER

18

While I was twisted up into a pretzel on the floor of the black SUV, wondering if I was going to pay for being so stupid, Dontay was busy pretending not to sweat it after Miracle Ruth called him and spilled as much as her hysteria allowed. Dontay described in detail later how freaked out Miracle Ruth had been when she'd called to tell him what I was up to and the scene he had to go through worrying over me and trying to cover at the same time.

"She what?"

"Nia snuck in the car—SUV—black SUV—the guy left the money—"

"Okay, hold on, Miracle Ruth. Let's give her a little more time. It's not gonna be dark for a while. I'll call you back. Don't do anything, Miracle Ruth, just wait. Nia's smart—I gotta go." His father had already called once about dinner being on the table, twice wasn't allowed. As Dontay told it, the talk over dinner was about Big Pete and the payback that might go down for his son's murder, which made it harder for Dontay to sit there with his father and Ahmad and act like nothing was going on.

"Something on your mind, son?" Dontay Jenkins Sr. asked his eldest son, sitting to his left.

"I'm all right, Pop," Ahmad said.

His father's fork paused midair. Dontay, seated on his father's right across from his brother, chewed a mouthful of corn furiously and concentrated on his plate.

Ahmad dropped his fork. "There's some noise on the street."

Dontay Sr.'s look narrowed. "About?"

"Little Petey."

Dontay's food immediately turned to cardboard in his mouth. *Little Petey.*

"What you hearing, son?" Dontay Sr. said. It was not quite a command, but not exactly a request either.

"Something's gonna go down. Not like we didn't expect it, right? I mean, you kill a little boy, that little boy . . . There's a lot talk about maybe who did it and the payback coming."

"This straight from the source?" their father asked shrewdly.

There was silence. Once upon a time, from the cradle until they got to the edge of adolescence, Big Pete and Ahmad played video games together in the very house in which they sat, had even eaten dinner at that same table and shot basketball at the neighborhood park. They dreamed together of music careers; Ahmad came up with beats and tunes, and Big Pete supplied the words. They both confronted the streets. Dontay Sr. faced them down with his son—there was a minute in his youth when he'd been out there himself on the edge of getting lost. He attempted to help his son's friend, too, but Big Pete refused to be deterred from the path he was going down.

Ahmad sat back in his chair and met his father's gaze. "Okay, yeah, I talked to him. That was his kid got killed, so I been in touch . . . tried talking some sense into him, too."

"How that work out?" his father had asked.

Dontay said he was gulping water to swallow his food because he was trying to play off how nervous he was and avoid looking at Ahmad and catching his father's eagle eye. Big Pete had been right there at the table, in Ahmad's seat, shot and bleeding, and they'd helped him without saying a word to their father. Dontay was going to hold it as long as Ahmad did, and with his brother, that was going to mean to the grave.

Ahmad did not respond to their father's question, just picked up his fork, and so did Dontay Sr. They continued eating the salad and smothered chicken Dontay Sr. had prepared with care, silent save for the sound of silverware clinking against the plate.

Dontay said it didn't help that Miracle Ruth called him during dinner. The rule at Dontay's house had been established when his mother was alive and his dad continued the practice—no phones ringing or vibrating, zinging, or texting during meals. His phone vibrated lightly against his thigh in the side pocket of his jersey shorts. The vibration stopped a few seconds, then vibrated and stopped abruptly. He and Miracle Ruth had a signal, two calls back to back with a pause and quick hang up in between. Luckily, Big Pete talk was a good distraction, so his pop and Ahmad weren't paying him any mind.

"He was my friend, Pop. My best friend."

"Son, we talked about this how many times? What he *was* and what he *is* now is two different things. You know this. You can't be this brother's keeper, you understand?"

"Yes, sir. I been knowing that a long time," Ahmad said quietly.

"Then don't you be forgetting. A bullet don't got nobody's name on it."

"Can I be excused?" Dontay asked, taking advantage of his father's current focus.

"You finished?" Dontay Sr. asked. Usually, Dontay didn't think about full until after two plates.

Dontay nodded and texted Miracle Ruth as he rushed off to his room. *A little more time, then I'll look for her.*

A few seconds later in his room, Dontay grabbed his Lakers cap and went to the window, where he turned the latch, and opened it just wide enough for him to slide through. He went back to the dining room.

"I'm going to walk Nia home from Miracle Ruth's."

His father nodded. He was raising gentlemen. He often told Dontay to watch out for Nia and Miracle Ruth.

Dontay went out the front door and down the sidewalk just past the house next door, then doubled back and cut around the side of his own house. He slipped his fingers under his bedroom window, raised it, and entered feet first, tiptoeing with his belly facing upward like a limbo dancer, just grazing the windowsill. His long legs barely touched his desk as his feet landed on the carpeted floor. He tossed his Lakers hat onto the shelf on the wall across from his bed. The second item on the shelf was his other most sacred thing—his first real camera, which his mother had bought for Dontay despite his father's complaints about the cost. The shelf was framed by a wall of pictures around it, all taken by him, including a shot of his mother at the stove, stirring a pot. He lay on his bed, the phone still on vibrate beside him. He knew I'd either show up outside his window or he'd get a call from Miracle Ruth or me confirming that I was at home safe. Good thing I did the first and fled to his house when I escaped the SUV. If I hadn't shown up when I did, Dontay said he would've been the one to call the police.

CHAPTER
19

While Dontay was buying me that time, figuring his house would likely be my first stop, I ran without glancing back or pausing until I got to the intersection with two street signs I couldn't see very well. I finally dared a look behind me. No Scary Face or SUV followed me. There were just normal things going on—some kids riding bikes, a young guy on a skateboard, and regular-looking people pulling into driveways in front of houses at the end of the street there. I still couldn't quite make out the faded street names on the signs. I looked hard to the left and right, then across the busy street and recognized the Everything a Dollar store I'd passed in the car with Mama many times. Jackson Street. I was just over the boundary between where the east side ended and the west side began.

At least I wasn't in one of the wrong sections of Hell Town, where Dontay had traveled to the night of the vigil. It was officially evening and almost dinnertime. I was supposed to be at Dontay's getting ready to fast trek it home from there. I ran, then trotted, then sprinted again, looking at cars and constantly glancing back.

When I neared our neighborhood, I didn't even think about going straight home for a possible confrontation with my mother. I was going to have to explain my whereabouts, which I couldn't, and I didn't want to tell a big lie. I figured a little lie was better. I could say I had been at Dontay's, which would actually be true, so I cut through yards and went straight around the house to Dontay's bedroom window in the back of the house. I didn't have to knock. He was lifting the window before I reached up. When I got inside, my body was shaking like it was winter outside or maybe I had a fever.

Dontay pulled me to him and spoke in low tones. "You all right, huh? You hurt? What happened to you? Miracle Ruth said—" His arms locked tight around my shoulders. He wasn't so skinny anymore.

I felt safe, finally. My left cheek was smashed into his neck. My nose took in soap and some sort of cologne. When had he started smelling like that? I also felt my damp T-shirt. I could smell my own sweat. My scalp tingled.

I pulled away, my elbows pushing against his chest. I had to. I looked a hot mess. There was no telling how Nana

Mae's braiding had collapsed. I was too embarrassed. That was not how those girls with the boobs you couldn't ignore from the park smelled, I was sure. Dontay dropped his arms and swallowed.

"You okay?" He didn't have his hat on. He looked more like Ahmad and his dad without it.

"Yeah. I ran most of the way. Your dad and Ahmad—"

"Yeah, they here, talking about Big Pete last I checked. We gotta call Miracle Ruth. Better hope she ain't already called the police," he said, reaching for the cell on his bed.

The police? I prayed again. *Please, Lord, don't let that be true.*

I could hear Miracle Ruth's scream of relief through the phone as Dontay assured her I was okay. "Yeah, yeah, she here. She fine for real." He held the phone to my ear.

"Miracle Ruth—" I managed to get out.

"Nia, are you okay? What happened? Why did you—"

Dontay spared me the avalanche. "Miracle Ruth, she'll call you later, okay? She's good. She'll call you later." He tossed the phone back onto the bed, then looked at me. His eyes darkened. He caught me by one arm and squeezed hard. "You don't get it. You know who those guys are?" he demanded.

I must've looked shocked and in pain, which I was.

He let go and stepped back. "This is going too far. You could've been hurt or killed. You think about that, huh? Now listen, we done with this stuff, okay. I followed them, you stowed away with them. That's far as we go, all right? No more dangerous stuff, Nia, all right? Or I'm out."

I was about ten seconds from tears. I had thought about this all the way home and while I was hiding underneath the stinky pile in the SUV.

"Okay" was all I could get out right then.

"Where did they stop?" he asked, easing off me a little.

"West side. Not where you were that night though. It looked a little like our neighborhood."

"The west side is all right in some parts. It's not like people are only over there walking around shooting at each other. But you lucky you didn't end up in Hell Town somewhere in the worst of it. You sure they were talking about Little Petey?" he quizzed.

"They had to be. Who else? The one who left the money, the driver, he was upset about it. But, Dontay, the other one . . . it was the guy in the Cadillac."

"Oh snap, dude with the face tattoos? You were in a car with that guy?"

"Yeah . . . Scary Face. I couldn't see the other one though," I said, applying my new nickname for our dollar-sign-tattooed suspect. I relayed the exchange I overheard.

"They said *all that*? And you sure it was about Little Petey?"

"Well, they didn't say his name or Big Pete's. But who else could they mean? It was about a little kid who got shot instead of his dad, the real target. I think Scary Face is the one that did it. I know it was him in the car, and they were talking about the guy coming after him for it."

"That might be sooner than he know," Dontay said. His Adam's apple bobbed.

"Why you say that?"

He shrugged and swallowed. I could tell he didn't want to tell me.

"Did Miracle Ruth tell you about the gun?"

"What? They had a gun?" He squeezed my arms, whispering loudly, "What gun? I was talking about something Ahmad said. What gun?"

"There's, uh . . . uh, a gun in the high bushes in Shayla's grandmama's yard in the back, right at the bottom just hanging there caught in the bushes, across from the back door."

A knock at the door interrupted. "Dontay? Nia?"

Dontay put a finger to his lips, "Shhh." When he opened his bedroom door, Ahmad, my former distant love, was there. I dropped my head. Even though I was over my little girl crush, seeing his fine self reminded me how I looked a hot mess.

He looked from his brother to me. "What'd you do, man, come back through the window?" He didn't wait for an answer and directed his attention to me. "We need to get you on down the street, Miss Lady. Your mom called Pops looking for you, which was a little confusing since Dontay said he was walking you home." Ahmad's deep voice sounded like this DJ that my mother listened to on some radio show at night. He only played old love songs that got Mama humming and singing. I bit my lip in response, and Dontay looked everywhere except at his brother.

Ahmad studied our faces. "Okaaaay. Whatever. You all right? Your mom sounded concerned."

"I'm good," I lied. My stomach groaned, not from hunger but at the thought of Mama mad and on my case.

"Well, I'll walk you home. You got kitchen clean up duty, my man," Ahmad informed Dontay, and ushered me right out of the room to the front door.

"Uh, bathroom, sorry, be right back." Truth was I really had to go, and I also wanted to delay the inevitable. I washed my hands twice as slowly as I could and dried them at the same speed, then reluctantly turned my self over to Ahmad and the walk to my house.

When I was about seven or eight, Daddy and I counted the number of steps between our house and Dontay's. I stretched my legs out and attempted to match my father's giant steps. I was so busy concentrating on stretching to copy his long stride, I lost count early in. Daddy said it was about one hundred seventy feet, and it took us over four hundred footsteps! That was something then. Now I wished the distance was much longer. I prayed for a miracle that would make Mama somehow forget to go off on me.

"You wanna tell me what you and my little brother are up to?" It was more a statement than a real question.

I couldn't get the right words to throw my used-to-be-fantasy-husband off, so I just studied how my stride was still so much shorter than his.

He laughed and threw his arm around my neck. "It's like that, huh? Well—" He tensed and stepped in front of me.

"Hey, Mad, what up?"

Lightning, aka Khalifah, a bandanna around his forehead as usual, rode up to us, standing on a red motor bike.

There was another hand greeting involving fist bumps and elbows before Ahmad continued walking slower, with me a step behind and Lightning rolling the bike alongside us with his feet.

"I ain't seen Big Pete since the last time," Ahmad said.

"Yeah, I know. He aw'ight. His thanks."

I caught a glimpse of the money roll Lightning held out to Ahmad.

Ahmad stepped back, his hands up. "Naw, no. I'm good."

"You should take it, man." There wasn't a lot of conviction in Lightning's urging. "He said you wouldn't take it. We bet." He grinned. "Now I owe him some money."

"You tell him to think about it. That's all. He can't undo nothing."

"Yeah, don't I know." Lightning sounded bitter. "Can't let certain things go down though and nothing happen."

We were almost to my house with Mama waiting on my behind inside.

Ahmad shook his head. His mouth opened. He turned to Lightning abruptly as if he was going to speak but then looked straight ahead. I just avoided stepping on Ahmad's heels.

"You not going to change what happened, but it ain't my business," Ahmad said finally.

Lightning paused over the bike. "That was my little cousin, man, family. Shouldn't have went down like that. I coulda stopped . . ." He trailed off and stared straight ahead.

I understood the blame game and felt sorry for him. I should've been on time that morning instead of too busy concentrating on my flat chest while Little Petey was on his bike waiting on me to come babysit. I was guilty of vanity and selfishness—two of the biggest sins they talked about at church. But right then my own impending pain at home with Mama was the major immediate concern.

I thought the Lord must have heard my prayer and saw fit to respond in my favor. When Ahmad left me to my fate at the house, Mama was not immediately in the mood for a whipping or her trademark long talk. We sat down at dinner like normal, though I caught Nana Mae peering over her eyeglasses at me every few bites. My legs were tired, and my stomach was still feeling shaky, but I was hungry and ate everything on my plate.

Mama waited to go in on me until I was standing at the sink washing dishes.

"I told you before, young lady, you not grown *yet*. I'm raising *you*." Whatever worrying she might have done was over. She was on to being pissed. Nana Mae offered no help. She sat right at the table, nodding. Mama stood over me while I worked, that one eyebrow going up and down, picking apart every dish I washed until it sparkled, then did the same as I cleaned the stove and swept the floor. She made me mop the floor, too, something she or Nana Mae usually did after I finished up the dishes.

"There will not be any more getting home later than you supposed to, period. Understand?"

"Yes, ma'am," I chirped.

"I told you, too much going on for you to be running around and I don't know where you are *at all times*." The left eyebrow rose higher. She sent me to my room with the note that I would be spending a lot more time helping her at Diva's, which was okay with me right then. Just thinking about being trapped in that car made me glad I was home and alive, Mama fussing or not.

CHAPTER

20

Instead of racing right up to take my shower, I lingered a few minutes on the stairs—not to eavesdrop, though I hoped they wouldn't come up with more restrictions for me. I liked hearing Mama and Nana Mae in their quiet times together, their voices melding like two people playing instruments on the same song the way Mama and Daddy used to be together as I dozed on Daddy's lap or sat in between them on the couch when I was little.

Nana Mae said to Mama, "Come on and sit down here a minute. Some lemonade left."

"I need something stronger dealing with that girl. Too bad I don't drink."

I felt a twinge. Last thing I wanted was to stress her. She had been through a lot, my mother.

Nana Mae chuckled. "Our girl is just growing up is all. She pretty good, but we can't expect not to have our nerves worked up now and again."

There wasn't any talk for several long moments. I started to step back and creep on to my room, but then Nana Mae said something I could never have imagined. "You know, Dot, I been meaning to mention something to you. Would it hurt you to try being a little friendlier to Officer Dele? He's a good man, not to mention our neighbor now. Try being a little nicer." There was a beat. "And he's pretty easy on the eyes, too, don't you think?"

Ugh, what?

"Uh-uh, no, don't you start that with me," Mama cautioned.

"Now ain't nobody trying to start nothing, love. I'm just talking to you. You getting awfully touchy over me just mentioning the man," Nana Mae teased.

"So you playing innocent?" Mama asked. "You never miss a chance to bring the man up. Ever since he moved in, you been 'Officer Dele this, Officer Dele that,' or 'Jay Dele said such and such.'"

"Dot, baby, you are still a very young woman."

"Now, Ma, come on. Please don't start with this again."

"Let me finish for once and I won't be starting again. I want you to hear me, good daughter. You know I love you. My son loved you, too. I thank the good Lord for blessing him to have such a beautiful family."

She paused. I imagined Nana Mae peering over her glasses at Mama.

"But you got to go on, baby—really go on. You a beautiful, wonderful woman. My son"—Nana Mae faltered—"is gone. We still here. I never will stop mourning my child nor my own man. But loving and being alive in the mind, soul, and *body*, that's something you can't shut down."

"Well, listen to you, ma'am. Where your second husband, Mae? Your great love? How long Mr. Barnes been dead, and you was not ready for no rocking chair then and not now either."

"Hmm." That wasn't a normal Nana Mae expression.

"You blushing?" my mother accused. I imagined her eyebrow arching up. "Something you need to tell me? Ma? Come on now, you sitting here blushing and hmmming."

"I have a friend. Someone I knew a long time ago when I was hardly older than Nia. He's a very nice gentleman, an old classmate of mine, in fact."

I was almost sorry for the bright idea of hanging around. Nana Mae had a boyfriend? It didn't even sound right.

Mama laughed and smacked the table. "You something else. All this time, we thinking you go down there and visit to spend quality time with your sister and the family and you down there . . . what the old folks used to call it? 'Keeping company.' Mae done got her groove back and didn't tell nobody."

Nana Mae laughed. "You hush now. Ain't no big thing. We only recently spent a little time together, just enjoying each other's other company. But we're not talking about me. Dot, you deserve a full life. Now, like I said, Jay Dele is easy on anybody's eyes and a decent man. I can tell—"

"Mae, I'm doing fine. I got my daughter and my business and you too. No thank you on Mr. Dele or anybody else. Besides, my mother-in-law trying to hook me up? That just ain't right in no way."

It sure wasn't, I cosigned silently.

"Of course you're doing well. What I'm talking about is—"

"Mae, for two years, I pulled myself up from sleeping on my murdered husband's side of the bed every day. I brushed my teeth, I put soap on my body, saw to Nia doing the same and her school work, handled my own work . . . and the whole time, I was on autopilot. There was not a day when the pain of losing him didn't press on my chest so I had to remember to breathe. I know you understand."

Strange hearing her admit this aloud. I knew exactly what she meant because it was the same for me.

Nana Mae didn't say anything as far as I could hear.

"Now, finally I feel my bones again," Mama went on. "I'm finding out what it is to be on my own, Mae, and that's not a bad thing at all. It's just how it came to be that I can never get over and if—and that's a big if—I was to ever get with another man, which I can't imagine 'cause I had the best as you know, it won't be with a cop."

She was dead serious.

I released the lip I was biting and held in my *yay* as I tip-toed backward up the stairs. My dad had almost become a police officer, but Mama and Nana Mae were happy he decided he didn't want to arrest people he knew and carry a gun that he would likely have to use to hurt or kill someone. He liked being strictly on the helping side.

Our Mr. Not-Jay-Z could look dopey at my mother if he wanted. She wasn't having it.

Good.

Wa alaykum as—salam.

Dear Nia, my friend,

I'm always so happy to receive your letters. It takes too long for them to reach my hands since I do not get them through the teacher at school anymore. I spoke of Zarqa's power to see ahead, which I do like, but I would not want her blue eyes or her fate.

I like the sound of Nzinga from your grandmother's story and look forward to hearing it when we can talk on our very own phones.

I once imagined what it would be like when I was older, and a teenager with things others people our age have around the world, like cell phones and access to the world with a click online. These were the things we took for granted before our town and our lives changed forever. As for the hijab, it is difficult to explain I think, but for me, I do not wear the hijab because it is something forced upon me to wear. I feel beautiful, connected to God, my people, my mother, grandmother, and the women before them and around me now in my village. Do you know what is terrible? When she was a girl, my grandmother was able to attend school only until she was ten before the War. But her mother educated her at home. School was for boys only. Can you imagine not going to school at all? I cannot. My mother said every child must have education, girls especially.

Alima

عَالِمَة

CHAPTER

21

"**Y**ou will NEVER—I repeat, *NEVER*—do something like that again." Miracle Ruth grabbed me and hugged my neck so hard the next day, I almost fell over.

You would've thought we hadn't seen each other for a year. I pulled away before I got too emotional. I was glad to see her, too.

"Here you go," she added, and handed me the book bag I'd left in her room when we'd gone spying in Shayla's backyard.

I felt bad thinking about how scared she must have been seeing me steal away in the SUV. Before I could say anything, Miracle Ruth went right on.

"I played it off. I just kept talking on my phone for like twenty seconds, but then that car got farther down the street with you inside and I was like, 'The Lord is my shepherd'—where'd he take you, girl?" she interrupted herself.

Adults at school and church congratulated Mrs. Torrence on having a granddaughter like Miracle Ruth to raise. Miracle Ruth would never be thoughtless enough to stow away in the car of a possible killer without thinking. Everybody said she was old beyond her years. I guess she had a lot of practice being with her grandmother in church 24-7, where the most important direction for children involved being quiet and sitting still. Miracle Ruth never seemed to get sleepy in church like I did during a long service.

I was lucky—or more like blessed, which is what Miracle Ruth, her grandmother, and the whole church would say—to have such a good friend as her. The three of us being together again in her pink bedroom felt good and safe.

"You don't even gotta worry about that," I said, and sat down on the floor next to Dontay.

"I want to know what happened." She sat cross-legged across from us, yoga-style with her hands on her knees. "I know you got home safe, but I couldn't hardly sleep thinking about what could have happened to you."

I filled her in on the conversation in the SUV. "See, I don't think the guy driving, the one we saw leaving the money—"

"Sad Eyes," Miracle Ruth interrupted. "I saw his face

for a few seconds right before he got in the car. He pulled his hoodie off and, I promise you, seemed like he was looking right in my direction. But it was like he didn't even see me." Miracle Ruth explained, "His eyes seemed familiar—but not the tattoo, or maybe it's a birthmark under his eye. Shaped like a teardrop."

"Sad Eyes?" Dontay laughed.

"It's not like we know his real name," Miracle Ruth countered.

Okay, I nicknamed Scary Face. Sad Eyes it was.

"Well, I didn't get a good look at his face," I said, "but now the other one, we've all seen him before, unfortunately. And I think he's the one who killed Little Petey. That's what it sounded like to me."

"You know this is serious for real. You found a gun . . . maybe THE GUN. We talking about dudes that killed a kid, and if we right, then . . ." Dontay's words hung in the air for a long minute. It was serious, especially if we were on the right track.

"We don't know if it's the killer's gun or somebody else's. We don't even have real names. It sure ain't Sad Eyes." *Or Scary Face*, I added silently. "If the killer is the guy who brings the money, why leave it in the bushes like that and take a chance coming there—leaving money, but not getting the gun?"

"Yeah," Miracle Ruth offered. "He didn't even look in that direction that I could see. Lucky for us," she added.

Dontay sighed. "I don't know, but a gun out there like that ain't a good thing no way. Some kid could find it."

"So what do you think we should do, go get it?" I asked.

"No, no way," Dontay replied. "For now nothing, okay? Let me figure it out."

Miracle Ruth reached under her computer keyboard and took out her little pink notebook. She ripped out a sheet and held it out to us. "Look at this."

Dontay took it, and we looked together. AL24090.

"It's a license," Dontay said.

"Miracle Ruth, girl, you got the license number? This is to the SUV, right?" I jumped to my feet, too excited.

"Yeah, but—"

"You are something else, girl. Now we can get a real name."

"That's what I'm trying to tell you. Just 'cause we have it don't mean we ahead. How we gonna find out whose it is?" Miracle Ruth said.

Dontay handed her back the notebook. "Online. You the one said you can find anything on it, remember?"

"Yeah," I said. "The internet."

Miracle Ruth shook her head at us like we were a lot younger than she was and didn't understand anything. "See, information like the names that go with license numbers, you don't just put it in, and somebody's name and address just comes up like that. It's a little harder than that."

The air went right out of me.

"So we got a license and can't use it," Dontay summed it up.

"It's the kind of information police have. Or if you work down at the license branch, something like that. There's websites that claim they can give it to you too. For a price."

"I don't think we know anybody down at the license branch like that," I said, almost hoping one of them did.

"Sure ain't gonna get it from the police." Dontay sounded as frustrated as I felt. "You sure you can't find it on the internet?"

Miracle Ruth poked her lips out in a pout. "What do you think I am, a hacker? I don't break into secure databases and steal classified information." She turned back to the screen. "I didn't say I wasn't gonna keep looking though." The girl did not like having her skills questioned.

I took the piece of paper from Dontay. "Okay, let's just see. You never know."

"'Faith is the substance of things hoped for and the evidence of things not seen,'" Miracle Ruth said. "That license number is in my phone and stuck in my brain. There's something else I did find, and it's scary stuff, but may help us."

She clicked on a screen and brought up Jabber, the latest most popular social media site on the planet.

I had an account, but with Mama's belief that what I

did on the web was her business at any point and her rules for what I shouldn't be saying or doing there and no phone to keep up, I hardly ever posted anything on it.

Miracle Ruth scrolled down a page that looked surreal. If Mama saw it, I'd never be allowed to say *Jabber*, let alone be on it.

The profile picture attached to the posts was a glittery dollar sign.

"It says *Scar* under the picture," I said. "Some kind of code name."

"*The Lion King*," Dontay explained. "The bad lion that kills Mufasa, his own brother."

The replies to Scar were from profiles with avatars of guns or a shoulder or some other body part with a tattoo of everything else you could name. Several posts featured short videos. In one, there was a group of young men, most of them naked to the waist, showing off torsos blanketed with tattoos. The others showed off sagging pants and T-shirts bearing the face of a dead rapper. Cigars or joints dangled between gold teeth, smoke slow curling into misty haze around them.

"Gangbangers," Dontay said, all Mr. Matter-of-Fact. "They online now like everybody else."

Miracle Ruth tapped lightly as the page loaded more. "Scary, right?"

"If your grandmother saw some of this, you might not get to see a computer again until you go to Spelman, Miracle Ruth." We all laughed, but I was telling the truth. Ms. Torrence wouldn't bother with parental controls if she got a glimpse of that stuff. She'd cut the internet off and sell the computer.

Another video mesmerized us from a post shared with Scar. It appeared to be at a funeral for a burgundy-haired girl the posts referred to as Po Gurl. An assortment of characters, girls and guys tattooed up to their necks, bandanas around their heads, took turns posing in front of the casket, throwing up finger signs, saying "RIP" between cussing.

It went on and on. Posts in English and in Spanish, with the strange emojis and block letters and abbreviated cuss words.

"Miracle Ruth, why you showing us this mess?" I asked.

"Hold on," she said, and scrolled down a bit farther. One post was from a profile picture we recognized. Big Pete's tag, a huge fist with diamond-studded rings.

"What's that reply to Big Pete's post say, Miracle Ruth?"

She clicked. The message was *CRY NOW MF Sed Yu Pay F wit Mine* 😈

"Let's see the profile . . ." Miracle Ruth said, and clicked. A face came up that I couldn't forget if I tried. Scary Face.

"Okay, all right," Dontay began. His Adam's apple rolled up and down. "So maybe it was him, but we can't prove it for sure."

"Yeah," I said, positive, "I know but everything points in his direction."

"You guys, what about that gun?" Miracle Ruth asked. "It could be . . . and maybe it's not, but it's still a gun . . ."

"And might be loaded," I added. "Anybody could come across it and—"

"Listen here," Dontay said, looking at Miracle Ruth, then harder at me. "You don't do anything. Hear me? Don't go back over there for nothing. I'll deal with the gun. Promise, Nia?"

It was not in my normal nature to accept a mandate from somebody my own age, especially any boy, even if it was Dontay. But a gun, possibly a murder weapon, was serious and he was serious. Also, I had already dodged a bullet, perhaps, stowing away in that SUV and living to tell about it.

"Okay" I promised, wondering what else could be done to get the answers we needed. Time was racing past. Summer break was almost over.

CHAPTER
22

The pre-orientation information session for freshmen and parents at the high school was on the first day of August. Me and Miracle Ruth rode with Ms. Torrence and Mama in our car. Dontay met us there with his dad. We sat together in two rows, our parents right behind us. Dontay immediately started playing games on his phone and texting in between. Who he was talking to that was so important, I didn't know. His dad tapped him on the shoulder and held out his hand. Dontay blushed red from the neck up. He swallowed and gave up the cell, then slouched down in his seat between Miracle Ruth and me.

Miracle Ruth got busy right away being a good student and school hadn't even begun. Right after the welcome, the girl started taking notes on her new digital notebook, which she had in a pink safety cover already. Mama was talking about getting another computer as part of my necessary back-to-school stuff. I prayed she'd come through with it. I needed my own device to communicate on instead of her aging computer that I mostly used for schoolwork and the house phone. I didn't know anybody else that had one of those except Ms. Torrence, and Miracle Ruth was never on it since she had her own phone.

Some of our future teachers and the principal spoke about everything from the rules to college placement classes. I missed pieces of it between thinking about Little Petey and visualizing the clues we had in my head. I scanned the gym, amazed at how many people were there, most of them around our age. The school was big, like two of our former middle school put together. High school was going to be way different. Miracle Ruth poked me with her elbow and slid her new notebook to me.

It read, *WE'RE IN HIGH SCHOOL!!!!* She had a purple glowing smiley face on the screen beside it.

I nodded and smiled.

An hour and a half after the orientation began, we were standing around waiting, while the parents spoke to one another and beelined for school officials to ask them a bunch of questions. Mama and Ms. Torrence steered Dontay's dad with them straight to the principal. I greeted a few kids we'd gone to middle school with and ignored the two Boob Crew girls from the vigil. They sashayed up to Dontay like he was all that, grinning and hugging him in their tight jeans and teeny tops that just barely reached to their waists. I didn't recognize Dontay. The boy grinned back, not fazed at all. His neck wasn't bobbing up and down or anything. He could have been his brother, Ahmad, coolly asking them what was up. He let them volunteer him to walk them to the door.

I turned to tell Miracle Ruth to check it out, but her attention was on something else. I followed her gaze. The crowd was thinning as more people made for the exit.

"I can't believe it. No, it can't be. Girl, is that—"

"What? Who?" I saw him the second the *who* left my mouth.

"Fernando. It is him." Miracle Ruth squeezed my left arm hard.

I didn't tell her to stop, though it hurt, because my eye was on the boy moving toward us. He was tall like Dontay but not as slender. He was suddenly right in front of us.

"You didn't forget me, I know! ¿Verdad?" His eyes went from me to Miracle Ruth back to me.

Neither me nor Miracle Ruth recovered fast enough.

"Same school again, finally." He smiled at us with pretty white teeth and a tiny gap on the bottom, politely ignoring that we were standing there like idiots, speechless. The room could have been empty or full of people for all I was aware.

Miracle Ruth gazed straight in his face like she was in a trance or he was a mirage. I couldn't blame her. The boy looked too good. Fernando had been cute when we were little, but now he was way fine, and tall with the promise of some serious muscles.

That moment outside the church on the day of my father's funeral came back to me. People kept coming up to Mama and Nana Mae, hugging them and saying sorry. The same men in black suits who had carried my father's casket into the church carried it back to the hearse, then went back and forth down the steps to the long, dark car where we stood, carrying the flowers from inside. One of Mama's arms had rested around my shoulders. A lady had come up and hugged her. Mama's arm dropped from around me as she turned and hugged the lady back. Then Fernando was there on the sidewalk in front of me. He'd taken my sweaty hand and tucked the folded paper in it. I'd looked straight into his deep brown eyes. He always did have a kind of quiet calm about him that made him seem older than the other boys, than all of us really. That day, by the car at Daddy's funeral, his eyes had been sad for me, sadder than I'd ever seen them.

Now, I was acting like a ventriloquist's doll, day-dreaming about the past and waiting to be given words to say.

I recovered. "Hey, Fernando. ¿Qué tal?" Stupid. I could not believe those were the words that came out.

Fernando had taught me them way back then, along with a few others. Not much of it stuck except that one line, which I'd worn out saying to him the whole of third and most of fourth grade until he left our school.

Thank God Dontay rescued us. He came back from walking his fan girls out the door. He and Fernando picked up as if no years had passed and shared one of those mysterious hand movements with a bump and a slap like I'd seen Dontay do a thousand times with his brother and other guys.

Dontay's father and Ms. Torrence returned, talking and laughing. Dontay's father gave Fernando the same handshake and Ms. Torrence hugged him and went on and on about how tall he was and how handsome. We moved across the aisle to the outer doors. Mama stood right outside with another lady. The woman leaned with two hands on one of those walkers that I've seen old people use, only she wasn't old. I'd seen her before. She had Fernando's dark brown hair and tanned skin. Fernando's aunt. They were smiling and talking fast, the lady sometimes mixing in Spanish.

"My sobrino is going here. Your daughter?"

"Sí," Mama replied. "Nia está aquí."

Fernando moved close to the walker and took the woman's arm. I felt a twinge in my stomach, a threat of bubbles on guard just as this weird déjà vu hit me.

A black SUV pulled up. *The* SUV. The driver side door

opened, and a young man got out and rushed around the back toward us. His eyes were sad even though he smiled. I couldn't do a thing except stare at the teardrop tattoo under his eye.

"We should talk," Fernando was saying. "See what's been going on the last four or five years, right?" He was looking straight at me and digging in the pocket of his shorts.

I couldn't respond. Miracle Ruth bumped my arm with hers, then pinched me. What? Right, a question.

"I don't have a phone." It came out before I could think about it. "I mean, not my own phone . . . I mean, at home I do." Like, I really wanted him to know my mother would not let me have a cell.

I desperately wanted to say something else, but the SUV and its driver, the anonymous young man in the hoodie who was leaving Shayla the money, were right there.

"No worries," Fernando was saying, "I'll catch you." A joke. When we were little kids in elementary school, he had never raced me or involved himself in the playground competitions at recess.

Miracle Ruth exhaled in shock as she recognized the SUV, too, and the driver she tagged Sad Eyes. A flash of hot pink hit the ground.

Fernando and Dontay both bent to pick up Miracle Ruth's phone. Dontay swooped the phone up and handed it back to her, but then it hit him, too. His gaze swung from me and Miracle Ruth to where ours was glued, on the newcomer and his SUV. He gulped.

"This is the other one, mi sobrino—nephew— Emeterio," Fernando's aunt was saying happily to Mama.

He spoke.

Voices ran together.

"Bye, be blessed now. Keep on trusting the good Lord."

"Take care."

"Estar bien."

Fernando's aunt, Mama, and Ms. Torrence hugged one another. The back door of the SUV swung open. Emeterio gave us a light smile as goodbye. The tear drop crinkled. He laid the walker across the backseat I'd wriggled across to get to my hiding spot. I flashed back to being folded up on the back floor, terrified. He shut the back door, then helped his aunt into the front passenger side.

Fernando smiled at us with the same eyes as his brother. He opened the side back door on the passenger side and got in, his feet taking up space where I had stowed away. The SUV pulled off slowly. We stood there with our eyes glued to the license plate on the back. AL24090. Not that I needed it to recognize the SUV I had been a secret passenger in.

"Why you standing there with your mouth open?" Mama asked. "You and Miracle Ruth didn't hardly speak to your friend's brother."

"Yes, ma'am." I realized a second after that it wasn't

a correct response. Miracle Ruth dropped her head and fiddled with the strap of her hot-pink purse.

It was okay. Ms. Torrence got Mama distracted by immediately directing her attention to trying find out all about Fernando's aunt.

"She got that MS, huh? Bless her heart. Look like she getting along though."

"She's fine. She was praising God. Talking about how he's blessed her," Mama said. That didn't shut down Ms. Torrence's nosiness.

"I always say," she went right on, "you know the Lord, don't matter what color you are, or where you come from or what language you praise him in, long as you know him."

"Look like that eldest boy doing all right." This from Dontay's father. It was a statement with a touch of something underneath.

"He takes care of her and works hard, the aunt told me," Mama defended, "and he's saving so his brother can go to college."

"Now that's a blessing," Ms. Torrence preached. "You can't find a lot of them like that these days, young but willing to take care of somebody else instead of running the streets."

"Well, she pretty much raised them boys—"

"Hmmph. The parents passed over there in Puerto Rico, right? The Lord giveth and the Lord taketh way," Ms. Torrence babbled on.

As far as me and Miracle Ruth were concerned, Ms. Torrence might as well have been talking to herself because we knew now who Shayla's secret money giver was—and the friend of the guy we suspected of killing Little Petey.

CHAPTER
23

DAMN. A million *damns*. Fernando's brother. Really? At Sunday school, they liked to remind us that "God knows everything, even our every thought," but I hoped he was too busy to pay attention to mine right then.

"You barely said a word since you got back from the orientation. That's not like you. And it's definitely not natural for you to mess around when it comes to eating my macaroni and cheese." Nana Mae lowered her fork and inspected me from over her eyeglasses as if they were in the way of her being able to see better.

I studied the food on my plate. "Yes, ma'am." That was all I could say back for the second time that day. Nothing had changed. I still couldn't tell her anything. So I just kept pushing the same forkful of the best macaroni in the world around on my plate.

"*Yes, ma'am?* That bad, huh?"

I put the fork in my mouth. I never knew a bite of Nana Mae's macaroni could take so long to eat. Usually, I'd already be on a second helping.

Nana Mae took a sip of tea and frowned.

There was a time when it would've been so easy to spill and tell her everything right then and see what sense she could help me make of it. Fernando's brother, Emeterio, and Scary Face, Big Pete and Little Petey, including the fact of me being late that morning he'd been killed. I wanted to give the whole thing over to her and let her figure out what to do.

"You ever . . ."

"Have I ever what, baby?"

"I guess it's kind of hard sometimes. How do you know which way is right and/or wrong when it could be both?"

Nana Mae smiled and sipped her tea. "Something's really weighing on your mind hard, ain't it, baby? You sure you don't want to tell me what's going on?"

I looked all around the kitchen except at Nana Mae and back down at my plate.

"All right, then. Well . . . sometimes it's a hard thing to figure. Yes, indeed. But it takes thinking about what's the greater good."

"The greater good?"

"The consequences and what's really right. Deep down, most of the time, I think, most of us know what's really right or wrong. Now sometimes, we can only do what we can with that, then trust the rest will work itself out how it's supposed to, with the Lord on the job." She grinned. "I'm sounding like Sister Torrence now, aren't I? Bless her heart. Well, like she says, *the Lord do know*. She's not wrong about that."

I mustered up a little smile. That was Ms. Torrence all right.

"Nana Mae?" I hesitated.

"Yeah, baby?"

"In that story, I wonder if Nzinga did the right thing running away and going on that path? I mean, she didn't know where it went."

"You sure got that story on your mind a lot suddenly," she said.

"I'd just like it if the story ended with her making it to freedom for sure. I know it's only a story and everything, but you always said there's truth in it."

"There is. A lot of our people ran away on some path or another. Many got there. Some not, and more never got the chance or died searching. There's another truth, too. Where they got to wasn't easy, most likely. But living hard in freedom was better than living hard in slavery. You know what I mean?"

I nodded.

"I got something for you I think will help you understand more than me telling."

She got up and headed upstairs. I contemplated the good macaroni and cheese on my plate going to waste and ate a spoonful.

"I was thinking I'd make this your birthday book gift this year," Nana Mae said as she came back with a book in hand. She set it on the table beside my plate. I always got a book or two on my birthday from Mama or Nana Mae no matter what other gifts I might get.

On the cover was the dark shadow of a Black girl and the title, *The Drennen Slave Girl Escape*.

Three knocks came from behind us on the kitchen door.

Nana Mae laughed. "Now who could that be? The other two musketeers?" She got up and let Dontay and Miracle Ruth in. I sprang up quick, too, planning to lead them straight to my room, but Dontay spied the macaroni cheese and sat himself right down in Mama's chair.

Nana Mae motioned Miracle Ruth to sit and got busy at the stove fixing their plates. She put some macaroni, green beans, and baked chicken on both plates and set them in front of Dontay and Miracle Ruth.

I sat back down and went to work on my food with better energy. The sooner we ate, the sooner we could talk.

"So how was the orientation? You all excited?" Nana Mae asked.

"Uh, yes, ma'am," Miracle Ruth said. She was eating like I was, slowly, pushing the food around the plate.

Dontay nodded and kept his eyes on his plate. He didn't have a problem eating. The plate was clean in two minutes as if there was no such thing as food at his house.

Nana Mae studied us from where she stood at the stove. "Hmph, you all too quiet. Now I know something is off."

Miracle Ruth started coughing and couldn't stop. Her eyes watered.

Nana Mae went over to her. "Slow down, child. Drink some of that water."

Miracle Ruth drank it and coughed a little more. Nana Mae half-patted and rubbed her back. The hacking stopped. Dontay paused long enough to make sure she wasn't choking to death, then went back to finishing his food.

"At least I can count on one appetite today. You finished?" Nana Mae asked, nodding at Dontay.

"Yes—" I went to say.

"No, ma'am," Dontay said.

Miracle Ruth and I shot him a dirty look. We didn't have time for messing around. We needed to talk ASAP.

We directed our attention to staring him down while he ate, but the boy didn't look up at all while finishing every last bit of the second helping of Nana Mae's macaroni and cheese.

Nana Mae let me off the hook with the dishes. Finally, the three of us were in my room, me sitting on top of my little desk and Miracle Ruth and Dontay like bookends on the bed across from me. We just sat there, not looking at one another, waiting for somebody to get us started.

Miracle Ruth, Dontay, and I made up this weird group. It wasn't only that we'd known one another for so long. Each of us was kind of missing a limb. Except it wasn't a leg or arm. My father had been killed. Murdered. Dontay's mother was dead because of a terrible disease. And Miracle Ruth, she had barely learned to run and walk before her mother left because of another kind of terrible disease. She hadn't ever known her father, either, who was also gone. And Fernando, he was like us no matter how many years it had been since we'd all been together. Back when we were in second and third grade together, he already had only the aunt and his brother. The brother, older by a few years, was just a shadowy boy who sometimes came over and waited from a distance by the door when their aunt came to pick up Fernando. Once Fernando talked about Puerto Rico for this report we had to do in class. He'd pointed it out on a map and showed pictures, and to the amazement of most of us in the class, explained that it wasn't another country. Puerto Ricans were Americans. One thing he didn't talk about, though, was his parents.

"I can't believe it." Miracle Ruth spoke first. "I can't take this. I mean, it's Teyo, Fernando's brother.

"Yep, Emeterio," I said.

"Who?" Miracle Ruth questioned.

"Teyo, short for Emeterio," Dontay answered for me. Back in the day, Fernando had always referred to his brother as Teyo.

"I still don't think Fernando's brother is like that. He don't seem like . . ." Miracle Ruth's voice trailed off. "The type to shoot anybody, especially a little boy—and he's helping Shayla with the money . . . but maybe he just feels sorry and guilty."

"It was probably like we been thinking. Maybe he was in the car driving. Maybe he didn't know any of it was going to go down," I said with a little hope.

Dontay shook his head. "Don't matter if he was in that car. You think the police won't see it that way? And Big Pete and Lightning definitely gonna see it like that."

His reality check was correct whether we liked it or not. If you are up to no good in the first place, Nana Mae claimed, you had some dirt on your hands.

"I got something else to tell you all. Too many ears were around to be talking before now. Earlier today, before the orientation, I went to Shayla's"—he paused—"to find the gun."

Miracle Ruth's mouth dropped open and my eyes got wide. "You did?" I asked.

Dontay nodded. "I wore gloves, and I couldn't find it—"

"You sure you went to the exact area we said under the bushes?" I asked.

"Hold on, let me finish. I crawled around almost the

whole clump of bushes—got the scratches to prove it." He pulled up the sleeves of his jersey shirt. Sure enough there was a patchwork of random scratches on both his arms.

"I crawled around under those bushes on that side after ol' boy left—"

"Who left?" Miracle Ruth asked.

"Teyo?" I followed.

"Uh-uh. Lightning," Dontay answered.

"Lightning?" Miracle Ruth and I said at the same time.

"You heard me—I got there and before I went to look, I surveyed the scene, you know, making sure nobody was around but there was. Lightning. He was leaving out the backyard."

"Not through the house?" I queried. "Why wouldn't he? I mean, he is Shayla's cousin."

"At the park," Miracle Ruth recalled, "Shayla and some other family didn't want him around. He hangs with Big Pete, and you know they think what everybody does. What happened to Little Petey was because of his dad."

"I don't know. Maybe Lightning saw the gun somehow and had the same thought we did—it's too dangerous to leave there or he knew whoever put it there," I reasoned.

"Or maybe he and Shayla are cool now and he was just visiting family, nothing to do with the gun," Miracle Ruth offered.

"Don't matter. He left. I went all up under those bushes and finally saw the gun," Dontay concluded.

"And what do we do now?" Miracle Ruth asked.

"Nothing," Dontay said, sounding like a grown man.

"But what—" I started.

"Nia, I took care of it. That's all you need to know. End of story."

I wanted to say something smart in response. We weren't supposed to hide information from one another. His tone, one I wasn't familiar with in Dontay, stopped me.

"Okaaaay," Miracle Ruth offered trying to smooth the tension. "Still, what now?"

I wasn't sure what that was. Every time I thought about it one way, another complication popped up. One thing was very clear. I didn't want anything to happen to Teyo because that would mean bad things happening to Fernando, too. "Maybe . . . we just stop?" I said, hating the words.

"What?" Dontay demanded. He rose and leaned against my desk, crossing his arms.

Miracle Ruth looked at me with her forehead crinkling. "I don't know. I just think Fernando's brother gotta be innocent. But like you say, if he look guilty . . ." She looked from Dontay to me. "Maybe you're right."

Dontay shook his head. His Adam's apple was jumping. "What? You the one got this whole thing started, talking 'bout we had to *do it for Little Petey* and *we can't just let this happen and not do nothing.*" He mimicked me, his voice going up an octave.

"Shhh, Dontay."

Nana Mae was downstairs, but sometimes she and Mama had bat ears and eyes in the back of their heads.

"You got us in this. I told you, we was getting into some trouble, didn't I?" He wasn't interested in the choir replying. "Tell you what we're not doing. We not just going to quit now. That's not the justice you was talking about when you started this. This is *all* we can do for him now. So put your little Nancy Drew cap on and . . . that's what we doing. 'Cause this"—he gestured with outstretched arms—"killing, man . . ."

Miracle Ruth took it as her cue. She nodded okay and clasped her hands together for prayer time. "Put on the full armor of God so that you can take your stand against the devil's schemes. For our struggle is not against flesh and blood, but against the rulers, against the authorities, against the powers of this dark world and against the spiritual forces of evil in the heavenly realms. Therefore, put on the full armor of God, so that when the day of evil comes, you may be able to stand your ground, and after you have done everything, to stand."

Okay.

"Let's sleep on it then regroup and figure things out." That was as good as I could muster up for the end of the sermon.

A cell vibrated. Dontay reached into one of his shorts pockets and tapped it.

"Okay" was all he said into the phone and put it back in the pocket. "Ahmad. I gotta go." He nodded at Miracle Ruth. "I'll walk you home."

We trooped downstairs to the kitchen, which didn't show any evidence of having been cooked in except for the containers cooling on the stove and counter. We could hear Nana Mae in the living room laughing at something on television.

"Oh, I almost forgot," Dontay said as they went out the door. He dug into the other pocket of his shorts and handed me a black USB with a short silver chain. "Here's that footage I put together so far. No sense not making something of it since we got it. There's a little more I have to do, but check it out."

I let them out the back door in the kitchen. The book about the slave girl was still on the table. I picked it up, went into the living room, and sat down by Nana Mae on the sofa. She was resting her legs on Pepto Bismol. She put an arm around me. A rerun of a criminal investigation series we both liked was on. The evidence was finally pointing in the correct direction in a murder case and the lead detectives were on the verge getting their guy. A commercial came on.

Nana Mae pointed at the silver chain I toyed with in my hand. "What's that?"

"The film we working on."

She nodded.

"I'm going to watch it on the computer before I go to bed," I said.

"A shooting on the west side tonight has left one dead and two wounded," Shandra Bell chimed in from the TV in a bright red puffy-sleeved shirt. "This brings the city's homicides to fifty for the year so far—" Her normally perky voiced dipped an octave.

I pecked Nana Mae on the cheek and headed up to Mama's room.

"Night, baby," Nana Mae said. By the time I made it up the stairs, the detectives were surrounding the killer and attempting to talk him down. That wasn't going to work.

I powered the computer on and inserted the flash drive. It wasn't raw footage anymore. Dontay had made a real short film in black and white. From the first image to the last, I was mesmerized. It began with short snippets of video and photos of Little Petey as a baby, and then cutting his birthday cake with Shayla and smearing chocolate frosting across his face. Dontay must have gone back and gotten the stuff from Shayla. In between, people talked. Mama, Ms. Torrence, people at the vigil and from around our neighborhood, including Dontay's dad and Ahmad and of course Mrs. James.

There was Shayla from the kitchen that day.

"You think it's possible to run out of tears, you know what I mean, like you just can't cry anymore 'cause you all out? But then you cry again."

He had even added news clips of the police talking about the murder and crime in the city. In between, there was more video of Little Petey, and photos I recognized from his grandmother's house. Near the end, there was me and Miracle Ruth playing with Little Petey outside right by where he was killed. Dontay had recorded us, I remembered, on his phone that day. We were teaching Little Petey how to play tag, but he kept running from us and laughing hard, wanting to be chased even when he was supposed to be doing the chasing. He was too funny. That scene faded into some words you couldn't see until they zoomed in large. STOP KILLING in white letters on the back of a boy's baby blue T-shirt.

The birthday picture of Little Petey, the one from his funeral, followed. A couple seconds later that faded into photos of other shooting victims in our city from the last few years. There were elderly men and women, grandmothers and grandfathers, teenagers, young men and women, an infant from a decade ago that I'd never known about, a police officer, and one last one, my father. He was in uniform and laughing. Dontay's dad had taken the photo, and it was one of those pictures buried among others on the mantel in his house.

I ejected the thumb drive and powered the computer off. I was upside down and balled up inside and couldn't untangle myself. I longed to go to the track and run and run, stretch my legs out in strides so long I'd break my mile record and run until my chest felt ready to burst out of my skin. Only then would the ball of stuff inside me perhaps unravel with the pounding of my heartbeat and the wind rushing past in my ears. But Mama was closing up the shop, and it was already dark out.

I brushed my teeth and flossed, then went to my room and changed into my pajamas—Daddy's old Medics basketball league T-shirt and some shorts. The book about the Drennen girl was on the bed was where I'd left it earlier. I flopped down and was twenty pages in before I knew it. The African girl was fourteen. One day in 1850, her enslavers, a white businessman and his wife, arrived with her at a fancy hotel in Pittsburgh. Later that night, the girl simply walked out of the hotel to her freedom. The businessman and his wife never saw the girl again.

Mama came in the house, and a few minutes later I heard her feet on the steps and knew she'd stop at my room. I placed the book by my pillow, closed my eyes, and slowed my breathing. Mama tapped on my door.

"Nia?" She poked her head inside, listened a beat, then turned off the light and closed the door gently.

I lay awake in the dark a long time after, my head busy with Fernando, Teyo, and Scary Face. Images from Dontay's film threaded through my mind. Then I took turns dozing and waking and something like dreaming in between. Little Petey and my father appeared alive and grinning. A girl by a stream, her back to the sun, looked down at the water, then stood and tiptoed across. She got to the other side. She turned, facing the direction she'd just come. She waved across the water with the same hand. *Come*, she motioned. *Come*. Another Black girl, barefoot, too, took hold of the branches. Suddenly, two girls stood together by the stream. The first girl pointed in the direction of the path, then moved toward it. She stopped and turned to the other girl, motioning to her again. *Come on*. The girl shook her head and stayed rooted by the stream. The first girl turned to the path again and bolted. The second girl started to run after her, but she couldn't get past the branches.

Everyone else filtered in as fragments—Mama, Nana Mae, Fernando, and his brother. Big Pete. Scary Face. Miracle Ruth and Dontay. They talked without making sense, gesturing. Then the girl running flitted through like a meteor, quick and gone. The channel kept changing, bringing a jumble of images, then paused.

The running girl's face came into focus. The face was mine.

Then she—I—was gone and Little Petey was on the floor, a Hot Wheels car in his hand, looking right at me, his mouth opening.

Why people diiive, Nia?

D-i-v-e?

Nooooo, dive. They go away.

Die. You mean die?

Yeah, why people dive?

He was on the sidewalk, eyes wide open, staring at me and me gazing at a red map spreading across his chest, soaking Batman.

I woke breathing hard, tears wetting up my cheeks with my nose running and stuffy. My T-shirt was drenched. I yanked it off and tossed it aside. The red glow of the alarm clock said 1:15 A.M. I squeezed my eyes shut tight against dreaming and counted to two hundred.

As-salamu alaykum.

Dear Alima,

I hope you got my last letter so you know what happened. I'm doing all right, getting by. I guess. How about you? I wonder if you and your family are, too.

I really hope so. I reread some of your letters sometimes until I get a new one from you. It's a good distraction for a minute. So there's something I've been working on with the two friends I told you about, Miracle Ruth and Dontay. It is a secret, but I hope to tell you about it someday. We have to stand up sometimes, right? Who can we count on to do it instead?

I think you would understand. I think about Little Petey and my father every day. I guess it's true what you wrote in one of your letters. Thoughts of your mom, sister, and brother keeps them close to you.

My dreams and thoughts are like memories. I wouldn't want to lose them because I don't want to forget them, but the thoughts hurt, too.

You know, I thought about how maybe we don't get to be normal teenagers thinking about our clothes and how they fit, and boys, music, and worrying over mean kids at school, our grades, and trying to get things we want from our parents. But then again, maybe we are. We live a world away from each other and share the most important fact in our lives. We don't have one parent because somebody killed them.

Sorry to sound so sad. Hey, I was looking up the weather where you are. It's summer here so it's hot, too, but I'm thinking, that it's a more intense kind of heat there.

Peace,

Nia

CHAPTER

24

The next morning, I stayed in my room longer than normal reading my new book, escaping thoughts of Little Petey and our Fernando/Teyo problem for a while. I heard dishes clattering from downstairs in the kitchen in the background. I got up when my stomach growled, demanding food, but I detoured to the computer in Mama's room before going downstairs to eat. I ignored the celebrity news tags and deleted about fifty sales junk ads in my email, then saw *New Message from QME. Go to QME?*

I clicked the link. QME was another social media site like Jabber that everyone at school seemed to use. I signed in and tapped the message. The minute I saw Fernando's avatar and profile, my stomach stirred. I flipped through his posted pictures. In one, he was sitting outside sketching. There were others of him with his aunt and a sketch he'd done with his brother. The teardrop tattoo looked like a shiny diamond under the one eye. Somehow his pencil had captured the faraway, tired something in his brother's eyes. Sad Eyes. If we did the right thing—or was it the wrong thing?—Fernando's life could blow up again. Teyo might end up being the one in prison, maybe for the rest of his life. Or dead.

I clicked again. My breath caught in my throat a moment. Little Petey laughed up at me in a beautiful black-and-white sketch. His eyes were huge and so alive, the same as Fernando had made my father seem on the page he'd pressed into my hand at the funeral. Fernando had drawn Little Petey reaching high up with a basketball bigger than his hand toward an invisible net or perhaps the sky. On the T-shirt hanging over his shorts, Batman crouched low on top of Gotham. Written in small block letters at the bottom underneath the red high-top tennis shoes that swallowed Little Petey's stick legs above the socks was *RIP* in the same style as the letters under the drawing he'd done of Daddy. *Rest in peace.*

Ding.

Fernando: Bout time. LOL.

The instant message surprised me. Right over it was Fernando's mischievous avatar picture. I hesitated a beat, then typed.

Me: Hey. What's up?
Fernando: Nada. You?

A lot. More than I could tell him, of course.

Me: Nada.
Fernando: We gotta catch up five years . . .
Me: Yeah.

Stupid.

It freaked me out thinking about being with him, know-ing how things were looking with his brother and Scary Face.

I could come over, I read.

Lord no, over to my house, with my mother and Nana Mae? It wasn't that they minded my friends coming over so long as that's all they were. And anyway, I didn't have company except for Miracle Ruth and Dontay. There'd be questions if Fernando suddenly started coming by. Mama might feel the need to make her embarrassing speech, possibly in front of him, about how I wasn't allowed to date yet when it wasn't even that anyway. I wasn't allowed to have unapproved company over when neither she nor Nana weren't home anyway, which pretty much meant unless it was Miracle Ruth and Dontay. Some laws of Mama I would never risk my life to break.

Bleep.

U OK? I read.

Yeah. I hit send and typed some more. *Not here.*

Park 11? he came back.

I did a quick calculation. I belonged to Diva's from 2:00 to 7:00, Mama's busiest hours during the weekdays. I paused before pressing return. The park. Yeah, it was close, but Mama's aversion for me being there unless it was for something like the vigil with, in her words, "an adult" stopped me.

Track @Carter. 10 A.M. Earlier was better. I tapped return, then hesitated. We'd meet, and then what? I'd tell him what was going on? No, but maybe I could learn something useful about his brother. Something that might lead to clearing him of anything that had to do with Little Petey.

CYA, 10:00 came several seconds later.

I was officially on edge by the time I took a shower, staying double the normal time allowed until Mama came banging on the bathroom door, yelling about the water bill. At the kitchen table, I concentrated on chewing my food to the tiniest particle. My stomach disagreed with the good eggs and turkey bacon. Concealing things from Mama and Nana Mae was too much pressure. Nana Mae at least helped by being so distracted with her charity drive notes instead of wondering why I was letting good food go to waste. Mama was not too busy rushing to leave to grill me.

"What're you up to until you come to Diva's? Your

grandmother's gonna be out most of the day, you know. She's running around for that drive."

See, that's why trying not to lie by not saying anything or avoiding lying outright was rough. Mama was a who-what-why-where-and-better-say-when type.

I chewed my eggs harder between side eye glances at the clock over the microwave—9:00 already. A bubble floated up and popped in my stomach in response. "Um, just hanging around here probably . . . I, uh, might go for a run." That was basically true since I was going to the track.

Mama grabbed her keys and bottle of water. She had an emergency client who'd called begging in the wee hours of the morning in full hair-crisis mode.

Her hand was on the kitchen doorknob turning, opening. "With Miracle Ruth?"

"Ma'am?" I stuttered. "Uh, Miracle Ruth, yes."

She was out the door.

I called Miracle Ruth to enlist her as soon as she and Nana Mae were gone. I had twenty minutes to figure out what shirt would hide my regressive chest and what to say to Fernando to maybe get information for the case.

Twenty-two minutes later, we glimpsed Fernando as we passed the building and crossed the grassy field separating the school from the outdoor track. Fernando sat on the top bleacher, leaning on his arms comfortably, his back to us.

"Girl, he's here," Miracle Ruth squealed excitedly, and grabbed my arm.

"I see him," I said, calmer than I actually felt.

"I been thinking and praying on it and I just don't believe Fernando's brother was mixed up in doing this. I really don't, Nia."

I didn't want him to be either, but I felt I had to reality check both of us like Dontay would, so it wouldn't be such a shock *if.*

"I told you what I heard in the car that day."

"I know, but you didn't hear him *say* he was with the other one when it happened. You don't know for sure, right? The car there that day wasn't any SUV, that's for sure. Have faith. Faith is the substance of things hoped for and the evidence of things not seen."

"Okay, all right, Miracle Ruth. Let's just see what happens," I cautioned.

Fernando stood up and took long-legged strides down the stacked seats until he was standing with us in white jersey shorts trimmed in blue, a Giants T-shirt and a matching cap that shielded his eyes. A short white towel hung around his neck. He wiped his forehead with one end.

Miracle Ruth was beside herself and so was I, but I willed my nerves not to react. My stomach quivered. I instantly regretted my shirt choice—red, short-sleeved and a little loose with stupid words, RUN HARD, emblazoned across the chest. I'd read somewhere online once that bright-colored, loose crewneck shirts with a pattern or design of some kind was better when you didn't want to draw attention to what wasn't there. Unfortunately, it didn't camouflage what was lacking on my chest.

To his credit, if Fernando was surprised to see Miracle Ruth there, it didn't show in his face or his greeting.

"Ladies," he said, and hugged Miracle Ruth lightly with one arm then me with the other. His arm went from my neck to sort of resting around my waist. One second, two seconds, then he stepped back, taking the scent of piney soap with him.

"It's getting hot out here already but trust you to choose here." He laughed and swiped the white towel across the back of his neck.

He looked so good.

His teasing loosened me up. I grinned back at him. "You can't hang, huh?" It was seventy-eight degrees and a cooler late morning at least than the string of ninety-five days we'd had up to that point.

"De nada. I play baseball out in the sun."

"Okay, it's on, then."

"You two go right on with all that," Miracle Ruth broke in. "I'll be right over here sitting, thank you very much." She headed straight for the seconds row of bleachers. "I'll be time-keeper while you race," she added with a too-pleased-with-herself glance over the shoulder at me.

"I'm thinking about running track this year," I said. I wasn't sure what prompted me to say it since my feelings were still so mixed on the subject.

I could feel Fernando's eyes on me as we walked side by side, his long legs reaching just a hair beyond me with each stride. I almost wished he wasn't so close. A side view of my chest was really not good. No shirt was hiding what I didn't have. How was he not going to notice?

"You should," he said. "Fastest girl in first, second, and third grade. You smoked everybody, the boys, too."

"Not you, though. You never raced me."

"Naw, against you? I already knew."

"Uh-huh, 'cause you didn't want a girl to beat you?"

"Nooo, I didn't need you to prove how fast you were and running wasn't my thing."

Okay.

We were soon three-fourths of the way into walking the first lap.

"Uh, Fernando." It felt weird to say and I hadn't planned to, but I needed to. "Thanks for giving me that picture of my father that day."

He pushed his hat back and dabbed his forehead with the white towel. Damp black curls adorned the edge of his hairline. "Your dad was a good man." He paused. "I know about bad things happening. That was messed up what happened with the little boy."

"Yeah." I didn't want to get in a direct conversation about Little Petey with Fernando, which made me feel like I was lying to him in a way because of the secret mission. "I liked that picture you drew of my dad."

I didn't know how Fernando's parents had died, none of us did. Scary Face and Teyo had mentioned them, but not the story of how they died. Back in second and third grade, we knew that he and his brother were born in Puerto Rico and their aunt Teresa had brought them back to Train to live with her. But that was all we knew.

"You still have it?" he asked.

"The picture? Yeah, of course." I would never get rid of his drawing of my father—though it lay in my drawer hidden away in my journal, 'cause it was harder somehow looking at that than the framed photo of me with Daddy by my bed.

Miracle Ruth looked up from her phone as we hit the mile mark and passed her. I knew she wasn't hardly that into whatever she was doing on the phone but at least she was pretending not to be paying attention to us.

"So . . . how's your aunt?" I asked.

"Tía Teresa? She's a beast. No matter what, you know, she just stays up. And keeps on smiling. The MS makes it hard for her, but she's tough."

"She must be. I mean, she took care of you guys."

"Yeah, she did. Teyo too. He's been looking out for me forever, too." *After their parents died*, he didn't have to say. I sped up, mostly because I felt nervous wondering how to ask him about something as awful as his parents' death. I avoided bringing up what happened to my father and hated explaining that he was dead to anybody. His legs were longer than mine so he just had to stretch a tad to keep up with the new pace I set. Both of us panted. The eighty degrees was on its way to ninety.

"Fernando"—I breathed in and out, taking extra seconds exhaling—"what happened to them? Your parents, I mean?"

"Car wreck in San Juan. I was three. Teyo was eight." He slowed his stride as he spoke. We were together on the beach, and then me and Teyo spent the night with our aunt Teresa and some cousins at this hotel she was staying at right there on the beach. So we weren't with my parents in the car . . . This guy was running from the cops. He robbed a store, shot somebody, and took off in a stolen car. He crashed into them and lived. They didn't. That was our last La Noche de San Juan."

I couldn't imagine that. Three years old and his mother and father both gone in an instant? I'd had my father for eleven years and it was too short. But I had known him. Until then, I'd gotten to grow up with him and Mama. Fernando never did. It was proof positive how much messed up stuff happened in the world.

"I'm sorry," I said, sounding as stupid as I had at the school.

He turned his head to me. "It's okay," he said softly.

Our eyes met. His were his brother's twin right then, a veil of sadness shading the deep brown.

"Um, La Nocheeeee de . . ." I butchered. Scary Face

had mentioned bad luck when Fernando's brother brought it up in the car.

"La Noche de San Juan. It's a big holiday celebrating the patron saint of Puerto Rico, Saint John the Baptist," he explained. "Every June twenty-fourth, right at midnight, hundreds and hundreds of people are on the beach and they walk backward into the—"

"Backward?" I tied to envision a bunch of people in the ocean in the middle of the night walking backward at the same time and couldn't.

"It's an old ritual that's said to bring good luck and get rid of negativity, but you gotta walk backward and dunk yourself at least three times," Fernando explained patiently.

That's why Scary Face said what he had about the bad luck and why Emeterio had La Noche on his mind. Then another thought hit me—June twenty-fourth had just passed a few weeks ago.

"I'm sorry," I said again.

"It's okay, Nia." He paused. "I guess it'll never be okay, right? But we can't change what's been. We can only be glad for what still is . . . mi tía says that. I think she might be right," he concluded.

We made the three-lap mark. I was sweating and running out of time with him. I hadn't found out anything useful to clear his brother or the opposite.

"Is Teyo in college now?" I asked innocently.

"No, he wants to make sure I go and get my degree.

I'm trying to get a scholarship for baseball and my grades so he don't even gotta try to handle it. Then he can go, too, or I'm gonna help him go soon as I finish."

"Does he want to?" I asked.

"He's working as like an assistant mechanic right now. But yeah, he does."

I glanced at him out of the side of my eye.

"Teyo's got mad skills. He can take stuff apart and put 'em back together easy and fix anything broken. He used to talk about being an engineer—" He interrupted himself. "This our last lap, right? A bruh can't be getting funky in the presence of ladies. Especially ones he hasn't seen since before he needed deodorant."

We fell out laughing. It felt good for about three seconds. Then Little Petey lying unmoving on the ground flashed in my mind. I dug in and looked straight ahead.

"Last lap," I agreed aloud. "So your brother works at an auto shop somewhere?"

"Yeah. Out on County Road Twenty. He pretty much works every day he can."

The car that Dontay said looked newly painted brown popped into my head. Was that where it had been re-painted?

We finished our lap and chilled a few minutes with Miracle Ruth, drinking water on the bleachers, reminiscing, and updating Fernando on kids we knew from early elementary years. Several times Fernando looked at me so intently, I swore he was trying to figure out how to draw my face or something. Or maybe he sensed that there was something we weren't saying. That thought generated a flush of heat and a flurry of bubbles in my belly. A patch of sweat broke out in the center of my chest.

We refused Fernando's offer to walk us home. It would be just my luck for Mama to happen to be out the shop for a quick run home or to the beauty supply store and encounter us or Nana Mae or Miracle Ruth's grandmother or anybody from the neighborhood or church. We left him staring after us as we walked away from the track.

"Well, find out anything?" Miracle Ruth asked.

"Maybe," I answered. I told her Fernando's brother worked out on one of the county roads.

"Where, though? What kind of business?"

"Auto shop," I answered.

We had a couple of hours before I had to be at Diva's for the usual hair sweeping and telephone answering for Mama, so we went to fill Dontay in on the latest.

"The question is, what do we do with this information?" Dontay asked when we told him. We were in the living room spread out on the couch with the TV muted.

"Well, we don't really know if that's where that car got the quick paint job," I said.

"And it's not good if it did," Miracle Ruth said.

"But if it didn't, that would be great, 'cause maybe

Teyo didn't have anything to do with what happened to Little Petey," I offered.

"It's not like we can call the shop and ask, 'Hey, we want to know, did you guys do a quick paint job on a gold Cadillac to cover up a shooting?'" Dontay could be really annoying when he wanted.

"Okay, okay, Dontay," I said.

"Yeah, like we don't know that." Miracle Ruth rolled her eyes at him.

"All right, all right. Maybe Fernando's brother was at work when it went down," Dontay said. "So he wasn't in the car. You said Fernando said he works a lot, right?"

"Yeah, but we still gotta find out. We can't call up and ask." I mimicked Dontay, "Hey, were you at work that morning?"

Miracle Ruth giggled.

Dontay ignored me. "I got an idea. And it's real simple and won't get us caught or killed messing around following people or stowing away in cars." He took his phone out of the pocket of his yellow jersey shorts.

"What're you about to do?" I questioned.

"Just wait," he said, swiping the screen several times. "Okay, so this gotta be the shop. It's the only one way out there, so . . . block the number and . . ." He cleared his throat. "Yeah, hey, can I holla at Emeterio? Yeah, Teyo." His voice hit two octaves deeper than it really was. "He told me to bring my ride in Friday morning and y'all hook it up."

Miracle Ruth mouthed, *"What. in. the. heck. is. he. doing?"*

I shook my head and shrugged. I was transfixed by the voice coming out of him.

"What? I coulda swore Teyo said he there all day on Fridays," the new Dontay went on. "Damn . . . uh-huh, right . . . He ain't tell me that. Uh, SUV, Tahoe. What don't it need? Oil change, spark plugs. I need like a thirty-thousand-mile tune up on a thirty-dollar budget package, you feel me? And I'm thinking about getting it painted, too." He laughed loud and fake. "All right, I'll holla back or might just bring the ride over there Friday when Teyo get in . . . Okay, thanks." He turned to us and slid the phone back in his shorts pocket.

"Monday through Thursdays, he comes in at one. Not on Fridays."

My stomach lurched. "Not on Fridays?"

Miracle Ruth bit her lip. "He's off on Fridays?"

Dontay smiled. "Fridays and Saturdays he goes in at eight . . . A.M."

"You play too much, boy." Miracle Ruth shook her head.

I picked up the square velour couch pillow behind me and threw it at his head.

"Chill, y'all need to be happy. At least Fernando's brother was at work, but . . ."

"But what?" Me and Miracle Ruth questioned in unison.

"If you want the shop to handle your ride getting painted, Teyo's the one you see to schedule it. Plus, he could've been off that Friday or gone in late."

"But let's assume that's not what happened," I said in a rush. All three of us wanted this to be truth.

But there it was. Teyo wasn't in the clear.

"What do we now?" Miracle Ruth asked.

We were back where we were before, wondering which way to go. I looked down at my hands on my knees instead of at my friends. Of course, we could still lay back and forget the whole thing, let Big Pete and Lightning or the police do whatever they might end up doing. That was A). But now Dontay was finally on the same page as us, and we couldn't be sure the police would ever find who the guilty one was. I still didn't feel like I could just leave it alone anyway.

Miracle Ruth continued slowly, "We could keep going until we get more leads to the truth." That was B).

"Or tell the police, like maybe your new next-door neighbor, what we do think," Dontay finished. C) That was a *no way* for two reasons: We absolutely couldn't go to Officer Jay-as-in-not-Jay-Z Dele 'cause that would be as good as telling our parents and the rest of the world what we'd been up to. And the other reason was that I didn't like the fact that he was my next door neighbor.

I did not say this part aloud as I pondered our situation. I thought of Nana Mae's words. *The greater good*, she'd said. I could see Little Petey's snaggle-toothed smiling face in my mind's eye. So I looked at my two friends. "I think . . . we gotta think about the greater good. I mean what's really right. We can't sit back and hope the police are going to do everything to find who shot Little Petey or wait until somebody else gets shot or killed, because Big Pete isn't going to stop probably until then. It's like you said before, Dontay, we shouldn't quit yet."

"Whoever knows the right thing to do and fails to do it, for him it is sin."

Of course, Miracle Ruth had another perfect scripture.

"Listen," Dontay said, standing and stretching out his arms at us like he was getting set to play defense. "I also been saying from the beginning, this right here ain't no JOKE. We can't be going off doing stuff and not sure what's what. We didn't see who did the shooting, remember? We're still guessing mostly, am I right?"

Of course, Dontay knew that he was. "We don't know for FACT that dude with the tattoos or Teyo or whoever else was the one. I know you heard what you heard, but that's not the same as facts. They what you gotta have, right? Forensics. *Evidence*. *CSI* show stuff, right? That gun might not have anything to do with what happened that day. Think about it. The shooters were in the car. Why would they come back and throw it away there?"

"Now, you sounding like you want to quit again, but a little while ago, you said we should keep going." It was satisfying throwing that on him, at least.

"We don't know where the gun is or who has it. We gotta be real careful and have facts, 'cause man, if we don't . . . " He shook his head.

"He's not wrong," Miracle Ruth said.

"Okay, we have to get something more concrete in our hands. It's still a big coincidence, don't you think, that gun is just *there* like that?"

Dontay stared me down eyeball to eyeball. "Don't even say nothing else about that. I told you, leave the gun alone, Nia. You know, you lucky things didn't go as bad they could've with that little joy ride you took."

His mentioning my dangerous adventure in the SUV got me back to thinking about the other vehicle, the car. "Dontay, you said that it looked like it was painted quick so if . . ." I trailed off, thinking.

"If what? We can't get them to tell us, or steal the car and inspect it ourselves," Dontay quipped.

"I think I got an idea," I said.

"Of course you do," Miracle Ruth encouraged me, just like Nancy Drew's best friends in the books.

Dontay was another story. He was looking at me all suspicious, frowning.

"It's low risk," I promised, "for the most part."

That night, after sweeping hair and tuning out the beauty shop chatter except Mama's directions, then dinner with her and Nana Mae, I got on the computer as soon as Nana Mae and Mama settled downstairs to watch TV. I typed *La Noche de Juan Puerto Rico* into the search box first and browsed through photos and a video of people indeed walking backward and plunging themselves into the water multiple times. Then I put *blue lights Puerto Rico* and lots of images and sites came up. I clicked one of the links. The page exploded with pictures of water lit up with brilliant blue neon shimmering underneath. The lights looked magical. Fernando was probably barely born when Scary Face's father had taken him and Teyo to see the lights, and then that one La Noche de San Juan had happened and Fernando and his brother had left Puerto Rico after their parents died. Fernando would've loved seeing those blue flickering lights in the bay. I hoped someday he still would with his brother. I closed all tabs and powered the computer off.

Back in my room, I lay on my bed mentally plotting out my idea for getting close to the Cadillac. My mind drifted, first to Alima, wondering what was happening in her world that very moment. Then the running girl in my dream who looked like me popped into my head, and Nzinga, the girl from the story who ran away like the real-life enslaved girl in the book. Neither knew where they'd end up.

When I ran track, I always wanted to win, even if it was against myself. I knew the finish line and kept it in sight whether it was a tree like back in second grade or a mark during a school track competition. I thought of Fernando. It had been great hanging out with him after so much time had passed. I wanted to see and talk to him more, but the last thing I wanted to do was tell him what we suspected about his brother and Scary Face. I wasn't sure about the greater good Nana Mae spoke about.

A blurry memory dogged me. I was on my bike and Little Petey was on his blue bike in front of me, looking back and giggling. I drifted off to sleep and slept hard for the first time in a long time with no more dreams replaying.

CHAPTER
25

The brown Cadillac was parked at the curb in front of the same house that Dontay had followed it to the night of the vigil. That was the fourth major thing that had to go right for us to carry out the plan I came up with. Me getting to spend the night at Miracle Ruth's without any hassle, and Ahmad working on music at his school in Chicago while his father worked late so Dontay could get out were numbers two and three. The first was Ms. Torrence being what you call a deep sleeper and sticking to that norm. Once she got off the noon-to-seven shift at the hospital, she took a "nap" until around one in the morning, when she'd get up, eat, then watch her recorded shows on the TV in her room. When she was asleep, you could just about throw a party, and it might not disturb her.

"Better pray she don't wake up this one time," Miracle Ruth fretted when we left her house. "Children, 'obey your parents in all things: for this is well pleasing unto the Lord.'"

Miracle Ruth prayed and continued to fret as we bicycled along. Dontay led with me in between him and Miracle Ruth, who was bringing up the rear. We traveled past the park where we first followed the Cadillac the night of the vigil. Dontay stuck to the sidewalk when he could, and close to the side of the street as we drew closer to our destination. A couple of times he pedaled too fast, momentarily forgetting me and Miracle Ruth, then slowed his pace until we caught up.

We're doing this. We're really going over there, I kept saying to myself, thinking of the house with the tattooed gang guys where Scary Face could be. The lighting got dimmer the closer we got. There was only one streetlight, fading and neglected at the intersection.

The plan was simple: Look like we were just some kids hanging out, riding our bikes having a good time. Dontay was to ride close to the car and reenact some fake bike trouble and try to get evidence suggesting the paint job. We split as planned as we approached the middle of the street by the house where the Cadillac was parked out front. Me and Miracle Ruth took to the sidewalk facing one side of the car. Dontay stayed in the street on the other side of it.

We slowed our cycling, me and Miracle Ruth attempting

to stretch out as we passed the house, while Dontay neared closer to his target, the car. We were about half a car length past the Cadillac. Dontay stopped right near the back end on the opposite side and stooped down.

Only something happened at the same instant, as if it was synchronized—but it wasn't part of our plan. The door to the house cracked open. A bright porch light lit up the house and halfway down its walkway. The tip of a gun peeked out the crack.

I knew what time it was. One of three things was possible for us:

A) Get shot dead.
B) Get kidnapped, then shot dead.
C) Get beat down almost to death.

There wasn't much hope that none of the above was in the mix.

The door opened. I almost crashed right into Miracle Ruth's bike.

A thick-necked guy wearing a black baseball hat, a white T-shirt, and black denim shorts that about swallowed his short legs stepped out onto the porch, gun hanging from his hand down at one side. Black shades hid most of his face, except for a large scar that lined one cheek down to the top of his lip. Tattoos snaked all over his neck and arms.

Miracle Ruth and I stayed on pause, standing over our bikes, dead center in front of the house and the car.

"God bless you, good evening, sir. We giving out Bibles from our church," Miracle Ruth sang out sweetly. She got off her bike, kicked the stand out, and slung her pink bag over her arm. "Would you like to get a Bible and make a donation?"

Say what? I was floored, but I got off my bike anyway, nudged the stand, and followed her into the light, halfway up the walk to the house. Had she really lied like that and moved closer to a guy holding a gun? Where Miracle Ruth had gotten the nerve, I didn't know, but there she was, at the bottom porch step by then, even closer to the dude with the gun. I had no doubt he was ready to kill upon suspicion. I was also positive other guns were in the house behind him, targeting us, too. Miracle Ruth held out her hand and offered him a peek into the bag. He glanced down. She reached in and, calm as you please, pulled out a miniature pink Bible.

The guy leaned back like maybe it was a trick Bible, but the arm with the gun in hand eased down to his side. His attention shifted to checking us out, Miracle Ruth in a black shirt with dark pink jeans capris, a perfect ponytail, and the same encouraging, holy expression the deacon-esses at church set on their faces when somebody lost in sin tracked bravely down the center aisle when the preacher did the altar call. He noticed me next and didn't seem to find my jeans and black T-shirt anything to regard more than a second.

"Dios." The dude actually laughed.

I couldn't believe what was happening, but if Miracle Ruth could lie like that on the spot, while holding a Bible no less, I sure wasn't going to be the one to get us killed no matter how much my knees were shaking. We wouldn't have been there if I hadn't come up with the idea. I ignored the rising gurgle in my stomach and concentrated on fixing my face to look as innocent as somebody collecting for Sunday school, standing by Miracle Ruth's side.

The guy peered out over our heads at Dontay. His clenched his gun and half-raised it.

Dontay had been still like he'd been laser tagged on the other side of the car. He was swallowing fast, I knew without seeing him.

"I got a flat," Dontay called out. Squeaked, actually. His voice hadn't sounded high like that in a good couple of years.

"He's with us," I spoke up. "With the Sunday school."

"¿Escuela dominica?" Scarface took the Bible from her. He laughed.

"Sí," I managed to say. "Escuela dominica." It didn't come out sounding natural like his.

"It's going to the Salvation Army," Miracle Ruth went on in her best Sunday-school-innocent voice.

"For the kids. The group with the most donations," I

said, matching her cool with a little bit of begging in it, "gets a trip to Six Flags. Uh, you know, Six Flags?"

A face leaned out of the doorway. "What's going on?"

The guy with the scarred face held the Bible up. "Just some kids getting donations. They got Bibles."

The other dude sported a shiny bald head like Scary Face, without the dollar signs. He stepped out the door. He wore a black tank and long blue-jean shorts like the other guy, and no socks or shoes. Both his arms from shoulders to wrists framed his body with a quilt of tattoos. He checked me and Miracle Ruth out, too, and eyed Dontay. The guy with the scar handed him the pink Bible.

The bald-headed guy seemed delighted with it. "I got a donation." He reached right into his pocket with the other hand, leaned down, and gave a green bill to Miracle Ruth. "A fuego. My niece, she loves pink! Or maybe I give it to mi abuela so she'll stop prayin' over me so much."

"Act civilized, man," the scarred guy scolded. "Salvation Army used to give us toys. Feliz Navidad."

He motioned to the guy with the Bible, who went on back into the house, laughing to himself, the small Bible still in his hand.

"¿Cuántos?" he asked Miracle Ruth.

Sweat curled the edges of her hair. She wasn't sure what he'd asked.

"How many Biblias you got, Ms. Rosa?" he asked impatiently.

Oh, Lord, now I lay me down to sleep, the Lord is my shepherd, our Father, who art in Heaven . . . The words jumbled up in my head, but it was praying time.

"Two," Miracle Ruth said.

"Dos," I said without thinking. Miracle Ruth glanced at me blankly. The guy's scarred face seemed to flush, but he didn't cuss me out. I was just nervous and wasn't trying to insult him in any kind of way. My better sense told me to hold back and say as little as possible. I bit my bottom lip instead.

Behind us, a low clatter broke the pause. We turned. Scarface frowned out. Dontay caught his bike before it toppled completely to the ground. Miracle Ruth dug in her book bag again. When her hand came out, she was holding two more pale pink Bibles. The guy tucked his gun in the back of his waist as casually as you please and reached into a pocket on his shorts. He took a bill out of his wallet and handed it her. Miracle Ruth gave him the Bibles. He waved his arm at us. We needed no translation. Miracle Ruth and I couldn't turn around fast enough, hit that sidewalk, and speed-cycled fast as we could until we were up the street under the dim light at the corner. Dontay followed right after us. It wasn't until I caught my breath that I remembered his flat tire. Somehow he had kept right up with us.

"Hey, your flat tire," I began.

"What flat tire?" He grinned and swished his arm in

a magician's reveal. A good-size chip of the car lay in his gloved hand. "I got the license number, too," he said, and tapped the side of his forehead. "Right up here. Now let's get the hell up out of here, please."

He didn't need to say it twice. We did just that.

CHAPTER
26

"**W**e have breaking news in a local murder investigation." Channel 4 broke into a show about a young rich woman doctor who practices in a poor neighborhood— one of those fill-in programs Nana Mae and Mama were checking out by default since their regular one wasn't back until September. The episode was almost over. The doctor was trying to save this homeless guy who had tried to rob her at the beginning. Mama groaned. The news had a habit of interrupting at that kind of moment.

Shandra Bell sat at her normal desk spot, looking Colgate-commercial ready as usual. Then Little Petey's picture was on the screen, the birthday-turned-funeral photo.

My stomach lurched and spun as I sat in Daddy's chair across from Mama and Nana Mae on the couch.

"There is progress finally in the case of a five-year-old's

murder that shocked the community. Petey Cantrell Barnes was gunned down in an apparent drive-by shooting on the east side in early June. Julia, what are you hearing?" Shandra Bell asked.

Julia, Shandra Bell's white twin, wore this bright daisy-yellow dress with a tight belt and neat blondish hair. The happy color didn't go right with what she was saying. She was standing outside on the sidewalk in front of the jail downtown.

"Well, I can tell you that the police have arrested Roberto Eduardo Garcia in connection to the shooting on the west side a few weeks ago, which they say is somehow connected to the murder of that little boy." So that was Scary Face's real name. In the SUV, Teyo had called him E. That was probably for his middle name, Eduardo. And the shooting on the west side, that was when Big Pete had been shot, but there was no mention of him. I made my face be blank in case Mama or Nana Mae studied it like they did so often. Not that they would know my secret deeds of the last few weeks, including the last one a couple of days ago.

I had conveniently positioned myself outside doing a task I only did when Nana Mae would say, "Come help me pull these weeds up." She had a small flower bed right under the window on one side in front of our house. I saw our postman of forever, Mr. Charles, coming along in his mail truck making the usual stop at the mailbox before ours. I quit my fake weeding, and with Nana Mae's gloves still on, raced to our mailbox by the curb, one hand discreetly out of sight.

"Well, if it ain't Ms. Nia. How you, young lady?"

"Fine, Mr. Charles. How you?" I parroted.

He was gathering our mail in the truck beside him—an assortment of bills and some cards, and what I was focused on underneath them, a whole pack of sales papers and coupon booklets. I let him hand me the stack. After he saluted, he took his usual perusal of the mail beside him that he was going to deliver next. I slipped the envelope I'd been sure to keep from view right in between the sales papers from a pizza restaurant, the dollar store, Burger King, and a half-off furniture outlet.

"Oh, Mr. Charles," I called sweetly and stepped forward. "This one isn't ours. Mama hates all this sales junk and coupons anyway. Remember, she said just keep 'em or just give 'em to somebody else." I handed the bunch to him gently, knowing he was going to unburden himself of it at the next stop next door. "Have a good day," I called out.

He was already rolling the mail truck forward with one hand while setting the bundle right on top of the mail in the seat beside him.

No, Mama and Nana Mae didn't have a clue. I focused on the TV news that was unfolding, transfixed by a familiar image.

Roberto E. Garcia—formerly Scary Face—appeared right there on the screen, the quilt of money signs decorating his face. His smirk defied the mug shot as if he might have been hanging out at Ronnie Shields Park with not a care in the world.

"What is that he got all over his face?" Nana Mae said, amazed.

"Tattoos. Look like dollar signs all over his face," Mama marveled.

"Ooooweee. Why? That don't make no kind of sense." Nana Mae shook her head.

The bubbling in my stomach began to creep up. I felt sick but didn't dare get up.

"There is an as yet unconfirmed report that there has been another arrest in this case. This comes as the result of an anonymous tip that led police to the gun used in the shooting." Julia couldn't quite hide her excitement. She was all breathy as if reporting on a winning touchdown for a big game.

Say what? My heart beat a mile a minute. Police had THE gun. The one that was in the bushes? Or was it another one entirely and who had given the police the tip? Lightning?

"One of the family representatives of the slain child

spoke with me briefly right outside the jail here shortly after that suspect was brought in about two hours ago."

Reverend Don King leaned into her mike. "The family is thankful the police have a suspect. We have said all along that it's not revenge we're after, but justice for the innocent child whose life was taken. And if it indeed was an anonymous tip, praise God if that's the case. It says the community is not going to stand by while our children are gunned down in the street—"

The camera cut him off and spun back to the news desk where Shandra Bell was ready with a news bomb. "Now, if this story isn't dramatic enough, we have just learned that the person arrested for allegedly shooting Petey Cantrell Barnes, the little boy who was killed this past June in an apparent drive by shooting—"

On the TV screen, a young man was being led away in cuffs. It was Lightning, Shayla's cousin Khalifah. He was pale, and it didn't look like any fight was in him. His head hung low toward his lightning bolt tattoo as the police tucked him into the back of a squad car.

What?

"—is reportedly a relative of the young victim," Shandra Bell went on. "The police are not releasing more details at this time. We will keep you updated as this story continues to develop."

I made my escape before Mama and Nana Mae launched into what I knew was coming—a whole dissection of what we'd just heard and seen. "I gotta call Dontay," I announced, and dashed upstairs.

I got on the phone next to the computer in Mama's room. I called Dontay and powered the computer up at the same time.

"Yeah," Dontay answered just as an alert dinged for a direct message on QME.

"Did you—" I began.

"I heard."

"Dontay, it was Lightning, and the police have the gun."

There was a long beat before Dontay begin to speak. "I didn't know it was going to turn out like that. I just thought . . . even though it probably had nothing to do with Little Petey, it's still a gun, and like you said, a little kid like him could end up getting hurt if he found it or maybe it was used in another shooting . . . I still didn't think Lightning—"

He was broken up about the unexpected outcome, I could tell. We didn't want the killer to be somebody we knew or somebody close to Little Petey.

"Only it was Lightning's gun." I flashed to that walk home with Ahmad when Lightning had tagged along. What had he said or started to say? "I could've stopped"— and now it was clear what he had almost let slip.

"Dontay, you did the right thing, okay . . . and the truth came out like we wanted."

"Nia, talk to you later, okay? Ahmad and my dad just came in." He hung up quick before I could reply.

I turned my attention to the QME message. It was from Fernando. I was afraid he'd be live and want to chat, but I wanted to see his message, too. I signed in and clicked. The first thing I saw over his avatar was that he signed off two minutes ago. I let go of the breath I'd been holding in.

"They got the guy. Good. Messed up still. You okay?"

He was right about that. It was messed up, and I couldn't answer yet about the okay part.

CHAPTER
27

Jay Dele as in not Jay-Z came over our house late morning the following day. He was off duty and came with coffees for himself and Mama, and doughnuts for Nana Mae. Luckily, Mama had already headed out since she had a stop to make before appointments. I swore his face fell a little bit when Nana Mae told him that, but she was thrilled at the sight of him as usual. She invited him to a seat right at the kitchen table and then trapped me into sitting with them with some remark about me and her being happy to keep him company with those doughnuts. She plopped saucers on the table for the doughnuts, and I was forced to sit there and listen to them go on and on. Jay Dele related his last long twelve-hour shift, how he had to chase a suspect on foot through the length of Ronnie

Shields Park; arrest one guy for indecent exposure and two rowdy ladies, one of whom spit in his face, then tried to kiss him; testify in court on another case; plow through a pile of backlogged paperwork; and the most memorable, he said, was this young man down at the precinct.

"You know, Ms. Mae, it's a shame. I see too many young men like him. The kid got picked up for stealing some one-hundred-fifty-dollar jeans from a store in the mall."

"Mmmph," Nana Mae encouraged him. "I hope he didn't end up in jail. Something as foolish as that ruining a young man's life? That's the shame."

"Well, we try to scare some sense into them. The minute I told this young man that we'd notified his parents, his whole demeanor changed. He was just a scared, decent kid wanting material things he can't afford and listening to some other knuckleheads. To tell you the truth, I went through something similar."

"I can't imagine you in no kind of police trouble." Nana Mae smiled while I took a bit of powdered dough-nut and wondered how many bites I needed to take before I could excuse myself.

"Oh no." Jay Dele laughed. "The reason I am the cop before you now had everything to do with how bad I messed up when I was that young man's age, fifteen years old and being raised right by both my parents."

It was a watch he had coveted and made the mistake of stealing. Attempted to, anyway. A boy he'd grown up with was always taking stuff—food from the grocery store, watches, cologne. He'd even managed to steal some pricey jeans successfully. According to Jay Dele, he'd let the boy's streak without getting caught and his encouragement go to his head. He tried to take the watch and was promptly busted by a security guard. When the white police officer arrived, he was handcuffed and put him in the back of the police officer's squad car.

"I tell you, Ms. Mae, all the way to the jail, I was about ready to burst. I'd never been so scared in my life."

"Mmmm-mmmm," Nana Mae replied.

He'd sat in the same interrogation room at the very same precinct where he was a cop now. When Jay Dele's father and mother were ushered in with the cop who'd brought him in, he almost peed on himself.

Nana Mae laughed. It was kind of funny, but I refused to let it show and took another bite of doughnut.

"My father said let's go, and my mother, she just stood there with her lips squeezed tight and tears in her eyes. She wasn't going to cry in front of the police. As soon we got in the car, she started to cry, but there wasn't any sound to it." He paused. "Tears were just rolling down both cheeks, and I couldn't do anything but watch from the back seat. Longest ride of my life, and no one said a word."

Nana Mae peered sympathetically at him from over her the top of her glasses. "What happened when you got home?"

"I tried to apologize to Mother. She wouldn't even look at me, and I went in my room and waited. I knew something was coming, just didn't know what. They let me sit in there three hours by myself waiting."

I was interested in what happened with his parents, though I stuck to fronting like I wasn't paying attention. I kept my eyes on my saucer and the doughnut.

"When my father finally came into the bedroom, he only had one thing to say. 'Son, tell you this right now and you best believe it, 'cause won't be no going back on this. You end up down there in the jailhouse again, me and your mama won't be coming to get you. And won't be no visiting you in nobody's jail. You on your own.'"

No punishment, I was thinking. Daddy would have never let me go with just that for stealing, and I didn't want to think of Mama's wrath in a situation like that.

"Then before he walked out the bedroom, he said, 'If I wasn't so mad, I'd whip your behind. Next six months, you home and school. That's all.' And he walked out."

He and Nana Mae laughed together. "I know that's right," Nana Mae said.

A decade later, after Jay Dele graduated college and a master's program, he shocked his parents and became a cop, a detective at that eventually, instead of heading to law school. He did go back to the jailhouse, all right, but on the other side of the law—and his parents had visited him there.

"You made a liar out of your father." Nana Mae smiled like she was his proud mother.

"Well, anyway, I remember that trouble I got into," Jay Dele finally concluded. "So I tried to put the fear of God in the young man and sent him home with his parents. I got a second chance, so hope he takes advantage of his." He took a sip of coffee. "And if that wasn't enough for one shift, I come home and find a mysterious package in my mailbox, evidence, and had to go back into the station."

I almost fell off my kitchen chair. I studied the table, the coffee cups and the saucers, the box of doughnuts, anything to keep from showing any change in my demeanor that Nana Mae or Jay Dele would be able to detect. Especially him, because the man was a cop. I'd watched enough crime shows to know that when it came to trying to unravel evidence, detectives were sneaky, always on the lookout for cues to people's guilt while looking like they weren't.

"In your mailbox?" Nana Mae was saying. "If it helps with a case, then good. Any idea who put it in there?"

I held my breath.

"No, ma'am, none, but like you say, it's hard to come by good evidence. If people choose to help us keep our communities safe by sharing information anonymously, well, that's fine. Better than everybody thinking it's about snitching when it's really about justice and everybody's safety."

"Uh, I'm going to my room," I snuck in right there. Before Nana Mae could shoot me one of her looks, I added, "Thanks for the doughnuts" as politely as I could.

"You're welcome," Jay Dele said as I took my saucer to the sink.

I fled as I heard Nana Mae say, "It's been a rough summer, but we thank God ya'll figured out who shot our baby Little Petey."

CHAPTER

28

It was a colossal should-never-have-happened. Early, early before the sun had thought about coming up on that awful day, Lightning drove Big Pete's yellow Hummer over to Shayla's. Big Pete left in it, but Lightning stayed and slept on the couch. He couldn't hang out like that over there when Shayla's grandmother was in town. It was Lightning that Mrs. James had seen so early in the morning in the front yard right after Big Pete left.

When Roberto Garcia—and others maybe yet to be found—allegedly drove by shooting, most likely to get at Big Pete and Lightning too, Lightning fired back from the window in the front room where he had been sleeping. He kept Shayla from running out. He wanted to get to Little Petey and get him back inside. As he tried making his way out the door, he was still firing back at the vehicle as it spun around to escape. So bullets were flying each way. Lightning likely panicked and threw the gun in the bushes that day as he ran out the back that morning. It had been a bullet from Lightning's gun that struck his cousin Little Petey dead as he rode on his bike. Lightning didn't know this and neither did Shayla. They assumed that whoever was shooting in the car fired the fatal shot, so Shayla wasn't going to be snitching on her cousin and saying he was there, trying to protect them that day. The bullet wasn't for Little Petey, but it hadn't known that or cared, just like it hadn't with my father.

The last afternoon my father spent on this earth, we had our carnival day. He laughed the whole time and made me and Mama laugh, too, though she tried to hold it in. He showed off by winning us tickets for more rides and games and finally won the biggest stuffed animal at the carnival.

"Hey, baby, yo' man gone hit that hammer so it pop straight to the top and win you that big ass lamb—or is it a bull?" He pumped his left arm until the muscles jumped.

Mama and me giggled. Daddy feigned seriousness.

"Black man," Mama mocked, "what I'm supposed to do with a giant stuffed pink lamb? Sure can't eat it. All we need is more junk at the house."

Daddy paid her no mind. He grinned at her and picked up the hammer. Some bystanders gathered nearby, watching.

"Where my little cheerleader at? You believe your daddy can do it?"

"Yes, sir," I shouted, my hand in Mama's. "Go, Daddy!"

He raised the hammer like John Henry in my old picture book about to tear a hole into a mountain.

CLANG. The disc zinged to the top. We stopped for pizza after the carnival and lugged the lamb Daddy had won home, laughing off and on the whole way. Mama sat Pepto Bismol in the living room by Daddy's chair temporarily until she could find somewhere else where the hot pink lamb wouldn't ugly the place up.

And that was the last day things were normal.

My father went to cover the shift for his friend that night, the same night this guy in Hell Town lost it, beat on his girlfriend, and held her hostage. It was very late, two A.M., and one of those nights when you turn into a ball of sweat if you're not lying under a fan or the air conditioning isn't going full blast as ours was. There hadn't been any fatal incidents or newsworthy fights on the west side for a couple of weeks, a rare interlude there.

When my father and the other paramedic arrived, it was pretty quiet except for a barking pit bull and a circle of guys on the porch drinking beer and cracking jokes several houses from the one where the deranged boyfriend was holding his girlfriend. A police car pulled up at the same time, but Daddy and his partner were out of the ambulance first.

Daddy was good at helping in situations like that. But that night he never got the chance to try. As he went around to the back of their vehicle, somebody shot him. The bullet came from somewhere in the dark, from one of the lone abandoned houses squatters had stripped, the police thought. They said Daddy wasn't the target. The police officers may have been, or someone was just messing around playing with a gun and it discharged. It was a case of being in the wrong place at the wrong time, as if that made any difference. No one admitted to seeing or knowing a thing. The girlfriend who was held hostage by her boyfriend was fine, and he ended up on the news being led away in handcuffs, saying he was sorry Daddy got killed. It was a few weeks before my twelfth birthday.

The whole thing went down a couple hours after Daddy had kissed me goodbye when I was half asleep and gone to cover that night shift for a co-worker friend of his. The next morning, I woke stretching and fighting the slits of sun sneaking through my window. There was no sound. None. The rareness of it struck me before I got out of bed. There were no clanging pots or silverware in the kitchen or the muffle of voices, no CNN keeping Mama company or the shower going in their bedroom bathroom. No coffee scenting the whole house, competing with breakfast. I got up and headed down the hall toward my parents' room. I heard talking, or so I thought, until I crept closer to the door and could just make out what sounded like somebody crying. I knocked like I'd been trained to do, but didn't wait for the "Come on in."

Nana Mae and Mama sat on the other side of the bed away from the door, their backs to me, holding on to each other and rocking back and forth. I turned right around, ran back down the hall, out the door, and down the street, barefoot, in my pajamas without stopping. I knew.

Mr. Carter intercepted me as I passed his house, or rather, I ran right into his arms. It was a weekday, not Saturday. Mr. Carter caught me and held onto me tight. I think he said, "I know, I know." The whole block knew the morning after Daddy was gone.

I was hollering and getting snot all over one of his favorite black army shirts. He cupped my face with his huge, callused hands on each side of my wet cheeks so I was forced to look him straight in the eyes.

"Ain't nowhere to run, little girl."

He carried me next door back to the house, his dog, Warrior, leading the way.

CHAPTER

29

The anniversary was upon us a week after the news about Little Petey's murderer broke. We counted down the last forty-eight hours silently amid all the ongoing news and gossip about Little Petey and his cousin Lightning. Mama came to my room and sat on the side of my bed where I was reading. Her eyes darted to the photo of me and Daddy but didn't linger.

"Well," she said, forcing a smile that turned her full lips up. "Time's moving so fast, your birthday will be here before we know it."

I forced a fake smile, too. I was thinking about what she skipped saying, though both of us had it lodged in our brains. There was THE DAY to survive first.

"I think I got the perfect birthday present for you this

year. In fact, I know it." This time the smile reached her eyes.

My stomach jumped—for once in a good way.

"What?"

"Something you been wanting."

"Mama—" I sat up.

"You gotta wait till your birthday, and that's just around the corner. That's all I'm saying, so don't be worrying me asking, but for now let's go and get on this school shopping."

Phone, please, I prayed. The computer I was supposed to be getting was not a secret and was a needed item for school. Finally, I hoped, I was going to be rescued from being the last teenager in my universe without my own phone. And she'd given me a definite cue, which Mama didn't normally do, probably because of the terrible summer. So many things had happened. Little Petey's murder and the mission to solve it, the children at the daycare, the reunion with Fernando, and then there was the hated anniversary that Mama, Nana Mae, and me had to get through again.

I got new bras during our shopping trip. I was out of AAA into A size zone at least. While I was occupied with more important things, my breasts had decided to grow just a little more so at least my chest looked less like flat bread. A letter from Alima came in the mail while we were out. I took it as a sign, a rare good one I really needed. When Nana Mae handed me the letter, I went straight up to my room and tore it open.

Wa alaykum as-salam.

Dear Nia, my friend,

I am sorry to hear of the little boy who died. I used to think America must be very different, not so much violence. A boy in our town was blown up by a grenade. He was fourteen. Abdul-Rahman Obeidallah was shot when he was fifteen.

Somewhere children must play in the sun with no bullets or walls to fear. My grandmother says hope is difficult sometimes, but one cannot live without it. She lived through the war of 1967 when her family was displaced and the Annexation so she knows.

Nahn jisr alsalam: We are the bridge to peace.

Alima

عَالِمَة

When our class started writing our pen pals, our teacher warned that it was hard sometimes to translate some meanings into English and have the meaning stay the same. That last line in Alima's letter was as good as one of those Bible scriptures that Miracle Ruth or Ms. Torrence could pull out at just the right moment, or one of any parent's or grandparent's right way to act type of sayings, like treat other people like you want to be treated.

I'd heard it a million times between church and home for years, but the first stuck out because my father had been disappointed in me for something that I'd done at school. I was in kindergarten back then, and I pushed a girl who was on the swing I liked best. She fell and hit her knee, crying hard when she saw blood. I felt bad and ashamed instantly but refused to show it and apologize. The teacher sent me to time out, which was a wooden bench where you got banished for misbehaving. Mama got news of the incident as soon as she picked me up from school.

She got busy laying out the punishments the minute we got home. "I am not about to raise no bullies up in here. No TV the rest of this week or park. You understand me? And you will be apologizing to the girl you hurt and to your teacher too understand?"

"Yes, ma'am."

Later, I did not run up to Daddy soon as he came in the door from work as usual. I was hiding in my room, knowing Mama would tell him about the trouble at school. When he came to find me, there was no "Bright Eyes" and one of his bear hugs.

"Your mom told me what happened at school. First thing I thought was, *What? Not my Bright Eyes.* You know what your daddy does all day?"

"Save people," I managed.

"I try to. A lot of times I'm helping people who been hurt by people up to no good—bullies, you know. See, there are people who love picking on folks they think are weaker, smaller, nicer. Kinda makes 'em feel bigger, but that doesn't make anybody big. It makes *them* small. Sometimes, it's a husband bullying his wife or his girlfriend or son or daughter." He paused. "Every now and again it's the wife being abusive or somebody's neighbor doing his best to keep the man living right next to him down. Or gangs bullying a whole community. Lots of people in this world—too many, Bright Eyes—are hurt 'cause too many people want to bully instead of helping."

I could hear in his voice how sad this made him.

"Listen to me now, Nia. You can always choose to do wrong or do right in this world. My father used to say that to me, and he was right, too. Now, while me and your mama raising you in this house, if you pick incorrectly next time, your butt is gonna be double hurtin'. But I know won't be no next time, right?"

I nodded. That he was disappointed in me hurt more than the thought of any spanking, which he hated to give and rarely did. I threw myself against his chest and hugged him as tight as I could. He kissed the top of my head and held me just as tight.

"That's my girl, Bright Eyes."

I could almost hear him, and it hurt.

I squeezed back the memory and placed the new letter from Alima with the others in the drawer. I got ready for bed though I didn't really want to go to sleep. The next day was coming whether I wanted it to or not. Little Petey's killer was behind bars, but Little Petey was still dead, and the children at the daycare were gone, too, like my father. He was never going to smile at me and hug me or remind me that I was special no matter what I looked like or what happened. He was never going to see me cross another finish line.

Sometime before the darkness gave way to morning and the birds got noisy singing songs I did not want to hear, I finally stopped tossing and turning and fell asleep. I dreamed again. *I hug Daddy. He lifts me close to him and rubs my back. I bury my face in his neck. He pulls away and kisses my cheek. His eyes and voice are smiling. "Love you. See you in the morning, Bright Eyes." Then he is gone. I reach and reach, trying to pull him back, because now I know. He will not be coming home again.*

Wetness seeped through my eyelids. The dream ended. I made a cave out of my blanket and lay there for a good while. Morning came. It was officially three years and seven hours since the last time my father was alive.

I picked up the photo of us, hoping to relive the moment in time it captured, and couldn't. As I placed the picture back in its place, my hand brushed against the drawer of the nightstand. I opened it and dug underneath the notebooks, random former treasures, and Alima's letters until my fingers found the last journal I had kept. A pen and Fernando's drawing of my father's face, served as the bookmark to the last entry I'd written before my father died. It was about our fun carnival day, how we rode the bumper cars, Mama and me in one, with me driving, taking on Daddy, how Daddy bumped into other cars trying to crash into us, how we ate pink-and-blue cotton candy, how Daddy had hit the hammer so high and won Pepto Bismol and then took us for pizza on the way home.

BEST DAY EVER!!!

A little girl's words from what seemed a lifetime ago. It was officially three years ago since that perfect day at the carnival. I picked the pen up and wrote.

August 17.
Someday, I will find out why, who. PROMISE.

AUTHOR'S NOTE

Many years have passed since one of my sister's best friends, Kimberly Renee Saxton, was murdered. Just twenty-four at the time, she was not the shooter's intended target, but the bullets didn't know that. Since then, many have perished similarly, including people I knew, like a childhood schoolmate who was a teacher innocently minding her own business, and a student gunned down mere weeks post-college graduation, and so many more as of this writing in schools, homes, stores, front porches, highways and streets, parks, post offices, movie theaters, night clubs, freedom protests, and seemingly everywhere on the planet, including my hometown. The people and events in this book are fictional, but our condition as human beings living within the constant threat of violence was very much the inspiration. However, neither pessimism nor acceptance is the way. *Nia.*

ACKNOWLEDGMENTS

Writing a book that you pour so much of your time and self into is a journey of challenges and reward smade rich by the people who support and cheer you on. While I cannot name all of those people, I must extend deep appreciation and gratitude for my biological ancestors known and unknown and the many writers who inspired me in early life and continue to do so. Thanks to my family—my true compass—Mama (Earnestine Watson), who always asked that important question, "Is the book done yet?" My late maternal grandparents Idene and Will Lee Ward; my sister Marisa (I see you); Katina (believe); and my play-real sista Lisa; Rita, Steve, and Bryant (always); my aunties (all eleven beautiful strong ones), uncles, tribe of cousins, the late Leon Dunn, Jerry Watson, and extended bonus family (Khadijah, Chad, Fatin, Jen, Gloria, and the rest of the crew). Lastly and not least, my loves and home—Nasir A. Muhammad and our son, Nadir. Many thanks to my super women editors Jessica Powers and Stacy Whitman for the eagle eye feedback and support, Lee Byrd and the Cinco Puntos team and Lee & Low Books for seeing the potential and publishing this book, cover illustrator Ashley Floreal, Razan Abdin-Adnani, and the workshop peer and mentor group feedback and encouragement in the early days of writing this book—Napa Valley Writers Tayari Jones fiction group (Summer 2012); VONA/Voices Evelina Galang fiction workshop group (Summer 2015); Shelly O'Connor, Mary Phillips, and Yvette Wigfall for reading early versions and believing, along with a cadre of other super friends— Tyeta Beattie, Avery O. Williams, Sheila Norman, Albert Turner, Harold Booker, Tonya Landon, Cleo W., Mark Anthony Neal, Beverly Guy-Sheftall, my supportive Morehouse community members including Leah Creque and the past chairs of English and creative arts, other supportive colleague-friends, and my creative writing class students who were reminders to me of my own "writers must write" mandate. My impactful former teachers (Dorothy Thompson, Jane Poe, Frances Beard, Samuel Longmire, the late Dr. Erskine Peters, and Gloria C. Edgerton).